TAMING THE BEAST

ALSO BY ALICIA MONTGOMERY

Shadow Wolf

A Touch of Magic

Heart of the Wolf

THE BLACKSTONE MOUNTAIN SERIES

The Blackstone Dragon Heir

The Blackstone Bad Dragon

The Blackstone Bear

The Blackstone Wolf

The Blackstone Lion

The Blackstone She-Wolf

The Blackstone She-Bear

The Blackstone She-Dragon

TAMING THE BEAST

BOOK 5 OF THE TRUE MATES SERIES

ALICIA MONTGOMERY

ABOUT THE AUTHOR

Alicia Montgomery has always dreamed of becoming a romance novel writer. She started writing down her stories in now long-forgotten diaries and notebooks, never thinking that her dream would come true. After taking the well-worn path to a stable career, she is now plunging into the world of self-publishing.

CHAPTER ONE

Sebastian Creed signaled to his favorite bartender as soon as he sat down on the long, onyx-colored bar. The young man spotted him instantly and nodded in acknowledgment. Soon, a glass of his favorite bourbon appeared in front of him, and he took a small sip. There were some days he still couldn't believe he was allowed in a place like this.

Luxe was the most exclusive club in New York City. He had to show his sizable bank statements just to be considered for membership. That was ironic, considering that growing up in a rundown trailer in Tennessee, he didn't even have two dimes to rub together. Money was power, he learned. And over the years, he had acquired lots of it. Of course, that came with women, too. Not that he had any problems before he became rich. It was always easy to find some chick for a one-night stand or even a quickie in the bathroom, especially when he was in uniform. All he had to do was walk into some dive bar or small-town roadhouse, and the women were eager to "do their patriotic duty."

As his wealth grew, however, so did the number of women who wanted him. Luxe catered to men and women like him, so at least here, he never had to worry about gold diggers. He only had to worry about the chicks who were too clingy or wanted to reform the bad boy. Those types he had learned to spot and avoid. He gave as good as he got but always left right after the deed. The sex, the skin-to-skin contact were the few times he *felt* something, but the moments right after left him cold and empty. Most days, he was just going through the motions as life had sucked the joy in him. He hadn't felt real emotions in a while. Not since Afghanistan.

He swallowed down more bourbon, enjoying the burn down his throat. Pushing those thoughts aside, he scanned the room for his next target. The blonde across the bar seemed promising. She had just sat down,and leaned over to give her drink order, showing off a fantastic set of tits. They were unusually perky, so she either had a good bra or an excellent plastic surgeon. He'd find out soon enough.

Without warning, the hairs on the back of his neck bristled, and years of combat training told him he was being watched. He swung around, instantly recognizing who it was, but not the two others with him.

"Well, hello trouble."

"Hello, Sebastian," the man said. "Alone for tonight?"

"Not for long." Sebastian turned his head towards the blonde, thinking about what color panties she was wearing under that silver dress. She looked back at him, her eyes flashing with interest. He knew that look. She could wait, though. He had a feeling this night was going to be interesting, which was a good thing. Sebastian was starting to get bored.

It was Grant Anderson, CEO of Fenrir Corporation. He'd met the guy a couple of times before and on his last visit to Luxe, even introduced himself. That night, he seemed like he had the weight of the world on his shoulders, and Sebastian figured it wouldn't hurt to give him his card, especially if it could drum up some business. He even expected Grant to do a background check on him and his company, which was standard in his line of work. Creed Security pinged them right back, and then he found out who his mysterious friend was. After that last time, though, Grant had stopped coming to Luxe. It was too bad, as he genuinely liked the guy, though they only spoke a few times. The last time they did speak, the Grant was apparently in trouble, but he didn't specify what kind of trouble. Now, maybe it was his chance to find out what kind.

He turned back to Grant. "But before I move on to tonight's entertainment, tell me, where have you been? What happened to you?"

Grant gave him a smile. "Something worse."

Sebastian laughed. So, some girl had gotten her claws into the CEO of one of the world's largest corporations. Lucky chick. "Really?"

"Oh, yeah. Baby on the way, too."

Ah, that was at least eighteen years of child support payments. Whoever she was, she must be happy as a clam. Of course, judging by that stupid grin on Grant's face, he didn't know what was coming. Better cheer him up while he could.

"Well, shit." He gestured to the bartender. "A round of bourbon for my friends here. On me. But we're not here to celebrate your doom, are we?"

Grant placed a manila folder on the bar beside him. "Sebastian Creed. CEO of Creed Security. You enlisted in the Marines as soon as you turned eighteen, went all the way to Spec Ops. Discharged honorably after ten years, then you started your security firm. Hit it big when you got some military contracts, and now Creed Security is one of the largest military and private security companies in the world."

Now comes the fun part. "You know when I take a shit, too?"

"I like to get to know my friends well, Sebastian."

"So do I, Mr. Grant Anderson, CEO of Fenrir Corp."

He waited for a reaction from Grant, but there was none, not even a blink. The man wasn't head of a major corporation for nothing.

"You've been doing some research, too, I see."

"You think you can run a background check on me and I wouldn't find out? Your guys are pretty good, but mine are better." Sebastian rose to his feet. He was taller than Grant and his companions, but then again few men reached or topped his 6'5" height. "Now," he said calmly, "What do you want?"

The blonde man to Grant's right spoke in a cool voice. "We want to hire your firm, Mr. Creed."

Any other man would have been intimidated, but he wasn't just any man. "And you are?"

"Nick Vrost. Fenrir Corporation's Head of Security."

He didn't feel inclined to shake the man's hand, and Vrost didn't offer his either.

"And you?" he said to the other man with Grant. This one was dark-haired and seemed more friendly. He also held out his hand.

"I'm one of Grant's partners, Liam Henney."

Sebastian shook Liam's hand, surprised at the unusual strength. He looked at all three of them, and for the first time, felt a strange sensation in his gut. There was something unusual about these three men.

"So this is business." Sebastian settled back on his seat. "So, let's talk business. What can I do for you gentlemen?"

Grant took the seat next to him. "We have a missing...asset. The asset was taken from us by force, and we need he— it back."

The hitch in his voice didn't escape Sebastian's notice. "So, standard corporate espionage stuff, huh? And you want me to retrieve your asset?"

"We will recover the asset. We're narrowing down its location, but we already know we'll need muscle to infiltrate the facility. Now, we've done research on your firm." Grant paused to give the bartender a nod as he accepted the drink, immediately taking a sip. "You're the best, and you're also discreet."

"Of course. Discretion is part of the game." Sebastian nodded. "But first you'll have to tell me what this asset is, and why it's so important to you."

"No," Vrost said in his cool as ice voice. "It's on a need to know basis only. My team will take care of retrieval. You just need to make sure we can get in and out safely."

Ice filled his veins. No fucking way. This was not how he did business. There were certain types of people who thought that just because they had money, they could lead him by the balls and tell him what to do. "Then we have no deal. Have a good evening, gentlemen."

"I'll pay whatever you want. Double what you usually charge," Grant said.

"Look, Grant." He wanted to be honest with the man, at the very least. "My company is used to handling secrets. Classified stuff, even, so you can be sure your secret is safe with me. But, I need to know exactly what I'm getting into."

"I've seen your record, Creed. Your company has run operations far more dangerous than what we're asking."

Hmmm...Fenrir's security people were probably top-notch if they knew what kind of jobs he'd done. "The answer is still no."

"You'd turn away millions of dollars to do one small job, just because we won't tell you what it is we want you to retrieve?" Vrost asked.

He would not let the man get under his skin. "Listen, Mr. Vrost, right?" Sebastian crossed his arms over his chest. "Money,

I got. Lots of it. But you know what I can't replace with money, Mr. Vrost? The lives of good men and women. If I went in blind, I'd be risking the lives of my employees. Good, loyal people who've been to hell and back with me. And for what? The prototype for a fancy new gadget? A miracle pill that promises weight loss without the hard work? No. That's how people get hurt, and I don't do business with anyone who would treat my people like disposable toys. So, goodnight, gentlemen." He felt disgusted, and frankly, disappointed that Grant Anderson was just like all the other rich bastards who wanted to hire him.

Sebastian walked straight to the blonde, leaning down to her ear. "Hey sweetheart," he whispered in a low voice. "Why don't you and me have a little fun on our own?"

The woman's blue eyes widened, her pupils blowing up as he traced his fingers down her back. "Sure," she said, standing up and following him.

He led her to one of the corner couches and moved over to give her some room.

"I have to confess, this is my first time here," she said, scooting closer to him. "But, well, I was thinking of a nice birthday present for myself when my trust fund came in and..."

Sebastian gave her an empty smile, and let her drone on about her hobbies. Something about dancing horses or some shit. He nodded, as if he heard her, though all he could think about were those long legs and how they'd feel wrapped around him later that night.

"Mr. Creed."

That was quicker than he'd thought it'd be. He glanced up at the trio of men, a bored look on his face. It was Liam Henney who had spoken. "Please, call me Sebastian."

"Call me Liam, then," the dark-haired man continued. "May we speak alone, Sebastian?"

He leaned down and whispered into the blonde's ear. "I really wanna hear more about your horses, sweetheart, but I have some business to take care of. Go over to the other couch, and I'll join you in a bit, okay?"

The blonde nodded, and with one last saucy look, she left.

Sebastian focused his attention back on the trio. "Okay, say what you need to say."

"We've talked it over," Liam said. "And we can tell you a little bit more about the asset. But not everything."

This shit again. "All or nothing," Sebastian insisted. "And if you fucking lie to me, I'll know."

Liam settled on the couch next to him, took his phone out of his pocket, and turned it on. He placed the device on the table and slid it over to Sebastian. "The asset."

"Oh, fuck me," Sebastian Creed said under his breath. He nearly dropped the phone in his hand but kept his grip tight. The air in his lungs rushed out of his body, and an unfamiliar feeling in his middle was gnawing at him.

The woman in the picture was beautiful. No, wait, that didn't even begin to describe her. She was breathtaking. Peaches-and-cream complexion that looked soft to the touch. Burnished brown hair that went past her shoulders. Delicately-arched, but thick brows that framed her face. Long, sweeping dark lashes over expressive eyes. He wasn't sure what color they were, but he thought they could be a very light green. And those lips. Pink, luscious and pouty, and he instantly imagined how they would taste and feel against his.

"Well? Will you help us?"

Sebastian looked up at the three men watching him. "Fine. Sit down, gentlemen." He leaned back into the couch and watched as the three men sat across from him.

He waited for one of them to speak. When it came to

negotiations, after all, the first one to talk was the loser. They needed him more than he needed them, that was for sure.

"Sebastian," Liam Henney began. "This asset...I mean, she's important to us."

He narrowed his eyes at the other man. Was she his woman? Something he hadn't felt for a long time —jealousy —clawed at his insides. Henney was the one who approached him after they walked away, and he probably took the photo of her. Fuck it all, if that was the case.

Tamping that feeling down, he spoke. "Who is she?"

"Dr. Cross is one of our leading researchers," Nick Vrost said. Vrost clearly despised Sebastian, but he seemed like a solid guy, someone you could rely on. He said he was Head of Security for Fenrir Corporation, but he didn't appear to have a hint of military experience. In fact, the pretty boy seemed more at home in a boardroom than a war room. He detected a hint of danger around the man, though. Vrost wouldn't have risen to such a position if he didn't earn it.

"What was she working on?"

There was a pause, but Grant answered. "Food. Food research."

Sebastian rubbed his jaw. Food R and D was a multibillion-dollar industry. Many manufacturers had better security than the Pentagon since the competition was fierce. Still, there was something they weren't telling him. He was tempted to walk away right now, but another glance at the picture had him rooted to the spot. "So, what happened?"

"Dr. Cross didn't show up for work this morning, which is unusual for her. She didn't call in sick, and we couldn't reach her phone. We had our HR department check her apartment, but she wasn't home," Grant explained. "Finally, we decided to send our security team to investigate. None of her colleagues or friends knew where she was. Then, we checked the video from the security camera in her building. She was walking home last night when she was taken."

Sebastian gritted his teeth. "How?"

"Two vans, about a dozen men, came and plucked her right off the street. She tried to fight them, but they must have drugged her," Grant continued.

"Where is she now?"

"We're working on finding her," Grant replied. "But we don't have enough people to retrieve her. We need extra reinforcements."

"Why come to me?" Sebastian asked. "Why not go to the police?"

The CEO hesitated. "We know the people who took her. Let's just say they're not the type of people the police could handle. She might get hurt, as well as other innocent people."

"Hmmm," Sebastian rubbed his jaw. "Mercenaries or some sort? Cartel? Hell's Angels?"

"Yeah," Grant nodded. "Mercenaries. Hired goons. Plus, you know NYPD handles dozens of missing persons in any given week. They'd take forever to get an investigation going, and who knows what'll happen to her if we wait any longer."

Sebastian knew how cops worked. Small town cops, big city cops. Most of them turned a blind eye, whether it was because they were crooked or simply too jaded.

"Also," Liam interjected. "We're not using legal means to find her. In fact, our PI is working with some hackers to find out her location. They can tap into security cameras all over the country and run face recognition software."

"Smart," he said. "But definitely illegal."

"This is why we're doing it on our own," Grant said. "Now, will you help us?"

Sebastian glanced at the phone, but the screen had gone

dark. Not that it mattered. The woman's face was burned into his memory, and he doubted he could forget it.

"All right. We'll have our lawyers sort out the details. I'm sure you have someone you can call at this hour. But we need to get started on this op."

"What the fuck is going on?"

Sebastian looked back at Aiden James, his right-hand man. "Fuck if I know."

He and Aiden had been in the Marines together, and as soon as Sebastian started Creed Securities, he knew the first man he wanted to hire. Aiden James was loyal and would go through fire for him, just as he would for Aiden. They had been through a lot together, and he was the only one who still talked to him after what happened in Afghanistan. Years of training and combat, however, didn't prepare either of them for something like this.

"Those, guys..." Aiden shook his head. "They're definitely military. Marines, and maybe a few SEALS. But it's like they got their fear switched off or something. Maybe they're using some type of experimental drug?"

Sebastian grunted in agreement. There was something fishy going on. He should have known. Seeing the "team" Fenrir had brought in alone should have warned him. Three women, Henney, Vrost, and a third man. Not that he didn't believe women could handle the simple retrieval op, but they certainly were a ragtag bunch. With all the money Fenrir Corporation had, he'd have thought they could afford some real muscle. Then there were the strange animal sounds he heard coming from the warehouse. They were faint, and none of his men seemed to pick up the sounds, but he was sure he heard them. They sounded like big dogs, barking and snarling.

Aiden shook his head. "This is not going the way we want it."

Sebastian was skeptical of their plan, at first, but it was a good one. His snipers took down the guards in the back, and then the Fenrir team went in. His team went out front and distracted the rest of the guards. They were expecting two dozen or so men, but it turned out they were hiding more. Did those men just appear out of nowhere? Their surveillance didn't show any additional forces, and there was no way they could have snuck in that many guys without them noticing.

"Where do you think those guys were hiding out?" Aiden asked as if reading his mind.

Sebastian thought for a moment. "Remember when we raided that farmhouse in Kundul?"

Aiden's eyes lit up in recognition. "They dug a basement," the other man stated. "I don't think their asset is anywhere near here, though."

No way. She was here. He didn't know how, but he knew it. *Find her.*

"What did you say?" Sebastian snapped his head back to Aiden.

"What, man?" Aiden gave him a confused look. "I didn't say nothin'."

Fucking hell. Sebastian gritted his teeth. His body was hot and cold all over at the same time like he had ice running through his veins and someone set fire to his skin. That voice inside him. Shit. He rubbed the bridge of his nose as a pressure began to build behind his eyes. He thought the voice was gone, long ago, thanks to a lot of medication and therapy. Memories flooded back into his mind. The hot desert air and gritty sand.

He gripped his gun so tight his knuckles went white. No, this was not the time to have another episode.

The voice from the communications unit in his ear interrupted his thoughts, and he was grateful for the distraction.

"One sec," he said to Aiden, lifting a finger. "Grant," he answered. The CEO was staying in their communications station, coordinating efforts with his team so that they wouldn't have too many voices in each other's ears. "There were more than the two dozen we expected..." he explained. Grant answered, saying his team hadn't found the woman. "I think they have a basement. They might be hiding her there, too. I'm gonna go in." He shut off the comm, not wanting to hear Grant tell him to stay away. The CEO was unusually protective of his little scientist, but Sebastian didn't give a shit. He was not going to stand down knowing she was still in danger and the Fenrir team couldn't find her.

"I think I found something, boss," Zac, one of his newer recruits, said as he jogged towards them.

Sebastian motioned for two more of his guys to follow him, Aiden, and Zac, then barked orders at the rest to secure the area.

Zac led them to the back of the warehouse. "I was searching for more of those guys, and I found this." He pointed to the ground, where there were metal doors buried underneath some recently-cleared gravel.

"Good job, Zac," Sebastian said as he reached down and grabbed the rope tied to the doors. With a firm tug, the doors flew open, revealing a set of rickety stairs. "Let's go."

The stairs creaked under his weight, so he went down slowly. They led to a tunnel, one that was crudely built, but still, it was large enough for two men to walk side-by-side. There was a light at the end, so he didn't need to flip on his night vision goggles. He turned back and signaled to his men to follow behind him, then crept forward slowly, his weapon at the ready.

His heart beat a tattoo onto his ribcage as he walked forward. He could practically taste the danger. As the end drew nearer, he breathed deeply, willing his heartbeat to slow down.

The room that the tunnel led to was larger than he'd imagine, and there was a single, swinging lamp overhead. His eyes immediately zeroed in to where the light was shining. On the floor was a small, curled up figure. Though he hadn't seen the figure's face, he knew who it was.

"Fuck!" he cursed as he strode towards the center of the room. His boots were loud as he clomped his way in. He normally moved much quieter, but he couldn't contain himself. The anger building up inside him was threatening to explode.

He knelt down and gently touched the tangled brown hair. Brushing it aside, he held a breath as he looked at her face for the first time. Christ, she was even more beautiful up close and in person. The picture didn't do justice to her incredible skin. The rage began to boil when he saw the bruise on her jaw.

"Boss..." Zac warned.

Sebastian's head snapped up. Ten men were approaching, their weapons trained on them. "Take them down!" he ordered.

His men raised their own weapons—the real ones, not the tranquilizers—and aimed. He closed his eyes, readying himself for the sound of gunfire. It was a sound he hated since it brought back all the memories of his time in the Marines, but he would endure it to protect her. He waited, but there was no sound of recoil or the blast of bullets. Instead, there were loud thuds as ten bodies hit the floor.

"What the fuck is going on?"

His men looked confused. Did Grant call in reinforcements?

A soft voice from across the room gasped. A small figure barreled past his guys and knelt beside him. It was one of the women from Fenrir. She had taken her helmet off, and strawberry blonde hair fell past her shoulders. She reached down and touched the woman's face.

"Jade..."

Nick Vrost had called her Dr. Cross. Was Jade her name? Beautiful. Just like her. Sweet Jade.

As Sebastian tried to move Jade, the rattling of metal caught his attention. His eyes trailed down to Jade's wrists and ankles. Thick metal cuffs were wrapped around them, connected to chains bolted to the floor. Something inside him roared with fury, and he wanted to tear those chains apart.

"Who the fuck would do this?" He tossed one of the chains aside. "Zac!" he yelled at the younger man. "Go find a key. The rest of you, see if there are any tools around we can use to break these chains."

He looked back at the women, and saw the redhead had Jade's head on her lap, tears rolling down her cheeks. They were obviously friends.

"You'll be okay, Jade. Don't worry, I'm here," the redhead said, then looked up at him. "Why isn't she waking up?"

Sebastian quickly looked around him and saw the syringe. No, wait, there were several of them on the ground. Fuck, were they trying to kill her? "Drugged, I assume," he said, feeling the distaste in his mouth. "Jesus, how much did they put in her system?"

Another woman had approached them. She was a short brunette, and something about her face and bright green eyes look familiar. "Is she..."

The redhead nodded. "She's...alive."

"I'll go ahead and get Dr. Faulkner," the brunette said before she tore out of the room.

"Boss!" Zac bellowed, running towards them at full speed. "I think I found 'em!" The young man tossed a set of keys at Sebastian, which he caught in his hands. He quickly unlocked the shackles with the keys, trying not to stare at the redness around her wrists. Something inside of him wanted to burst out of his skin and tear the place apart.

Gently, he picked her up and lifted her into his arms. His skin prickled where their bare skin touched, and his nose was suddenly filled with a heady scent. Vanilla, mixed with cherries, like his favorite milkshake from his childhood. It was delicious and made his head buzz for a moment. She let out a soft moan, and the sound of her voice shook him out of his reverie and soothed him. Her head rolled back, her soft cheek laying on his chest.

"Hey, what are you doing?" The redhead grabbed his arm, but he ignored her. Sebastian continued to stare down at his precious package. Someone pulled the woman off him, and another soft moan from Jade made him shake his head. The doctor. Fenrir had a doctor standing by. He had to take her to him.

Sebastian walked out of the basement, towards the hallway where the Fenrir team must have come from. He brought Jade closer against his chest, but not too tight. She was so small and fragile, he feared he would break her. He took his time, not just because he didn't want to jostle her in case she was injured, but also because he was dreading when he would eventually have to let go of her.

Outside, the scene was chaotic, but he didn't pay them any mind. He went straight to the van where the doctor was waiting. The older man in glasses was already preparing his medical equipment.

A younger man approached him, reaching for Jade. "Let me help you with her, sir."

"Fuck off," he growled, whipping Jade away from him. He didn't want anyone else touching her.

"Mr. Creed, I'm just going to bring her to Dr. Faulkner," the other man said, raising his hands in defense. "Mr. Anderson said he'd like you to come in for a quick debrief."

"It's all right, Miller," Dr. Faulkner called to the other man. "Mr. Creed, will you bring Dr. Cross, here, please? I'm her doctor. I need to examine her and make sure she's metabolizing the drugs they put in her. Otherwise, I'm going to have to start detoxing her system."

He nodded, but his teeth were still gnashing at the thought of letting go.

"Place her here, please...that's it, just be gentle when you lay her down," the doctor instructed.

Sebastian deposited her on the bed carefully, slipping his arms out from under her.

"Thank you," Dr. Faulkner said. "Now, I believe Grant is waiting for you?" He looked at Sebastian meaningfully.

That was his cue to leave. It took all his strength, but he pivoted away from them, but not before he took one last look at Jade. Even as he walked away, he could still smell her cherry and vanilla scent.

CHAPTER TWO

"I can't believe you talked me into this," Jade said with a frown. She was not happy. The dress she was wearing was too tight, the thong panties were riding up her behind, and the heels were too high. Oh, why did she let Meredith do this to her?

Meredith rolled her eyes. "You're here. Get over it." She gave Jade a once over. "And you look hot."

"Meredith! Jade?" Lara said as she came up behind them. "Um, wow!"

"I know, right?" Meredith gushed. "You're welcome." The blonde gave an exaggerated bow.

"It's just that...I've been asking you for months to let me give you a makeover!" Lara pouted. "And now I miss it!"

"Well, you were a little busy," Jade retorted. "How is Liam?"

The witch blushed at the mention of her fiancé. "You know I had to...spend some time convincing him to let me have this bachelorette party."

"Don't be jealous, Lara," Meredith said. "I had to twist her arm to let me strap her into that dress and put some makeup on her. *Et voila!* My masterpiece."

The Lycan scientist was wearing a peach lace bustier dress that pushed up her breasts without being vulgar. While the lace went below her knees, the underskirt stopped about halfway, giving a teasing view of her thighs, while the sky-high heels not only added height to her petite frame but also elongated her legs. She wore minimal makeup, just enough to emphasize her thick brows and pouty lips, while her long, brown hair was styled in sexy waves down her back.

Lara looked like she still couldn't believe her eyes. "Jade, you look gorgeous. You've been hiding this the whole time?"

The scientist gave her outfit another pained look. "Yeah, well, don't expect me to wear this every day now. I only did it because it was a special occasion."

"How did you convince her, exactly?" Lara asked Meredith.

"I promised her I would stop singing the song that doesn't end if she'd let me give her a makeover," Meredith explained.

"And then how did you get out of Fenrir?"

"Oh Lara, don't you know? They let me out now if I'm good!" A few weeks ago, Meredith broke into Fenrir Corporation's offices hoping to steal some new tech or corporate secrets to sell to the highest bidder. Unfortunately (for her), she was caught and detained by the New York Lycans. They gave her a choice: be shipped off to the Lycan Siberian prison or stay in New York and serve the clan. As a Lone Wolf, Meredith had no clan to call her own anyway. So, instead of living out the next ten years in the wastelands of Siberia, she decided servitude to the New York Lycan clan was a better option. Currently, she was helping protect Jade, who had been the target of a kidnapping attempt by their enemies.

"But you're still wearing your ankle monitor, right?"

The blonde Lycan stuck a foot out. The ankle monitor was

there, but tonight, it was decorated with sparkly pink Princess-themed stickers. "Yeah, I can't do anything about that. And I can only go out if Jade needs protection and no one else can take her. So, I decided she needed protection on the way to this boutique on 5th Avenue and the makeup store."

"I don't know why I let you do this," Jade grumbled. As she attempted to walk, she nearly stumbled and had to grab onto Meredith. "It's impossible to walk in these things!"

"Oh shush. You're a woman, you'll figure it out."

"Ladies," Frankie Anderson came up to them, dressed in a cute, vintage-style red dress and matching heels. As she looked Jade over, her mismatched blue-and-green eyes sparkled. "Oh wow, Dr. Cross? You look great!"

"Thank you, Lupa," she replied, using the traditional honorific for the female heads of Lycan clans. Frankie was married to New York's Alpha, Grant Anderson, but she was also Alpha in her own right to the New Jersey clan.

"Alynna and I are already at our table," she said warmly. "Let's go."

Frankie led them to a VIP table cordoned off in the corner, where her sister-in-law, Alynna Westbrooke, was already waiting for them.

"There's the beautiful bride!" Alynna waved happily at Lara, and immediately put a tiara on the other woman's head and draped a sash that said "Bachelorette" across one shoulder. "Let's get this party started!"

"I think someone's already started the party," Meredith said, making a drinking motion with her hands.

"Hey! I'm a new mom, and this is my first time out in months!" She took a swig of red wine. "Woohoo!"

"How many have you had?" Lara asked, shaking her head.

"Two!"

"Two glasses?"

"Two bottles!" She grinned. "Lycan metabolism, you know! I need just that much to get me happy. But I'll burn it off in an hour or two when I have to go back to the ol' ball and chain!"

The rest of women settled down, and a handsome Lycan waiter brought them more drinks (including non-alcoholic ones for Frankie and Lara) and snacks. It was early yet, so Blood Moon wasn't very crowded.

"Here you go, ladies!" Alynna moved over to the other couch and sat between Jade and Meredith. She passed them both shot glasses filled with a clear gold liquid. "I'm afraid with these two knocked up," she motioned to Lara and Frankie, "it's up to us to try and bankrupt Blood Moon tonight. Don't worry, though, I hear the owner's loaded!" Blood Moon was a well-known hotspot, at least for Lycans, and Fenrir Corporation was actually a silent partner of the club.

Jade gave the glass a delicate sniff. "What is it?"

"Oh my God, this is top shelf tequila!" Meredith exclaimed. "Oooh, we're gonna get smashed tonight!"

"Put those metabolisms to good use ladies!" Alynna raised her glass in the air.

"I don't think—"

"Oh, come on, Jade," Meredith placed the glass to the other Lycan's lips. "Live a little."

Jade wrinkled her nose. "This smells vile."

"You've never had tequila before?" Meredith asked incredulously.

The brunette shook her head.

"Oh, you're in for a treat." She gave Alynna a wink. "Ok, here's what you do. First, put some salt on the back of your hand, grab one of those lime wedges..."

Jade's nose wrinkled as she followed Meredith's instructions.

"...And then you lick, shoot, and suck!" Meredith

demonstrated with a flair, spitting the lime wedge over the couch.

"Eww!" Lara gagged.

"C'mon, you try, Jade!" Meredith urged her on and refilled her own shot glass. "Let's do it all together now." She nodded at Alynna. "Ok now...lick...shoot...suck!"

Jade did as she was told and winced as the liquid burned a path down her throat. She nearly threw up, but suddenly, the warmth pooling in her belly felt good. The sourness of the lime was a good way to end the shot, too.

"All right!" Meredith cheered her on. "How was that?"

"That was actually...pleasant," Jade remarked.

"Let's do another one!" Alynna raised the bottle.

They did two more shots, and Jade simply shook her head when Alynna tried to pour her another one. "I think...I'm going to pace myself." The warm, pleasant feeling in her stomach felt nice, but something told her she should probably slow down. Surely, people didn't do more than three shots of tequila in a row, right?

"Well, hello, ladies." A tall, handsome man with broad shoulders and chocolate brown eyes approached their table. "Have room for one more?"

"Get lost, loser," Meredith snapped. "This is a private party."

"Aww," the man looked at Frankie. "I don't get points for being related to the owner's wife?"

"She's right, Enzo," Frankie smirked. "This is a private party. And you are a loser."

Enzo put his hands over his heart. "Ouch, such words from my own sister!"

"Wait!" Meredith exclaimed. "You're her brother? But you're a..."

"Handsome young man?" Enzo finished. "A charming and smooth guy?"

"I was gonna say jackass," Meredith retorted. "And human."

"I like her," Enzo said to Frankie, who shook her head and laughed.

"Meredith, this is my half-brother, Enzo Moretti," Frankie introduced. "Don't worry about being nice to him. I can confirm, he *is* a jackass."

"Nice to meet you, Meredith," Enzo flashed her his best smile.

She gave him a raised brow. "Same here."

Enzo turned his attention to the rest of the party. "Hey, Alynna, Lara...who's this...Dr. Cross!" Another smile spread across his face. "Is that you? You clean up nice!"

The look he gave her made Jade blush from head to toe, and Meredith gave him a slap on the head.

"Ow! Are we in that stage of our relationship already?' Enzo said, rubbing his head. "'Cuz I was hoping you'd take me out to dinner first before we started the spanking."

"Enzo, what are you doing here?" Frankie asked.

"It's Tuesday night, sis, my night off, so I thought I'd check out this place," he said. "I'm also meeting up with some buddies, so I'll see you ladies later." With a smile and a wink, he walked off towards the bar.

"I think it's time we headed out too," Frankie declared as she stood up.

"Awww, Frankie," Alynna protested as she took a shot of tequila. "Noooo...."

"C'mon, now." Her sister-in-law took her by the arm. "We've got husbands and you have a kid waiting for you at home. No more drinking. I don't want to bring you home stinking like a sailor!"

"Fine," she pouted. "Enjoy the rest of the night ladies. Just order whatever you want, on us!" She grabbed her purse and followed Frankie towards the exit. "And don't do anything I wouldn't do!" With a final wave, both women left the club.

Meredith shifted her attention back to her two remaining companions. "Now that our chaperones are gone," she began. "Let's talk about where we're going next. I know this great strip club—"

"No strippers!" Lara protested.

"Why not?" Meredith asked. "Aren't pregnant women supposed to be horny all the time? I bet some hot, gyrating male bodies and six-pack abs are what your hormones need right now! Don't you have urges?"

"I don't need strippers," Lara said smugly. "I get my urges satisfied plenty. Four times before I came here."

Meredith groaned. "Fuck me. No, I mean it," she put her hands on her face. "It's been way too long since I've had sex." She turned to Jade. "How about you, Jade? When was the last time you..." She looked meaningfully at Jade's crotch. "Got your grass mowed?"

"Meredith," Lara warned.

"What?" The blonde Lycan looked at her, then turned back to Jade. "C'mon, Jade, spill!" She took another shot of tequila.

Jade blushed a bright red. "That's none of your business!"

"Don't evade my question!" Meredith warned. "Has it been that long? I promise not to laugh. Your dry spell can't possibly be longer than mine."

"I don't think so," Jade said, looking at her shoes.

"Try me, Jade."

"Well, um, twenty-four years."

"That's not—HOLY CRAP!" Meredith's eyes widened. "You're a vir —"

Jade slapped a hand over the other woman's mouth. "Shush!"

Meredith looked from Jade to Lara, who also seemed shocked at the revelation.

"Jade," Lara began. "I didn't know. I mean, you never talked about it, but..."

It seemed impossible, but Jade turned even redder. "I'm just...it's not...you see..." She dropped her hands to her lap. "I'm not a weirdo who's saving herself for marriage or anything," she said defensively. "I've just...never had a chance! And I gave it the good ol' college try."

"Wait, weren't you like fifteen when you went to college?" Lara asked.

"Fourteen, and it was an academy for gifted youngsters," she corrected. "And I let Jeremy Goldsmith get to second base...er, maybe one point five base? What's under the shirt, over the bra?"

Meredith rolled her eyes and Lara clamped her hand over the other woman's mouth so she wouldn't hurt Jade's feelings.

Jade sighed. "Look, it's not like I want to stay a virgin. I've put some thought into it and I'm ready. I even started birth control, just in case. I just need to...find the right person."

"What have you been doing?" Meredith asked. "Tinder? Online dating? Going to bars?"

The scientist looked at her with wide eyes and shrugged.

"Oh my God! Nothing? How are you supposed to meet guys?"

"I haven't figured that part out yet," Jade retorted.

"What are you looking for in a boyfriend, then?" Lara asked.

"Other than a penis, I haven't really thought about it yet."

Jade's bluntness sent both Lara and Meredith sputtering their drinks.

"Holy crap! Jade, you whore!" Meredith said as she cleaned up the tequila she spit out all over the table. "I knew you had it in you!"

"Jade, honey." Lara put her hand on top of the other woman's. "You can't mean that! I mean, you don't want to just... lose it to some random guy, do you?"

"I've decided I'm not cut out for a boyfriend or relationships," Jade declared. "I'm too busy with my work. I don't want distractions."

"Then why did you say you're ready?" Lara inquired.

"I just want to give sex a try, and get it over with and see what the fuss is all about. Like an experiment."

Meredith looked at Jade with a raised brow. "Well, that escalated quickly."

"C'mon now, Jade," Lara said. "Is that really what you want?"

"Why would I want a boyfriend anyway?" Jade said in an exasperated voice. "Emotions and feelings are way too messy. I don't like it. I prefer real things, like facts and hard evidence, things I can quantify."

"You said hard," Meredith snorted.

Jade shot her a warning look and continued. "Tell me, how am I supposed to act when I don't know what to expect?"

Lara shook her head. "Honey, that's not what life and love are about. It's not science."

"Have another shot, Jade," Meredith handed her a glass. "Maybe you'll start making more sense."

Jade threw back the golden liquid. "Besides, you never know who you'll meet on these dates! Do you know that fifty-three percent of people lie on their dating profiles? I mean, what if we meet for dinner and he chews with his mouth open or breathes too loudly? Or what if he's the type of person who licks the cream off the cookie, then puts it back in the package?"

"You're right, Jade." Lara rolled her eyes. "Anyone who does has got to be a monster."

"I'm being serious!"

"What do you care, though?" Meredith pushed another shot at her. "As long as he licks your cream?"

Jade took the shot glass, contemplating the amber liquid. "I want to know what I'm getting into before I get into it! Is that too much to ask? I'm not even asking for 100 percent certainty. I'd be happy with...eighty percent. Maybe seventy-five."

"Oh wow, Jade, don't go too crazy now," Meredith said sarcastically.

Jade knocked the shot back. The burning was actually starting to feel good now. "Argh. Never mind, I don't want to talk about this anymore."

"Aww Jade, I'm sorry for making fun of you." Meredith rubbed the other Lycan's arm. "Maybe we can help you find someone to pop your cherry! Let's start with the guys you know."

Jade sighed, grabbed the bottle from Meredith, and then poured herself another shot. How many was that now? Her thoughts were growing fuzzy.

"No one?" Meredith asked incredulously. Her eyes drifted over to Enzo Moretti, who was at the bar, talking with Sean the bartender and a bunch of other guys. "There's one! Enzo Moretti."

"Ew, no," Jade took the shot. "He's a man whore. Who knows what he's carrying."

"Jade, you're a Lycan, you can't get STDs," Meredith pointed out.

"Jade likes his twin more!" Lara giggled.

"I do not!" Jade protested loudly.

"He has a twin?" Meredith's eyes grew wider.

"Yup," Lara said, popping the p. "He's the total opposite of Enzo, though. Smart. Likes to read. Works with computers."

"Oh, so he's a male version of you!" Meredith said to Jade. "Boring!"

"What?" Jade asked. "He's not boring!"

"Yes, he is. You were yawning while you two danced at the Alpha's wedding," Lara pointed out.

"Oh, hell no," Meredith shook her head. "You want someone who's exciting. And experienced."

"What about Gabriel from Marketing?" Lara suggested. "He's cute and French, plus he's been flirting with you in the cafeteria for weeks!"

"Ooh, sounds promising!"

"We both work here and I don't want it to get awkward," Jade countered. "Besides, I like the lemon curd muffins at the cafeteria. I'd have to stop going there if things went south with him."

Meredith shook her head. "Really? Lemon curd muffins are more important than your lady muffin?"

"I'll buy you some next time, and then tell me what you think is more important." She pouted. "I should probably face facts here. Who would want to have sex with me?"

"Jade!" Lara admonished.

"Oh shut up, biatch," Meredith said.

"No, you shut up," she said. "That's easy for you guys to say." She motioned to Meredith. "Look. At. You. You're tall, blonde, and gorgeous, plus you've got legs 'till Connecticut!" Then she shot a look at Lara. "And don't you even start with me! You're marrying that sex-on-on-a-stick Alpha who gets all growly and protective whenever he's around you."

Meredith sighed. "You are so completely fuckable, Jade. Trust me. You'll find someone. Let's keep going down your list."

"What list?" Enzo said as he popped up behind Meredith.

"Jesus Christ on a cracker! Are you sure you're not Lycan?" Meredith exclaimed. "No one gets the drop on me!"

He flashed her a smile and then a wink. "Pretty sure, babe. But I heard I'm built like one where it counts."

Jade giggled.

"Hey, pretty doctor." Enzo slid into the booth next to her. "How are you? You look real nice."

"Where's Matt?" she asked.

"Ouch. Really? You want hanger steak when you can have filet mignon?"

"That doesn't make sense," Jade slurred. "You're twins. You have exactly the same DNA. Don't you know that monozygotic twins develop from the same fertilized egg and—"

"Have another one, Jade," Meredith shoved a shot glass at her.

"Whoah, there," Enzo frowned at Jade, his voice turning serious. "Jade, are you okay? What's wrong? This doesn't seem like you."

Meredith opened her mouth, but Jade shot her a warning look. "I'm fiiiiiiinnnne, Enzo, really I am." She drank the shot. "I promise, this is my last shot of tequila!" She shook her head. "Wow, I feel...great!"

"Sounds like the tequila talking," Meredith stage-whispered to Lara.

Jade sighed. "I just wanna have some fun."

Enzo took the shot glass away from her. "If you want to have real fun, Jade, you don't need alcohol." He stood up and took her hand. "I'll show you how."

———

Sebastian Creed slunk back into the booth, taking a slow sip of his bourbon. As the gorgeous waitress stopped by for the umpteenth time, he waved her away before she could ask him if he wanted anything again.

Oh, he knew exactly what she was offering, and part of him was tempted. The young, blonde waitress was leggy, tall, and had a mouth that looked like she could suck the chrome off a bumper. He could probably have her quitting her shift early for an evening romp with him at the hotel across the street. But, another part of him was just not cooperating. Not anymore. Not since her.

He narrowed his eyes, looking around him. Blood Moon. Not the strangest name for a club, but still, not the type of place she would frequent. She never even left the 10-mile radius around her apartment and her workplace.

Yes, he knew her habits. Where she went to get her coffee, the supermarket where she shopped, even the Chinese takeout place she stopped at on Wednesdays. Once, he had already been waiting inside the small, greasy little takeout place, standing in the corner, his hoodie covering his head. She entered, gave her name to the old man who worked the cash register, and got her bag of food before walking out without a care in the world. All the while, he had been standing there, waiting for a glimpse of her pretty little face and a whiff of her perfume that reminded him of cherries and vanilla.

Jade Cross. She worked in the R and D department at one of Fenrir's food subsidiaries. That was about as far as his soft background check on her went. Her records had a big gap, due to the fact that she moved to England when she was twelve years old. She finished her two PhDs at the age of twenty, and then started working for Fenrir Corp two years later. Still, he couldn't imagine why she was kidnapped, drugged, and locked up like some animal. The memory of her chained down still made his blood boil. He wanted her safe, and he couldn't feel at ease knowing anything could happen to her. Yeah, that was it. That's why he kept following her around.

Fucking hell, what's wrong with me? His hand gripped the glass so tight, he thought it would break. This wasn't him. Never in his life had he actually stalked a woman. He felt like a fucking creeper. Yes, it definitely wasn't him doing this. It was the—

"Are you sure I can't get you anything else?" Tall, blonde, and leggy asked as she stopped at his booth again. She leaned down so far he could see the edge of a nipple over her low-cut blouse.

"I have all I need here, sweetheart." He gestured to the bottle of bourbon. "But," he said as he slipped two, one-hundred dollar bills into her palm. "That's for you. Now, come back here when I call for the bill, and not earlier than that, okay? There'll be more where that came from."

The waitress' eyes grew wide at the generous tip. "Uhm, yes...sure sir, whatever you say!" She hopped away, a giddy look on her face.

Sebastian took another drink. *Where the heck was she?* Just a second ago, she was sitting in the booth with her girlfriends. Now, the booth was empty, except for one of the women, who he recognized from the night of the rescue. The redhead was not what he'd expect from a member of Fenrir's security team, but he knew better than to judge a book by its cover.

His fingers curled tight into his palms. Just before she disappeared, he saw that young, arrogant prick slide into the booth next to her, putting his arm around her shoulder. Imagining that kid's hands all over Jade was driving him insane, especially since Sebastian had yet to touch her since that night.

Christ Almighty, he had gone crazy. Crazy for some chick. And they hadn't even spoken to each other.

He pushed the glass away from him, his keen eyes sweeping over the crowd, looking for her. A few minutes passed and he still couldn't find her, and *something* in him was itching. Scratching.

She's here.

"How do you know?" he muttered under his breath. Really? He was talking to it now? He shook his head.

A loud whoop caught his attention and he saw the tall, blonde one—another one of Fenrir's security team, though he could tell this one actually had some combat training—on top of the bar. She reached down and pulled something up.

Jade.

Sebastian recognized the slinky dress, watching with envy at the way it touched her body. Jade usually dressed conservatively, always in long-sleeved shirts and pants or long skirts. Tonight, though, when she walked into Blood Moon, he almost didn't recognize her. Gone were the glasses that were usually perched on her tiny, pert nose. She didn't really need any makeup on her perfect, peaches-and-cream skin, but she wore just enough to enhance her already gorgeous features. Her long hair hung around her shoulders in waves, covering her back. He wondered what it would be like to thrust his fingers through the soft locks and wrap it around her hands while he—

Oh fuck, now she was dancing on top of the bar. Earlier, he saw one of them—the brunette with familiar green eyes from the rescue op—order a bottle of tequila, along with the wine she had already drunk. They were probably celebrating—likely a bachelorette party, based on the tiara and sash on the redhead. As Jade danced to the beat of the music, his eyes trailed from her delicate ankles, up slim legs, over the delectable swell of her hips that nipped into a tiny waist, to the curves of her breasts. Her soft tits weren't overly large, just right, and he imagined his hands could cover them entirely. Fucking hell, his dick was so hard, his zipper was practically imprinting on it. Despite his best efforts, he couldn't turn away, and his gaze continued up to her neck and to her face.

That goddamn pretty face that got him into this mess in the first place. She was even more beautiful than in that picture

Liam Henney had shown him. And when he saw her lying on the dirty floor of that basement, rage burned through him and he wanted to kill something. Jade had looked so fragile and beautiful, despite the healing bruise on her jaw.

Finally, the song ended, and Jade hopped off the bar with her friend. The strobe lights in the dim room blinded him for a moment, and he lost her again. Tamping down the urge to look for her, he poured himself some more bourbon, watching as the golden-brown liquid spilled out of the bottle and into his glass.

Maybe he should call the waitress over. She was just his type, not that he had one, exactly. If he did, it certainly wasn't brainy little geniuses with juicy, blowjob lips. It had been weeks since he'd had his dick stroked, and the waitress would be a much easier catch than the women at Luxe. She'd appreciate the attention from a man like him, and she probably wouldn't be too clingy. But the thought of sleeping with any other women left a bad taste in his mouth.

The mental clock in his head ticked the minutes away. His head shot up and he scanned the room again. Jade wasn't anywhere in the room, and it had been too long since he saw her last. Looking towards their table, he saw the redhead, the blonde, and that cocky kid, but not Jade. The redhead stood up, waving her hands and looking around them.

A bad feeling in his gut hit him instantly. Jade was gone, he could feel it. He shot to his feet, slapped a couple of bills on the table, and quickly slid out of the booth. He remained calm, years of training teaching him that in emergency situations, he had to keep his head on straight or he'd risk losing it. His heartbeat slowed, and his breathing evened. *Think.* Out of habit, he staked out all the exits and entrances as soon as he entered the club earlier that evening.

Sebastian wasn't sure where it was leading him, but he followed that feeling in his gut. He remembered seeing an exit near the back. He stalked towards the hidden hallway behind the stage, which led to the dimly-lit alleyway behind Blood Moon. Opening the door slowly, he sharpened his ears, listening for any strange sounds as he quietly slipped out.

"You're so beautiful, baby," a voice said. "And so sexy."

There was a soft groan. "No, don't...I'm not feeling well... can we go back to my friends, please?"

He wasn't familiar with Jade's voice, but something told him that was her.

"C'mon, baby, don't be like that," the male voice replied. "Just one kiss..."

White hot fury filled his veins and Sebastian stalked towards where the voices were coming from. His vision sharpened as he approached them.

The man had one hand braced against the wall, his body leaning forward. He was blocking Sebastian's view, but he didn't need to see her to know she was there. The scent of her perfume was unmistakable.

"What are you doing?" he asked, trying to keep his voice even.

"Nothing that concerns you, buddy," the man said, turning his head to face him, his features obscured by shadows. "The lady and me were just looking for some privacy. Move along, now."

"Are you sure she wants to be alone with you, *buddy*?" He shot back. "I don't think she's sober enough to be making decisions like that."

The other man turned around, leaving Jade behind him. He swayed slightly as he stretched up to full height, though he was still at least half a foot shorter than Sebastian's. "Look," the man said. "Why don't you just be a bro and leave us alone." He fished his wallet clumsily from his pocket, opening it to take out some bills. "Now, how much will it take to—"

"I suggest you choose your next words carefully," Sebastian warned, crossing his arms over his chest.

"Aw, c'mon—"

"Hey! What's going on here?"

"Jade!" a female voice cried out, followed by the clacking of heels across the concrete.

While he was distracted by the newcomers, Sebastian took the wallet out of the other man's hand. Of course, the man was so drunk and probably high, he could hardly protest.

"Let me repeat my question. What the fuck is going on here?" It was the cocky bastard who was cozying up to Jade earlier. The young man was almost as tall as him, but built on the slim side. Deep brown eyes narrowed at Sebastian. "Who are you?"

"The name's Sebastian Creed," he said, then took out a plastic card from the other man's wallet. "And this is...Mr. David Ronson. 235 West 75th Street, Apartment 4B." He gave the other man a feral smile. "Mr. Ronson was taking your friend out for some fresh air and I think he got a little carried away."

David's face paled and he slunk back. "Hey, it was all a bit of fun. And she wanted it—"

"Remember what I told you about choosing your words carefully, David?"

"Y—y—yes," he choked out. "I mean...shit...fuck this shit! She's not worth the trouble anyway." David shook his head, and looked over towards Jade's direction.

"Don't look at her," Sebastian said, his voice scarily even and cold. "Don't think about her, don't even dream about her. Got that?" Sebastian flashed him an angry look.

"Jesus!" David jumped back, his face twisting in fear. "What's wrong with your...never mind! I knew that new stuff I got from my dealer was shit! It's making me see things!" He rubbed at his eyes and blinked several times.

"Go," Sebastian commanded. "And never show your face here again."

David backed away slowly, and then turned around, picking up his pace as he disappeared down the alley.

Sebastian watched him leave, calmed himself, and then turned around. The redhead and the young man were helping Jade up, as she had slunk down to the ground. Her eyes were half closed, and she was tripping over the ridiculously high heels.

"I'm fine," she muttered. "Just fine." She blinked several times.

"Jade, you're not fine!" The redhead shook her head, pulling at her friend's arms. "If it wasn't for..." She swung her gaze over to Sebastian. Green eyes widened in recognition. "Mr. Creed! What are you doing here?"

"I—uh." He cleared his throat. "I was inside the club and I saw your friend go outside with that man," he quickly explained.

"You guys know this man, Lara?" the tall guy said.

"Yeah, he's...uh..." Lara stammered.

"I'm a contractor with Fenrir," Sebastian said. "I've worked alongside Miss..."

"Chatraine," the redhead said. "Lara Chatraine."

"Yes, sorry. We didn't have time for an introduction that night."

"Yes, we were all quite busy with work," Lara said.

"I'm Enzo. Enzo Moretti," the younger man held out his hand. Sebastian shook it. "Thanks, man. If you hadn't thought to come out here, who knows what would have happened?"

"She and that guy were dancing and then they just disappeared," Lara explained as she wrapped one of Jade's arms over shoulders. "Sorry, she's never been drunk."

"I'm not drunk!" Jade slurred, her head popping up. She

blinked a few times at Sebastian. "Hey..." Luminous light green eyes peered at him. Even in the dim light, he could see the flecks of gold in the middle. "Who are you?" she asked, disentangling herself from Lara. Jade slowly lumbered towards him. "Do I know you?"

Her voice was sexy and low, with a slight English accent he found irresistible. It sent blood straight to his cock, and Sebastian was glad the alley was dim. "We haven't been formally introduced yet, darlin'," he drawled.

"Too bad. Because you are...hot," she said, poking her finger at his chest. "Like, ridiculously hot. And you make me feel all tingly. And you smell good, too. Say," she said, tracing her fingers along his left forearm. "How far do those tattoos go?" Her touch sent shivers over his skin. He didn't think his dick could possibly get harder, but he was proven wrong.

"Uhm, Jade," Lara warned.

"And you are hot, too!" She turned to Enzo, who was standing behind her.

Enzo gave an amused smile. "Oh yeah?"

Sebastian's eyes narrowed at the younger man, his fists clenching.

"And you're always flirting with me," Jade giggled. "You do it on purpose, to make me blush. But I think your twin brother is hotter if that makes sense. But you," she swung back to Sebastian. "You are one sexy son of bucket and I want to climb—"

"Jade!" Lara grabbed her friend and slapped a palm over her mouth. "I think it's time you went home. Before you say anything you'll regret in the morning."

"I'll take her home," Sebastian offered.

"Are you crazy? I'm not letting my friend go home with a stranger!"

"I meant I would take her to her apartment, of course," Sebastian said. "And I'm hardly a stranger."

"But you don't know where she lives."

Sebastian bit his tongue before he could answer, *Yes, I do.*

"And you won't know how to take care of her, either." Lara let out a long sigh. "I'm going to call my fiancé and have him pick us up. I'll stay with her tonight. Enzo, take care of her for a minute. And where is Meredith? If we lost her, Grant will have—" She stopped short as her eyes flickered towards Sebastian. "Um, I'm gonna make that call now," she said, taking her phone out of her purse and turning around as she spoke softly into the receiver.

"C'mon, Jade," Enzo said, putting an arm around the petite woman and guiding her towards the door that led back into Blood Moon.

"Enzooooo..." She blinked at him and then giggled. "Filet mignon. Your DNA is the same as filet mignon," she hiccuped.

Enzo rolled his eyes. "No more tequila for you, young lady."

"But it's sooooo good. That's why I finished the bottle!"

"She finished the whole bottle?" Sebastian roared at the other man. "How is she not dead?"

"Um...good genetics?" Enzo offered. "C'mon, Jade, let's go back inside and find Meredith. Maybe get you some water."

Sebastian frowned as he watched the other man take Jade away. Enzo was way too close to her, and it sent an unfamiliar, tight feeling into his chest, like a fist squeezing around his heart.

"Mr. Creed." Lara caught his attention. "Thank you again for your help."

"Nothing to it. I was just at the right place, at the right time."

"Yes, lucky us, then," she narrowed her eyes at him. "Well, I guess I'll see you around." She turned to walk away.

"Will she be okay?"

Lara gave a small laugh. "She'll sleep it off. My fiancé's on the way, and I'll stay with her tonight so she's not alone."

"She's got good friends," Sebastian remarked. "Especially considering what happened to her."

"Indeed." Lara shrugged and walked away. He detected a hint of hesitation in her voice. Or was she hiding something else?

"Wait," he called and Lara stopped in her tracks. "I know something's going on here." There was the gut feeling again, and he was listening to it this time.

A gust of wind blew through the alley, ruffling Lara's hair. "I don't know what you're talking about."

"Since this began...all of this...it's been fishy. And I'm going to get to the bottom of it. I always find the truth."

Lara huffed and turned around. "Really, now, Mr. Creed?" She crossed her arms over her chest. "Tell me, do you like your life now? The way it is? The reality you live in?"

He shrugged.

"Because, if you do and you don't want things to change, I'm warning you now—stay away from Jade. Stop trying to look at what's beneath the surface." There was a chill in her voice and another gust of wind blew his way. "If you knew the truth, then your world would never be the same."

CHAPTER THREE

J ade opened her eyes slowly as she began to wake up. She was having an amazing dream, but she couldn't remember what it was now. *What time was it?* She yawned and stretched her arm out.

"Ouch!"

Jade was startled by the presence of another body next to her. "Lara?" She blinked twice. Her best friend was on the other side of her bed. "What are you doing here?"

The young witch was rubbing her arm. "Jeez, Jade, you don't remember? Wait, aren't you even hung over?"

She frowned. "Hmm...my head feels kinda...light." She shrugged. "Was I drinking last night?"

"Argh!" Lara sat up, brushing her reddish-gold curls out of her face. "Must be that Lycan metabolism. You drank the rest of the tequila, got stupid drunk, and started dancing on top of the bar with Meredith."

"I...what?" Jade's eyes went wide. "I did not!"

Lara laughed. "Yes, you did! How far back do you remember?"

Jade searched her memories. "Well, we went to Blood Moon

for your party...Meredith had me wearing ridiculous heels...and then there were shots..."

"And you told us wanted to lose your V-card."

"I did not!" Jade's face turned crimson as if someone had set fire to her cheeks. The conversation was slowly starting to come back to her.

"Don't worry. It was just Meredith and me!" Lara assured her. "And how come you never told me about that before, huh?"

"Well, it's not something I bring up in casual conversation!" She tossed a pillow at the other woman, who blocked it with a wave of her hand.

"Don't be embarrassed, Jade. We were all virgins once!"

"Yeah, but to be one for over 24 years is pathetic!" She sighed, then looked over to her bedside table. "Mother Fluffer! It's almost 10 a.m.!" She got to her feet. "Why didn't you wake me up earlier? We're late!"

"Relax, Jade," Lara said, lounging backward on the bed. "You're the boss of the lab, right? And you don't exactly have any other assistants working for you."

"But I have too much work to do!" Jade exclaimed as she rushed into the bathroom. She came out 15 minutes later, a towel wrapped around her. Lara had left her room, so Jade quickly dressed, putting on a long-sleeved white shirt and a khaki skirt and swept her hair up into a neat bun. Grabbing her glasses from her nightstand, she put them on and went out to the living room.

"I borrowed a dress," Lara said as Jade came out. She was wearing one of Jade's long-sleeved floral dresses that came down below her knees. "And I'm meeting Liam at Fenrir."

"Why aren't you with your fiancé by the way?" Jade asked as they left her apartment.

"Well, you could hardly walk home. Liam came to Blood

Moon and then brought us here. I told him I would stay here and take care of you."

"I couldn't walk?" Jade said incredulously.

"Yeah, you lush!" Lara laughed. "Don't you remember what else happened last night? And Sebastian Creed?"

"Who?" Jade blinked in confusion. The name sounded familiar. Was he a famous rock star or something?

"Jesus, Jade!" The witch let out a sigh of exasperation. "Let me refresh your memory." As they left Jade's apartment building and walked to the Fenrir Corporation headquarters, Lara recounted the story of what happened the night before, including their run-in with Sebastian Creed.

"Wait," Jade stopped and faced Lara, adjusting her glasses. "So, I've met this Mr. Creed twice now? And I don't remember?"

Lara's jaw dropped. "Jade, he literally saved you twice."

"Well, apparently, I was drugged the first time and then drunk the second." Jade shook her head. "Anyway, it doesn't matter. I probably won't be running into him. Can you imagine how embarrassing that would be? I don't even remember what he looks like!"

They walked into the Fenrir Corporation lobby and headed straight to the private elevators that would take them to Jade's lab on the 33rd floor. The doors were about to close as they approached the elevator.

"Hold the elevator!" Jade cried as she sprinted forward.

"Jade, we can wait!" Lara called after her friend.

But the Jade didn't want to wait. She was already three hours late and was eager to get back to work. She slapped her palms against the doors to stop them from closing. Unfortunately, she tripped on the gap and went flying into the elevator. In vain, she tried to regain her balance, but ended up on the floor, her ass sticking up. As if it couldn't get any worse, she saw two sets of shoes inches from her nose.

"Jade!" Lara gasped as she saw her friend flat on the floor. "What the he—llo, Mr. Creed. Liam?"

Jade kept her head down, banging her forehead once on the floor.

"Um, sweetie?" Lara bent down to check on Jade.

Jade closed her eyes. "Dear Lord," she muttered. "If you strike me dead now, I promise in my next life I'll devote myself to you. I'll become a nun and do good deeds..."

"What are you doing?" Lara whispered.

"Shhh...I'm praying."

Lara rolled her eyes. "Are you going to get up?"

Jade cracked an eye to see her friend. "No, thanks, I'm fine down here. Hey!" A large pair of hands settled on her waist and picked her up. "Put me down! Stop manhandling me, you brute!" She stumbled away from her attacker as soon as she steadied herself, and then brushed the dust off her outfit. Liam and Lara were standing to her right, their faces a mix of shock and amusement.

She turned her head left, ready to give a dirty look to whoever had pawed at her; however, she was faced with a massive chest. Pushing her glasses up her nose, she looked up at the gigantic man who was staring down at her. Jade held her breath. He was quite possibly one of the most handsome men she'd ever seen—good-looking; masculine features with an edge of roughness; short, dark blonde hair; high cheekbones; and a straight nose. His strong jaw and cheeks were covered with a reddish-blonde beard that was neatly trimmed. He was big, but not in the scary, 'roid rage way. The man was built like a lumberjack, his shoulders and arms straining against his navy suit. Jade was lost in the depths of the dark gray eyes that stared down at her.

A discreet cough jolted Jade, and she took a step back. Lara was biting her lip, trying to hide her smile. "Uh, Jade...this is..."

"Creed. Sebastian Creed." The giant man offered his hand.

"Dr. Jade Cross," she said, hoping her voice didn't sound too breathy. She took his hand, surprised by its warmth. The touch of his skin sent electricity up her arm, making her shiver. His hand engulfed hers and his grip was firm, but she could tell he was holding back. A faint, familiar scent wafted to her nose. Something masculine. Like leather and musk and paper. It reminded her of when she was a child and spent hours reading books in her grandfather's library. *How strange.*

His face broke into a lazy smile. "Nice to finally be formally introduced, darlin'."

Sebastian Creed's drawl sent desire pooling in Jade's belly and the reminder that they had met previously heated her cheeks, as if someone had set them on fire. "Uh, yeah." She nodded stupidly.

Thankfully, the elevator dinged, indicating they had reached the 33rd floor.

"Well, looks like we're here," Jade announced as she sprinted out of the elevator. She made her way to the entrance of the lab, using her code to bypass the retina scanner. It was too slow, and Jade wanted to get away from the elevator as quickly as possible. As soon as she entered the lab, she braced herself on the wall, her chest heaving as she tried to catch her breath.

"What the heck was that?" Lara asked as she followed behind Jade. "Are you okay, hon?"

Jade swallowed a gulp. "Never better," she murmured, brushing past her friend.

"Hey you, late birds!" Meredith called. She was sitting on one of the office chairs, spinning around while waving her arms. "Where have you guys been? I've been waiting for hours.

Look!" She spun again, raising her feet off the ground. "I invented something new. I call it 'Office Chair Ballet'."

"How can you both still be standing after the amount of liquor you had?" Lara asked in an exasperated voice.

"Lycan metabolism," Jade and Meredith answered in unison.

"Ugh, I wish I had one of those back when I was younger," Lara sighed. "Anyway," she turned back to Jade, who was creeping up to her inner lab. "Jade! Tell me what's going on!"

"What's going on?" Meredith asked, pushing herself closer to Jade.

"Ugh." Jade put her hands up. "You are never taking me drinking again!"

"But you were such a fun drunk. We both were!" Meredith pouted. "I was hoping we'd have girls' night all the time now."

"Oh no." Lara shook her head at Meredith. "You are never touching alcohol again! Where did you disappear to last night, after we couldn't find Jade?"

"I checked the bathrooms and then went out front!" the blonde Lycan said defensively. "So, what happened anyway?"

Lara recounted all the events of last night and this morning. Jade's face turned a crimson color as she relived all the memories of her most embarrassing moments in front of Sebastian Creed. Of course, last night didn't compare to her humiliation of this morning, especially after he caught her obviously ogling him. She couldn't help herself. The man was gorgeous, like a sexy lumberjack in a suit. Frankly, she always thought nerdy intellectuals were more her type, but this man who oozed sexuality through his pores set her body on fire. And that voice, that sexy drawl, was enough to make her panties wet. God, she was mortified. He must think she's some spinster nerd who'd never seen a man before. All she needed were the cartoon eyes that popped out of her head.

"Shut the front door! Sebastian Creed is here, and you flashed him your undies?" Meredith howled with laughter. "Were you wearing sexy ones at least? Oh, please tell me you weren't wearing your granny panties."

"I didn't flash him my pants!" Jade protested.

"Just your ass," Lara said as she tried to keep from laughing.

"Shut up," Jade growled and stomped up the stairs to her inner lab and office. She tossed her bag to the side, and sat at her desk in the corner, angrily tapping on the keyboard to boot up her computers.

"Jade," Lara began as she and Meredith entered the inner lab. "We're sorry for making fun of you."

"Yeah, Jadey-girl," Meredith continued, walking up to her. "I'm not being mean, you know. We were just teasing you."

The scientist put her face in her hands. "God, I'm never drinking again."

"Aww, Jade." Meredith patted her back. "C'mon, you're not a quitter, are you?"

Jade looked up at her, her eyes shooting daggers at the other Lycan.

"Now, now, Jade. Don't worry about Sebastian Creed. I'm sure he's seen lots of asses; he won't remember yours."

Jealousy dug into Jade's chest, and then disappointment. Of course, a man like him has probably been with hundreds of women. She pushed away those thoughts.

"So, how's the wedding planning?" Meredith asked Lara.

"We're not doing a big ceremony," the witch replied. "But we've decided on The Conservatory at the New York Botanical Gardens for the reception."

"Oh, that's lovely," Jade said, her face softening. She was really happy her best friend had found happiness with Liam.

"Are we gonna be bridesmaids?"

"Who said you're coming?" Lara teased.

"Aww, c'mon Lara. You need me there to get the party going. I'll be saving up all my good behavior points." She looked at Jade. "And Jade's coming, right? So that means she'll need me there."

"I'm not having bridesmaids for the ceremony, but I supposed you could be unofficial bridesmaids."

"Yay!" Meredith whooped. "We should go dress shopping!" When Jade paled at the mention of shopping, she shook her head. "Oh no, Jade, you're not going to wear just any old thing to this wedding! We're gonna go out at lunch and pick dresses with Lara. Something sexy that will show off your assets!" She motioned to Jade's body.

"I don't think—"

"Besides," Meredith interrupted. "Weddings are the best places to get laid!"

Jade buried her face in her palms and let out a groan. "Oh no..."

"We're on a mission, lady," the other Lycan said. "Let's call it...Operation: Pop That Cherry! PTC for short!"

"Meredith," Lara warned.

"C'mon, Lara, be more helpful! Do you have any cute cousins? How about Liam? Any single friends coming to the wedding? We need to start making a list."

"Can't we forget what I said last night?" Jade groaned. "I don't want my...cherry popped anymore!" At least not just by any man, she added silently. Images of a certain very large, very male body tangled up in hers flashed through her mind, and she felt her face go red again.

"But this is an important mission!"

"Look," Jade sighed, massaging her temple. "I have a lot of work to do. If you guys leave me alone now, I promise, I'll go dress shopping at lunch, OK?"

Meredith's pretty face broke into a smile. "Yes!" she said,

raising her fist in triumph. "Let's leave the good doctor to her work then." She grabbed Lara by the arm and dragged her out of the inner lab.

"Finally," Jade muttered to herself. With a deep breath, she pushed aside all thoughts of Sebastian Creed and started her work.

———

Sebastian's gaze followed Jade's retreating form as she scampered away like a scared rabbit.

"Honestly, I don't know what's going on with her today!" Lara Chatraine exclaimed.

"Did she sleep okay, sweetheart?" Liam Henney asked the redhead.

"She wasn't even hungover." Lara pouted. Liam laughed, and they shared a look that conveyed a silent message.

Sebastian cleared his throat. "Ms. Chatraine, nice to see you again."

Lara gave him a smirk. "You too, Mr. Creed."

A heavy feeling suddenly filled the elevator, and Liam stepped closer to Lara, placing a protective arm around her. "You've met?" he asked, electric blue eyes trained on the other man.

"Don't you remember, Liam?" Lara said. "When you picked us up last night, I told you someone scared away the douche bag who cornered Jade. Didn't I mention it was Mr. Creed who saved her?"

"No," Liam frowned. "You forgot to mention that. What else happened during this bachelorette party of yours?"

"I'll tell you another time." She gave him a kiss on the cheek. "I'll see you later." She left the elevator, the doors closing behind her.

Sebastian gave a sigh of relief as the tightness in his chest lightened. So Liam Henney was the fiancé Lara Chatraine was talking about. That at least answered one question—Jade was definitely not Liam's woman. Since he'd been following her around, he knew she wasn't seeing anyone else either. The thought that she was free sent his mind whirling. Seeing her today, with her pert little ass sticking up the air, made his dick hard as steel. Her outfit and those glasses made him think of dirty librarian fantasies. And to think, he'd already jerked himself off in the shower that morning when his morning wood hadn't let up. He thought of Jade, of driving into her sweet body, and he didn't last long. Fuck, he hadn't blown his load that fast since he was a teenager, yet the image of Jade, naked in his bed, sent the cum shooting from his cock so hard he went dizzy.

"Sebastian? We're here," Liam said, interrupting his thoughts.

Sebastian adjusted his belt, glad he wore his suit jacket closed, or Liam would have noticed the erection he was sporting. He wondered if it was in poor taste to jerk off in a potential client's bathroom.

The two men walked out of the elevator and into the penthouse offices of Fenrir Corporation. Sebastian was surprised to get a personal call from Grant Anderson himself, asking if he was available to meet today about a another possible job. Sebastian was glad he asked his assistant to cancel all his meetings so he could make it, especially since he was finally able to meet a conscious and more sober Jade Cross.

"Mr. Henney, Mr. Creed." The young man waiting outside the main office doors greeted them. "I'm Jared, Mr. Anderson's admin. He's ready for you, but can I bring you some water or coffee?"

"No thank you, Jared," Liam said, while Sebastian shook his head.

"Very well, please go right ahead."

Liam opened the doors to Grant's office. The room was enormous and had floor-to-ceiling windows with a view of Central Park. Sebastian didn't pay attention to the view, though. Out of habit, he checked how secure the room was, how many possible exits there were, and the ways his enemies could sneak up on him or use any of the items in the room as weapons. Satisfied he had covered all the bases, he turned to the desk in the middle of the room, where Grant Anderson was sitting. The other man stood up and walked over to them.

"Sebastian, glad you could make it," Grant said, offering his hand to the other man.

"I was intrigued," Sebastian admitted, shaking his hand. "I wasn't sure you'd want to work together again."

Liam and Grant looked at each other, and Sebastian's brows knitted. Did everyone at Fenrir have some secret language? He couldn't help but feel like they all knew something he didn't.

Grant motioned for them to sit on the chairs in front of his desk. "Well, Liam, Nick, and I were talking about it, and after our last operation, we realized we could use a firm like Creed Security, and someone like you, on our side."

"Not getting into more trouble, are you?" Sebastian asked with a smile.

Grant let out a short laugh. "Oh no. We're just short-handed, that's all. And it's just not feasible for us right now to invest in our own security force."

"I see." Sebastian leaned back and rubbed his jaw. "Well, we can sort out the details, I'm sure. I'm actually not too involved in the business side of things."

"But you are very hands-on when it comes to the security part," Grant said. "Which is what I like. It would be nice to know you're personally taking care of any of our requests."

Sebastian nodded. "Of course."

"Great," Liam said. "The first job we need you to do is help secure my wedding reception."

"Sebastian's not into weddings," Grant quipped.

"It's not the wedding, it's the idea of marriage," Sebastian corrected. "But I'm happy for you, Liam. Ms. Chatraine seems to be a lovely young woman."

"She is," Liam answered with a grin.

"Are you expecting any trouble at your wedding? Afraid of old boyfriends or girlfriends crashing it and stopping the ceremony?"

Liam laughed. "No, no, nothing of the sort. But we do have some VIPs. My family from San Francisco is coming, plus some business associates, partners, venture capitalists, you know. I'd like to feel confident they'll all be safe and secure."

"Simple enough job," Sebastian said. "Nothing we haven't handled before. In fact, we've done two celebrity weddings in the last year. My partner and I will oversee it personally. I'll also have some of my guys blend in with the guests, if that's okay?"

"You do whatever you need to do to keep us safe," Liam agreed.

"I'll have my lawyers contact yours, and my assistant can work out the other details."

———

Jade tapped her fingers on her chin as she looked at the old, yellowed texts projected on her screen. Vivianne Chatraine, Lara's mother and head of the New York coven of witches and warlocks, had sent over some books from their private library for her to study. However, most of the texts were so old and worn, Jade instead decided to scan all the contents and keep digital copies. It was also much easier to catalogue them, though it had taken weeks. Now that that the last of the volumes had been scanned, she could breathe easier knowing she could return them to Vivianne. The books, after all, didn't just contain knowledge of magic, but were also heirlooms and historical artifacts of the New York coven.

She sat back in her chair, rubbing her tired eyes. Jade never thought she'd end up here. After finishing her two PhDs in biochemistry and bioengineering, she had been surprised to get a call from Grant Anderson, her Alpha. Technically, since she was born in New York, he was her Alpha, even though she moved to England with her mother after her parents divorced. She was twenty years old then, and Grant had an interesting proposition for her: come back to the States and help them study magic.

At first, she had been skeptical. As a Lycan shifter, she knew magic existed and it was not very different from science. However, she wasn't sure where to begin to study magic. Witches were very secretive and everyone knew they would never share their knowledge, especially not with Lycans. While she didn't say yes right away to Grant's offer, she didn't say no either. After all, she had just finished her PhDs and had never had any real-life working experience. So, she worked at a bioengineering firm in London for the next two years.

The whole time, however, the Alpha's offer kept niggling at her, always at the back of her mind, until, one day, she decided to take it. She moved to New York and helped set up the 33rd floor lab dedicated to studying magic. At first, she was hitting walls. She collected as much knowledge as she could from just reading books, journals, old newspaper clippings, whatever she could get her hands on. But without any other sources, or any witches willing to talk to her, she couldn't further her research.

All of that changed, however, when Alynna Westbrooke (or Chase, before she married Alex) came into the picture. It turned out Alynna was the secret love child of Michael Anderson, New

York's former Alpha, and his True Mate, Amanda Chase. The one downside to being a werewolf shifter was that their kind was not very fertile. Most couples didn't have any children, and if they did, few had more than one. Also, Lycans who mated with humans didn't produce Lycan children.

The one exception was True Mates. When a Lycan found his or her True Mate, they were guaranteed a child the first time they had sex without any physical contraception. Alynna grew up not knowing she was a Lycan, seeing as Michael had died before he could introduce Alynna to the clan. Alynna suddenly showed up at Blood Moon one day where she met Alex, who also turned out to be her True Mate. After she got pregnant, they discovered one more interesting thing about True Mates: the unborn children protected their mothers, making them indestructible. Alynna survived a poisoning attempt by an assassin.

This also started the trouble with the mages. Mages were former witches who used Blood Magic. As much as witches did not like Lycans, the mages hated them even more. They plotted to destroy the Lycans and even stop True Mates from finding each other. When the mages kidnapped Cady Vrost, her aunt Vivianne and cousin Lara teamed up with the Lycans to rescue her. That was also when the Witch and Lycan alliance began. Jade's research and study flourished, especially since she had Lara to help her with her experiments, as well as Vivianne's knowledge. Her studies into magic were still a secret from the Lycan High Council and the Witch Assembly. The two governing bodies had a tenuous truce, but they were slowly starting to work together, especially with the mages now growing bolder. The mages now had figured out how to control humans and had recently built an army of human slaves to do their bidding.

Jade gave an involuntary shiver and immediately shut down

the screen. She was the target of the mages, after all, and her time as their captive was still muddy in her mind. Her assistant had been feeding the mages information about her work, which is why their leader, Stefan, had her kidnapped. She was taken, put in a van, and then drugged. Actually, she didn't remember a lot of her time in captivity, which was, perhaps, a small blessing. The Lycans worked to get her back, of course, and apparently, Grant has asked Sebastian Creed for help in rescuing her.

Sebastian Creed. She cringed, thinking of him. God, it was embarrassing and such awful luck on her part. Oh well, she shouldn't dwell on it. It's not like she'd ever see him again.

"Jade!" Meredith called.

"What?" she asked.

"You said we can go shopping at lunch! It's now exactly 12 noon!"

"Ugh!" Jade exclaimed. "Fine. Let's go." Let the torture begin.

CHAPTER FOUR

The guests gathered around the entrance to The Conservatory, cheering loudly as soon as the doors opened and the happy couple strode in. Lara looked especially lovely in her simple white dress, and she blushed prettily as Liam wrapped her in his arms, dipped her, and gave her a kiss. The crowd burst into applause and whoops, stretching on and on as Liam refused to let go of his bride.

"Congratulations!" Jade greeted as Liam and Lara walked over to her a few minutes later. She wrapped her best friend in a tight hug and gave the groom a kiss on the cheek. "You take care of her, now, you hear?" she teased. "Or you'll answer to me!"

Liam laughed. "I promise. And if I don't, I'll hand myself over to you on a silver platter."

She gave him a playful shove. "All right, go and greet your guests!"

As they left, Jade let out a sigh and looked around her. The reception was gorgeous, and it was fitting. Surrounded by nature, it was the perfect place for a witch and a Lycan to celebrate their union. She shook her head. When did she become so poetic?

"Jade?" a familiar voice said from behind.

Spinning around, she found herself staring into friendly, chocolate brown eyes. "Matt!" she greeted. "How are you? Did you just get here?"

Matteo Moretti nodded and flashed her a shy smile. "Yeah, just got here with Enzo," he nodded his head across the room where a bunch of women were surrounding his twin brother. "He loves weddings."

"I bet," Jade giggled.

"Do you want to get a drink or something?" Matt said, offering his arm.

"Sure," she said, placing her hand on his arm as they walked towards the bar. When they got there, the line was three deep, and they waited their turn.

"You look real nice," Matt remarked, his eyes roving over her before settling back on her face. Gentleman that he was, his eyes never lingered too long on one spot.

"Oh, thank you," she said with a blush. She had to admit she was glad she went shopping with Lara and Meredith. Initially, the other Lycan wanted matching dresses, but Jade was sure what would look good on Meredith wouldn't look good on her. So instead, they decided on matching colors—a pretty pastel yellow that complimented both their skin tones. Meredith had chosen a strappy and daring dress that was slashed up to her thighs, showing off her long legs. Jade, on the other hand, had chosen a flowing, off-the-shoulder chiffon dress with a sweetheart neckline, which she paired with low-heeled sandals. Meredith styled her long, brown locks into cascading waves down her back and put on some of the makeup they bought for the bachelorette party. When the other Lycan was done and she looked at herself in the mirror, Jade hardly recognized herself. She actually felt attractive, and judging by the stares she'd been getting all night, other people, men in particular, thought so, too.

"You look nice too, Matt," Jade said. Tonight, he was dressed more casually in a light gray suit jacket with matching pants and blue shirt opened at the collar to show off the olive-toned skin at his throat. The last time she saw him at Frankie and Grant's wedding, he was wearing a formal black tux. She thought he was kinda hot then, and though he certainly looked handsome, something was different about him tonight. His hand over the small of her back didn't even do anything to her. He was just...Matt.

"Hey, bro," Enzo said as he bounded over to them. "Ooh! It's the hot doctor! She's back!" he joked, which made Matt send him a warning look.

"Enjoying yourself?" Matt asked his twin.

"Of course! I love weddings! It's the best place to score!" Another glare from Matt made him laugh. "Sorry...I mean, you know! These chicks, surrounded by all this wedding shit! They love it! Gets them all fired up!"

"Sorry about my brother, Jade." Matt shook his head.

Jade laughed. "Don't worry about it."

"Yeah, so..." Enzo began. "I'm talking to these two chicks, right? And guess what? They're twins!" he said excitedly. "But they don't believe me when I tell them I'm a twin too!"

"What's your point, Enzo?"

"You gotta come with me and show them!" Enzo begged. "Please?"

Matt gave Jade an expectant look.

"Um...Go ahead, Matt," Jade said. "I'm going to get a drink and then check on Lara. See if she needs anything. I am her bridesmaid, after all."

Matt flashed her an apologetic smile. "All right. I'll find you later, okay? Maybe we can dance or something."

"Sure," she said, putting on her best smile. Enzo tugged his brother by the arm, and as soon as they left, she gave a relieved sigh.

What the fudge was wrong with her? She shook her head. Matt was obviously interested in...something. This was what she wanted, right? Matt Moretti was kind, handsome, and she thought he was hot. Well, thought, as in, past tense. Now, he seemed so...brotherly. Maybe it was the idea that seeing Matt naked would mean she would also see Enzo naked, which was just plain weird. She wondered what it was like for people who married a twin.

"Miss?" the bartender asked. The line of people in front of her disappeared. "Did you want anything?"

"Oh yeah...uhm, how about a margarita?"

"Sure thing." The bartender turned around to make her drink.

"Starting a little early, aren't we?" A low voice behind her said.

Jade felt the hairs on her arms stand on end. She'd only heard that voice once, but instantly knew who it was. Slowly, she pivoted towards the voice. "Mr. Creed." She nodded. She quickly turned back to the bar, though it was a feat of strength to not ogle him. Dear Lord, he looked impossibly handsome in his dark navy suit and white shirt, she thought.

"Ms. Cross."

"It's Dr. Cross," she corrected, doing an about face to look at him straight in the eyes. How dare he question her choice of drinks! She was an adult. Or was he reminding her of their unfortunate first (or was it second?) meeting?

"Doctor, then," he said, as his eyes raked over her.

Unlike Matt's polite perusal, Sebastian's gaze was anything but gentlemanly. His dark eyes were the color of storm clouds now, and Jade could feel the heat in them as he lingered over the curves of her body. She gave a huff, ignoring the way his bold appraisal sent thrills of excitement through her.

"Did your date leave you?" Sebastian continued. "I think he's talking to those blondes over there," he cocked his head towards Enzo and Matt, who were, indeed, chatting with a pair of gorgeous blonde twins. "Doesn't seem right to leave a lady like you all alone."

"He's not my date, and it's rude of you to insinuate he would be so uncouth as to leave me by myself if he were," she bristled. She grabbed the drink from the bartender and took a delicate sip, the cool liquid a contrast to the sudden anger she felt. "Furthermore, I'll thank you to never remind me of that night at Blood Moon. I was very happy for my friend, and we were celebrating. I'm sorry you judged me to be some lush who can't control her drinking, but that's not who I am. Now, have a good evening, Mr. Creed." Jade slammed the glass down on the bar and sauntered away, suddenly losing her taste for the drink. She heard a soft curse behind her, but she kept on walking. What had gotten into her? What he said and the way he said it put her on the defensive. It was like he was angry at her, but she didn't even do anything. For fox's sake, she hardly said two words to the man before tonight. And the way he looked at Matt was frightening.

"Jade! Wait!" Sebastian called, but she ignored him, walking out one of the glass doors that led into the main gardens.

The sun had just set, leaving pink and blue streaks in the distance and she followed the path around the pond filled with water lilies and lotus plants, not sure where she was going. Heavy footsteps followed behind her and she picked up her pace. By the time she reached the end of the pond, the footsteps were right at her heels.

"Jade, stop!" Sebastian's voice boomed in her ear, and a warm hand wrapped around her upper arm.

"Let go of me!" She tried to pull away, but his grip was too strong.

"Look, I'm sorry!" He let go of her, sending her toppling backward. She regained her balance on her own, and he rubbed his face in a frustrated manner. "Shit. Fuck, shit! Motherfucker, I didn't mean...fuck!"

"Mr. Creed, if you're trying to apologize, you're doing a poor job of it."

"Fuck! I mean, Jade..." he paused and took a breath. "Look. About what I said. I'm sorry, I was out of line."

"You sure were, Mr. Creed," she said in a cold voice.

"Sebastian. My name is Sebastian," he said.

She paused. "Fine. Sebastian, I accept your apology." She turned around, intending to head back to the party. Then she realized she was going the wrong way and froze in her tracks. *Oh fiddlesticks.* She stepped back, hoping to make her way back to The Conservatory, but collided with Sebastian instead.

Two warm hands grabbed at her shoulders, brushing her hair aside. "Hey, I—" Sebastian stopped, and his hand stilled. "Is that a—"

Jade cringed, realizing what he had seen. She whipped around, brushing her hair over her back. "Don't, please," she whispered, turning her face away from her.

"Jade." He moved closer to her, slowly, as if he were approaching a wounded animal. He tugged at his left sleeve, revealing the beginnings of a sleeve tattoo.

Something about the tattoo seemed familiar. Had she seen it before? A flash of a memory came back to her. Oh Lord, she remembered asking him how far it went.

"Show me yours?" he asked, cocking his head to the side.

Jade frowned. "That's rather...forward, isn't it?"

He shrugged and said nothing, but waited for her answer expectantly.

She should walk away now. She had never shown anyone the tattoo on her back, and always wore shirts or dresses that covered it up. The memories were just too painful.

Sebastian waited patiently. With a sigh, she brushed her hair over her one shoulder and turned her back to him. It was an intimate gesture, and as a Lycan, she knew showing someone your back was no small matter. He was human, though, so he probably didn't understand the meaning of such an act.

Warm, rough fingers traced the whorls and lines of ink on her back. The dress revealed only the top part of the design, covering the rest of it, as well as the shameful scars the ink was hiding.

"What is it?" he asked in a low, rough voice, the rough pads of his fingers lazily stroking her skin.

"It's the Tree of Life, but it's done in lines," she said. His fingers were branding her as they touched her, sending heat straight into her core.

"What does it mean?"

"Well, the Tree of Life is a symbol from different mythologies and religions—"

"No, Jade," he said, his lips moving close to her ear. "I know what the Tree of Life is. What does it mean to you? All tattoos have a meaning."

She opened her mouth, then stopped.

"It's okay." He pulled away and brushed her hair back in place. "You don't have to tell me now."

They stood in silence for a moment before Sebastian spoke up. "I wanted to say sorry for being a jackass and make it up to you."

She raised a brow. "How?"

He flashed her a smile, the first she'd seen on his face. Slipping his hand into his coat pocket, he took out a bottle filled with honey-colored liquid.

She laughed. "Did you steal some liquor from the bar?"

"Don't worry, I tipped the bartender generously to look away," he said, his eyes twinkling.

"Are you sure you want to get me drunk?" she asked wryly.

"This isn't about getting drunk, darlin'."

God, his voice sent shivers through her body, and the way he called her darling made her want to melt into a puddle. Was everything the man did sexy? "Then what is it about?"

"Just enjoying the taste of good bourbon." He took her hand and started leading her away from The Conservatory.

"Where are we going?"

"Somewhere we can enjoy this more," he said cryptically.

Jade allowed him to drag her off, though she had to take longer steps to keep up with him. When Sebastian noticed her struggling, he gave her an apologetic look and walked slower to match her strides.

They didn't go very far, just farther south of The Conservatory, to a row of smaller glass houses. Sebastian opened the door to the first one.

"Are we supposed to be here?" she asked, looking around.

"Do you always follow the rules, Doctor?" He looked at her with a devilish smile, then flipped on one of the switches beside the door.

Jade gasped as light filled the greenhouse. They were surrounded by a multitude of orchids and tropical plants in different colors. "It's beautiful," she said, her eyes going wide. "Oh, my! Some of these plants, I've only read about!" She peered at one of the orchids, a delicate-looking flower in purple and yellow. "Thank you," she said, looking up at him gratefully.

"I'm glad you like it," he said. "Now," he opened the cap of the bottle. "This is top shelf bourbon. I don't have a glass, so we'll have to make do. Have a sniff and tell me what you smell."

Jade pressed her nose to the rim of the bottle. "Hmmm..."

Her sensitive Lycan senses picked up several notes immediately. "Vanilla...a hint of caramel. Figs?" She shook her head. "No... dates. Some black pepper and cinnamon. And maybe...oak?"

He gave her a surprised look. "Wow. That's pretty good. Have you had bourbon before?"

She shook her head. "No, I don't drink a lot. I have the occasional wine with dinner and uh...the tequila from that night. That's about it."

"You must have a good sense of smell then," he remarked.

"Uh, yeah." Maybe she shouldn't have shown off. Humans weren't supposed to know about Lycans, after all.

"Now comes the fun part." He pushed the bottle lower. She hesitated, but then pressed her lips to the rim. He tipped it and let a small amount of liquid dribble into her mouth.

"What do you taste?" he asked in a rough voice, his eyes trained on her lips. "Just swirl it in your mouth before you swallow."

Heat spread through her body, and she was sure it wasn't just the bourbon. She let the liquid flow over her palate before she drank it all down. "Uh...it's like...toffee and butter. It's a little on the sweet side, but also some spice."

He a sip himself, and she couldn't help but stare at his lips wrapped around the rim, and the way his Adam's apple bobbed as he swallowed. "Good," he said, putting the bottle down. "I agree. Definitely sweet and a little spicy."

The temperature around her spiked and Jade stumbled, her back hitting the empty shelves behind her. She took a deep breath, and got a whiff of his delicious scent, like a mix of musk and leather.

"Jade," he said in a hoarse voice as he moved closer to her. His hands braced themselves on either side of her, trapping her like a caged animal.

She tried to open her mouth, but nothing came out.

"Tell me something." He leaned down close and whispered in her ear. "How many people have seen that tattoo of yours?"

"Just two people, including myself," she answered. "And the artist. So that's three, I suppose."

"You mean four," he said with a low growl.

She tried to turn away as his head moved towards her, but his large fingers dug into her hair, forcing her still. His firm mouth, hot and wanting, landed on hers and she felt all the air leaving her lungs. The small hairs of his beard tickled her delicate skin, making her shiver all over. She sighed against him, and he used the opportunity to slip his tongue between her lips. He tasted like the bourbon, a mix of toffee and caramel, and something else that was male and spicy.

His hands grabbed her hips, lifting her up as if she weighed nothing and perched her up on the shelf. Spreading her knees apart, he moved between her legs, pressing his hips against her. She gasped and then moaned as something hard pressed against her core. Sebastian let out guttural sound as he began to grind his erection against her.

Jade whimpered, suddenly hating all the layers of fabric between them. She wound her arms around his neck to pull him closer, wanting to devour his mouth and tongue.

Sebastian pulled his mouth away and traced it down to her jaw and her neck. One hand crept up her ribs, then higher to cup one of her breasts. She moaned as his hand tugged down her dress, exposing her to the cool air. Rough fingers rolled her hard nipples, and she bucked against him, crying out as his erection brushed against her just right.

"Sebastian," she mewled, rubbing against him harder. Her body tightened and pleasure spread through her. Her panties were definitely soaked and she angled her hips, seeking that delicious friction against her hardened clit.

"Fuck, Jade...you're so fuckin' sexy," he growled against her neck. His tongue darted out, licking the soft skin right where her neck and her shoulders connected.

"Please, Sebastian." She wasn't sure what she was begging for, but her body felt so good.

"Jade...Sweet Jade..." he whispered over and over again. He grabbed a fistful of her skirt, tossed it up, and shoved his hands between her legs.

"Yes!" she cried out, her fingers threading through his hair.

Sebastian captured her mouth with his again, devouring and tasting her as his hand shoved her panties aside. He traced his finger against her soaking slit, pressing against her nether lips. Slowly, he pushed against her, and she let out a moan as his finger entered her.

"So wet and tight...Jesus, Jade!" he rasped. "How long since...?"

"Hmmmm..." The pleasure buzzing in her head and her body made her feel drunk. "Never," she moaned.

"Jade..." He pressed his lips against hers, but suddenly, his eyes flew open and he froze in place.

She whimpered in disappointment and pushed her body against his. Her body craved his warmth and the pleasure he gave.

"What?" He pulled away from her, his eyes growing dark. "What do you mean?"

"Please," she begged, pulling him closer, but he was like a statue, unmoving. The blood in her veins cooled, and she suddenly felt like someone tossed a bucket of cold water over her. "Sebastian? What's wrong?"

"Are you a...You've never..."

Her cheeks reddened in mortification. "I..." What was she supposed to say? *Yes, Sebastian, I'm a virgin. Sorry about rubbing myself all over you, I couldn't help myself.* Unable to speak, she nodded.

"Jesus!" His eyes widened, then he shut them tight. He backed away, burying his face in his hands. "Why didn't you tell me?"

"I just did!" she exclaimed. "What's wrong?"

"Fuck! I can't...I'm sorry. This isn't going to work." He pivoted and walked away, the door to the greenhouse slamming behind him.

And just like that, she was alone. The sudden silence in the greenhouse made her ears buzz. What the heck was that about?

Jade hopped off the shelf, brushing the skirt of her dress over her legs and then pulled up the front over her breasts. The humiliation was too much. Her insides felt like they were breaking apart. The sting of Sebastian's rejection and the look on his face when he found out she was a virgin was branded in her mind. Hot tears pooled in her eyes, but she brushed them off, letting the rage burn through her instead.

"Bastard!" she cried out and then covered her mouth in surprise. She hardly ever cursed, but she supposed it was warranted. Sebastian Creed *was* a bastard. She should probably thank him for running away before he did get a chance to take her virginity.

Straightening herself up, she walked out of the greenhouse with her head held high. Screw Sebastian Creed. Or rather, don't screw him. He could rot in hell for all she cared.

CHAPTER FIVE

"Master?" Victoria Chatraine called quietly.

"Come in," Stefan said. His back was turned to her, and he was gazing outside. "What news do you have for me?"

"Our two remaining puppet masters are hard at work," she said, referring to the mages who had the power to control their human slaves. "But we will need to find more men to launch any type of attack and to protect us."

The sound of breaking glass pierced the air as Stefan flung his wine glass across the room. "Do it then! Find me more men!" He turned around, his red-tinged eyes blazing at her.

"I'm doing my best, Master," Victoria cowered. "But I'm not...I mean, I don't have Daric's powers."

"But you have other talents, right my dear?" he sneered. "I don't care what it takes."

Victoria nodded. "Yes, Master. But, about Daric."

"What about him?" Stefan asked.

"We know he's probably either at Fenrir or The Enclave. Aren't we going to try and rescue him?"

"I supposed. But he's good where he is for now. He may be of use to us."

Victoria's brows knitted in confusion. "I don't understand, Master."

Stefan laughed. "That clever little Lycan scientist thought she dampened his powers. And she did, but Daric is much more talented than they think. He has powers beyond that of blessed warlocks. Soon we will be able to put our greatest plan in place yet."

Victoria gasped. "You mean...you're in contact with him?"

He gave her a sly smile. "The connection between us is not as strong as it used to be, but it's there. The Lycans were able to diminish his active abilities, but not his innate ones."

"You don't mean...Daric is a seer? But I thought those were myths!"

Stefan shook his head. "No my dear. There are two left in the world."

"Even more reason to get him back!" Victoria hissed. "The Lycans might discover his powers and use it against us. Don't forget, they have Marcus, too."

"Yes, our most talented puppet master. Too bad he let his ego get in the way. We could have had a major victory against the Lycans if it weren't for his incompetence," Stefan spat.

"What's our next move, Master?" Victoria asked. "Marcus is probably giving them our secrets. He definitely gave them our last location. And with Daric in their hands too...that clever little scientist of theirs and my sister might figure out how we're controlling the humans."

"That's why we need more of our puppets," Stefan sneered. "No more games. Get rid of the Lycan scientist first. Her loss will tear them apart and make them sloppy. Then, once Daric is ready, we can take him back."

CHAPTER SIX

"Jade! Shut the music off!"

The faint sound of pounding on the door was enough to jar Jade out of her trance. "Music, off!" she commanded to her voice-activated assistant. The music immediately ceased, and she shot up from her desk and stomped over to the door, flinging it open. "What?!" she exclaimed.

"Really, Jade? Metallica?" Meredith asked, her arms crossed over her chest.

"It helps me think!" she said impatiently. "What do you want?"

"My, aren't you grouchy?" the other Lycan smirked.

Jade tapped her foot impatiently. "Well?"

"Aren't you done yet? Don't you wanna go home?"

"No, I'm not done. It's only..." She looked at the clock. "Eleven p.m.?"

"That's right. You've been locked up in here for over 12 hours! That's the longest yet this week!"

"I have important work to do," Jade huffed.

"Well, you're not going to be doing much work if you're fainting from hunger and exhaustion. Now, let's get you home."

Meredith tugged at her arm. "No one else is around to take you back, and I need to return to my cell and get my beauty sleep."

Jade winced inwardly at the word "cell." She sometimes forgot Meredith was practically a prisoner at Fenrir. That was partly why she let the former thief bully her and take her shopping. Of course, the other Lycan did deserve the punishment for trying to steal from Fenrir, but after getting to know her, Jade realized Meredith was a good person and she actually liked her. She'd been meaning to ask Alynna if it was possible to move Meredith out of her cell at Fenrir and maybe to The Enclave, the New York Lycan's headquarters and home base where most of the clan lived. That way, she could feel less like a prisoner.

"Fine," Jade said with a sigh. "Let me close up, okay? And I am kinda hungry. How about burgers and fries at the diner on 3rd Avenue?"

The blonde's eyes lit up. "Alright! I'll check in with security and let them know where we're going. I'll be downstairs."

Jade gave her a faint smile and went back to her desk. She reached up over her head, feeling the muscles in her back stretch. Lord, had it been over 12 hours? Did she even move? Her stomach gurgled. Her last meal was lunch.

She gave another sigh as she saved her work and turned off her computer. Work was the only thing that helped keep her occupied. To keep her from reliving that night. She drove herself to exhaustion each day so her mind was too tired to think. It hurt too much, thinking about Sebastian's rejection. The bastard didn't even look at her, and then ran away.

Jade wished she could talk to someone about it, but it was too humiliating. Besides, she had to move on. Maybe it was better for her to concentrate on work and forget about sex and men. She had been right all along—emotions just muddled her up and were too complicated. She should just live the rest of her life surrounded by her books and experiments and data. At least she could rely on them.

"Jade!" Meredith's impatient voice rang out.

"Coming!" she replied, grabbing her purse.

Meredith was waiting by the foot of the stairs. "C'mon, those burgers aren't going to eat themselves!"

"Yes, yes," Jade said as she took the steps two at a time. "Let's go."

They locked up the lab and went straight to the elevators. The Fenrir lobby was quiet this time of night, and they waved to the lone guard sitting at the reception desk as they left the building. They walked east, heading towards the diner on 3rd Avenue and 35^{8h} St.

"What's going on, Jade?" Meredith asked as they walked along the quiet streets of Midtown. The area was mostly offices, so at this time of night, there weren't a lot of people around.

Jade was dumbstruck by her question. "What do you mean?"

"Look, I know I'm not Lara," she said. "But, you can...talk to me, you know?" She gave Jade a small smile. "I didn't have female friends...or any friends growing up. And well, I'd like to think we're sort of...I mean, kind of...friends."

Jade stopped and looked at Meredith. She never asked about the other Lycan's background or what her childhood was like. All she knew was Meredith was designated a Lone Wolf, which in the Lycan world meant she had no clan and had to wear a mark to show her status. There weren't a lot of Lone Wolves, but it was sometimes necessary. Some clans were too small and eventually died out since Lycans didn't reproduce so easily. If there was one or two left in a clan, they either had to join another clan or become Lone Wolves. Most clans were eager to accept new members, but it wasn't always easy.

"Jade?" Meredith frowned.

"Yes. I mean, yes, we're friends," Jade declared.

Meredith gave her a big smile and linked their arms together. "Great! Now, will you tell me what's going on with you?"

Maybe it would help to talk. "Fine. But let's get some food first. I'm famished!"

They laughed and continued to walk with Meredith chatting away as Jade listened. As they rounded the corner near their destination, Meredith suddenly stopped.

"What's wrong?" Jade asked.

Meredith's eyes turned dark and then began to glow. Jade froze and as she held onto her friend's arm. With her own enhanced senses, Jade could hear what set off her friend. Footsteps getting louder. Several sets of feet, but how many, Jade couldn't say.

"Jade, listen to me carefully." Meredith's voice was barely a whisper. "When I say run, you run, okay? Head back to Fenrir and alert the security team. They'll know what to do."

She held onto Meredith's arms tighter. "I'm not going to leave you."

"I can handle this," she assured Jade. "But, if you get cornered, you give them hell!"

"What?" she blinked in confusion.

"You know...shift into your badass she-wolf and protect yourself. Don't let them take you again."

Fear gripped her, and her body froze. "Meredith, I can't," Jade cried.

"Yes, you can," Meredith said. "Don't worry. The clan will take care of everything if someone sees you. One drop of confusion potion and our secret stays safe."

Jade shook her head. "That's not what I mean. I can't shift." And there it was. Her dirty little secret.

"What?" the other Lycan exclaimed. "What...shit! They're here!"

Half a dozen men wearing black fatigues approached them from up ahead. They moved slowly, in unison, their heavy boots pounding on the pavement like thunder as they moved closer.

"Fuck!" Meredith cursed. "Run back to Fenrir! I'll hold them off!"

"But Mer-"

"Go!" Meredith pushed her away, and then she advanced toward the group of men. "Run, Jade!"

Heart pounding in her chest, Jade swung around and ran as fast as her two legs could take her. The sound of heavy boots coming closer was like drumbeats hammering in her ear, and her lungs burned as she tried to suck in more air.

Despite having lived in New York for two years, the city confused her. She never left midtown, and she only went to work, her apartment, and the surrounding areas. She thought she was smart, trying to lose her pursuers by weaving up and down the nearly empty streets of Manhattan; however, Jade realized she was lost. The large, unfamiliar buildings loomed overhead, and as she turned a corner and walked down a dark alleyway, she saw a tall, chain link fence ahead. Her heart suddenly stopped, and her brain registered the direness of her situation. She was trapped.

The footsteps grew closer and louder. As Jade made an about-face, she saw a man in black stalking towards her.

God, she was pathetic. She spent years denying her she-wolf, pushing it deep down inside her until she could no longer hear it or feel it. Tears sprang to her eyes. Jade had betrayed her wolf, and now when she needed her, she couldn't even summon a whimper or cry.

Jade gasped in pain as he grabbed her arm and pushed her to her knees, her skin scraping against the rough concrete. She bowed her head down and felt cold, hard steel press against her temple. Dear Lord, the mages weren't going to kidnap her. They wanted to kill her.

The gun cocked, and Jade took a deep breath, waiting for the blackness of death. Her enhanced hearing could pick up everything. The man's breathing, the pressure of his finger on the trigger, the sound of approaching footsteps.

Suddenly, Jade fell over, a heavy weight pushing on her as her back hit the ground. She screamed and rolled away, then scrambled up onto her feet.

Two figures were struggling on the ground, their arms over their heads as they fought for the single gun. They were moving fast, and Jade was confused. One of them grabbed at the other's shoulders, pushing him down as he grabbed the weapon.

She let out another scream as the man on top brought the gun down on the other, clocking him on the head. Her attacker didn't make a sound, but instead, rolled his head back and went still.

The other man cursed and got to his feet. He swung over to Jade, and began to walk towards her.

"Stay away from me!" she hissed.

"Ma'am, no!" The man shoved the gun into his jacket and then held his hands up. "I'm here to help you, Dr. Cross!"

"Who sent you?" she said, scrambling to her feet. "And how do you know my name?"

"My boss! I mean, our company was hired to keep an eye on you, ma'am." The man stepped closer, and Jade squinted to try and make out his features. He was tall but young, probably a couple of years younger than her. His head was shaved, and he wore a black leather jacket and jeans.

"Ma'am." He put his hands down. "Are you hurt?"

Jade shook her head. "I need to go home." She started shivering, and she rubbed her arms to try and keep warm.

"Dr. Cross," he began. "I think you're in shock. We should go to the hospital and have you checked out."

"No!" she cried. "I'm fine. I wasn't hurt."

"Your knees, Dr. Cross."

She looked down and saw the bloody, torn skin of her knees. She didn't even realize she was hurt, but now that she had seen it, the pain began to creep in. "Argh," she cried out and stumbled forward.

The man caught her. "Dr. Cross, can you walk? Do you want me to carry you?"

Jade shook her head. "I'm all right. I just need to get home."

"I can't do that," he said. "My boss'll have my ass if I don't bring you to a doctor."

"I am a doctor!" she lashed out.

"The hospital, then." He put an arm under her armpits and helped steady her. "If you can walk, we can go back to the street, and we can take a cab to the nearest hospital. Or I can call an ambulance."

"No, I—Meredith!" She struggled to get away from him. "My friend! She might be hurt, too!"

As if on cue, she heard a familiar voice call her name. "Jade!"

"I'm over here!" she replied.

The blonde Lycan ran toward them, her arms reaching out to grab the man.

"No! Meredith!" she cried. "He helped me! Stop!"

Meredith skidded to a halt, crouching low to stop her momentum. She narrowed her gaze at him. "Is that true?"

The man nodded. "Yes, ma'am. I was sent here to watch over Dr. Cross."

"Who sent you?" Meredith barked.

"Your boss! I mean, your boss, Mr. Anderson, hired my boss' company. Creed Security, ma'am." He turned to Jade. "I was there, Dr. Cross. The night we rescued you from that warehouse. I gotta tell you, you got some scary guys after you."

Jade was speechless. The Alpha hired Sebastian Creed's company to guard her? Why didn't he say anything?

"Oh my God, Jade!" Meredith was staring at her knees. "You! What's your name?"

"Zac, Ma'am."

"Zac! Go get us a cab and we'll head straight to Fenrir. And stop calling me ma'am!"

"I can't do that, ma—I mean, Miss," he shook his head. "I need to take Dr. Cross back to the hospital."

"We have a doctor back at Fenrir. He can patch her up."

Jade suddenly felt dizzy, and her knees buckled under her.

"Jade!" Meredith made a grab for her friend, but Zac was too fast. He scooped up Jade into his arms.

"Ma'am," he began. "You can go home or follow me. But I'm not leaving you alone. I'm taking Dr. Cross to the hospital now."

"I'm fine!' Jade snapped. "Let me go, or you'll regret it!"

The young man gave a chuckle. "I don't think what you'll do to me can compare to what my boss'll do to my balls if I don't take you to the hospital."

Jade crossed her arms over her chest. "Fine." Damn Sebastian Creed. He can't even leave her alone while staying away from her.

CHAPTER SEVEN

The pain was unbearable today.

On most days, he could grit his teeth and bear it. But today was brutal, and he nearly passed out from the stinging pain across his chest.

He struggled against the bonds, but he was too weak. How long had he been in this hell hole? Days? Weeks? Months? Time lost all meaning in the darkness of his cell.

His eyes were closed in sleep, but as soon as he heard the creaky opening of the rusty door, they flew open. There was shuffling, and he knew who was coming. The man. Maybe he was a man, he couldn't tell. He wore brown robes, sported a long beard, and had cold hands. But other than that, Sebastian couldn't see his features.

The man entered his cell, and he knew what was coming.

The sharp steel cut into his skin, moving from his left wrist up his forearm, digging deep into his flesh. Then, the man poured a liquid over the wounds. It was hot. No, it was cold. He couldn't tell; all he could feel was pain. His eyes rolled back. The man was chanting in a deep, mesmerizing voice that put him in a soothing trance.

The language he spoke was strange. It wasn't Pashto or Dari, but it was like a dialect. He could pick up a few words here and there, but the rest was gibberish. Alive...come...beast.

Sebastian woke with a start, but his body was still paralyzed with sleep, and he struggled to move his limbs. Slowly, he regained the feeling in his body, and he sat up, rubbing his face with his palms. The soft mattress and silky sheets were a reminder he wasn't trapped in that cell anymore. Most guys who came back from war had a hard time adjusting to soft beds and covers. As soon as he got home, however, he bought the most luxurious sheets and most expensive mattress he could afford. That way, he knew the nightmares weren't real and he wasn't trapped back in the cell. Fisting the one thousand-thread-count Egyptian cotton sheets, he tossed them aside and padded across the hardwood floors to the bathroom.

He ran the tap, the sound of rushing water giving him some comfort. The cold water felt good against his skin, and he splashed some on his face. With a deep breath, he slowly looked up at the mirror. With an angry growl, he punched the glass, the smooth surface breaking under his knuckles.

"Fuck!" he cursed and ran his hands under the tap to clean off the blood. He grabbed a towel and wrapped his injured hand. He looked at the mirror again. *It* was here. His eyes, normally the color of slate, were now a burnished gold.

This always happened after he dreamed of Afghanistan. Actually, as he learned later, the people who took him were from a tiny border nation: Zhobghadi. Few people knew about the tiny separatist state, and the Afghan and Pakistani governments mostly left them alone, as both countries had too much to deal with in their own backyards.

Sebastian was doing a scouting mission near the border when he was suddenly surrounded by a group of local men. He was better armed, but there were simply too many of them to fight off. When they managed to grab his weapons, they bound and gagged him, then made him walk for hours under the heat of the sun. Finally, they arrived at their destination, some cave system deep in the mountains. First, they put him in a cell with nothing more than a loaf of bread and some water. He spent all night trying to find a way out, thinking of a plan to disable his kidnappers and escape.

The next day, they came for him. He tried to knock them down, but they bound him again, then brought him to another cell. Then, they strapped him to a cold, stone slab and left him. He waited for hours, it seemed. Finally, the rusty door opened and the man in robes came.

The torture began immediately. They weren't using any of the techniques he'd learned during training. The man used a curved knife to cut along his left arm, moving all the way up to his chest, over his heart. He would do this over and over again. Then he would pour this godawful liquid all over the wounds and begin to chant over and over again. It would have driven most men insane, having them beg for death. But he was a Marine. He was trained to fight and to endure torture. He just had to hang on and find a way out. Stay sane. Keep calm.

It was a month later when help came. Sebastian's troopmates, of course, realized he was gone and his CO had done everything in his power to rescue him. After doing their investigation, they eventually found the cave and raided it. The man in the robes was in the middle of his ritual when one of his troopmates came in and shot him in the head.

He spent weeks in the hospital after that ordeal. Physically, everything was fine, no permanent damage, unless you count the web of scars he now had running from his left wrist up to his chest. But, mentally, he was changed. The nightmares would come every night, and he would wake up screaming, his chest burning, like something big was trying to claw its way out. Roars and screams would ring in his ears at random times, and then the voice in his head began to talk. He would ignore it, at first, but it became louder and louder. Then, it started talking to him directly. Telling him to do things. One night, he was out having drinks with his friends, and some asshole was trying to start a fight. Usually, he would have just walked away, but the voice inside him was telling him to kill the other man. He did his best to ignore it, but when the asshole tried to take a swing at one of his friends, he lost it. He nearly killed the guy, and it took three of his buddies to pull him off. It was the voice that made him do it. The Beast.

So, to protect himself and his troopmates, he decided to take an honorable discharge instead. He focused on building his company, using all the money he had saved up and the connections he made. He got help, and the meds dulled down The Beast. Driving himself to exhaustion made Creed Security the top private security and military contractor in the United States. He was richer than he'd ever imagined and at the top of his game. The work seemed to calm The Beast, too. He began acquiring houses and apartments all over the world, cars, clothes, everything he had never thought he could buy growing up in a trailer in the middle of buttfuck, nowhere. He also purchased an old factory in Tribeca and turned it into his home. He filled it with artwork, luxury furniture, and all kind of toys. His favorite things and treasures, he kept locked up in a secret vault in his room.

Despite all the money, the power, the riches, he still felt numb. The women helped, and they were coming in droves. Maybe it was because they could sense his brokenness or his bad boy vibe. Sex, the contact, and the feel of bare skin gave him temporary bliss. In the moment, it made him feel more human. Afterward, though, the act always left him empty, but he couldn't do anything. He felt like his life was going in circles. Work, make money, sex. Over and over again.

Until her.

Ever since that night at Blood Moon, The Beast started talking again. The voice was getting louder and louder each time. Sebastian tried to get his doctor to up his meds, but the damn man refused. He considered turning to the bottle but didn't want to wind up like his old man. Never. The nightmares were coming back too. Over the years, he was getting them less frequently, but this was the third time in the last weeks, the first one came right after the rescue op to save her.

Jade. Sweet, innocent, and pure Jade. He could never forget the image of her that night at the reception. The combination of the yellow dress with her pale skin, dark hair, and light eyes were stunning. Seeing the other man with his hands all over Jade had driven him crazy. He couldn't help himself, and even though he was on the job, he went to her. The urge to touch her was great, and finally, he gave in.

She was his every wet dream come true, and kissing her was about a hundred times better than he'd ever imagined. Jade was soft in all the right places and tasted sweeter than any dessert. And her body, the way it responded to his touch was incredible. He was getting hard just thinking of her perky tits and her small, pink nipples. And her drenched little pussy, the way it sucked greedily at his finger. What he wouldn't do to just sink into her...

No, he had to forget her. He couldn't let The Beast taint her. She was good and perfect, untouched. When she confessed she was a virgin, The Beast roared, telling Sebastian to take her right then and there. Mark her. Claim her, it urged. Fuck her. *Make her ours*, The Beast hissed.

Fuck it all. He'll force his doctor to give him a stronger prescription or find another way to get his hands on more meds.

Hell, he'd drink himself to death first before he'd let The Beast have Jade.

The ringing of his phone jolted him out of his thoughts. Calls after midnight were standard in his line of work, so he wasn't surprised. He ran back to the bedroom to get his phone and frowned when he saw the Caller ID.

"Zac," he said in a gruff voice.

"Boss," the younger man replied. "You gotta come to Mount Sinai Hospital. Now."

"What's wrong?" Zac was watching Jade tonight. Sebastian couldn't follow her around anymore. Not when The Beast wanted her so much. Not when he wanted her so much, and couldn't even touch her. But he didn't want her vulnerable, so he had Zac do it instead. If she was in the hospital...

"She's been hurt, boss. Some guys—"

"I'm on my way," he said, not even letting Zac finish. Inside him, The Beast screeched in anger.

———

"Is he still out there?" Jade asked, peering around the curtain. She was sitting on the hospital bed, wearing an awful, scratchy medical gown.

"Yeah, he hasn't moved an inch."

"How are we going to get out of here?"

"I tried everything, Jade," Meredith said. "He won't go away."

Jade sighed and looked down at the bandages on her knees. The doctors in the ER patched her up pretty quickly, so hopefully they didn't notice the wounds were healing as they cleaned them. But they needed to get discharged now or try to sneak out before anyone else tried to look at her knees. The pain was gone and she could feel the skin scabbing. By morning, it should be all healed. But now, she was trapped in the hospital ward as Zac refused to let them leave until they got the all-clear from the doctor.

"I called Nick Vrost from your phone and he's on his way," Meredith said, referring to the New York Clan's Beta and Fenrir Corporation's Head of Security. As Grant's second-in-command, he was in charge of such things and would know what to do.

"Thank God," Jade said. The Beta should be able to get her out of the hospital.

"I don't understand it." Meredith shook her head. "The mages are after you again? Does Grant know? Is that why he had an additional guard on you?"

Jade shrugged. "I'm just as clueless as you are. Why wouldn't the Alpha tell us?"

"I don't'—"

The curtain dividing Jade's bed from the rest of the room suddenly flew open and both of them whipped their heads towards the figure standing in front of the hospital bed.

"Holy fucking crackerjacks, you're huge!" Meredith exclaimed as she craned her neck up at the intruder.

"Sebastian?" Jade said in an astonished voice. "What are you doing here?"

"Yeah, and did you Hulk-smash your way in here?" Meredith quipped.

Sebastian ignored Meredith and lumbered over to Jade. "Are you hurt?" he asked in a gentle voice.

"Like I told your lackey," Jade huffed. "I'm perfectly fine, but he insisted on bringing me here."

"Good," Sebastian said in gruff voice. "Now, tell me what happened."

"I will not!" Jade crossed her arms over her chest. "Please leave."

"Stop being stubborn!" Sebastian growled and took a step towards Jade.

"Hey, hey!" Meredith stood between them. "Just who do you think you are?"

"I'm protecting her, I need to be debriefed on the situation."

"I'm sure you can do that once Mr. Vrost gets here," Meredith began. "Fenrir is your client right? He's in charge of these things as Head of Security. But you should maybe step back a bit and give my friend some room? She looks like she's going to pass out from all the testosterone you're flinging around."

Jade's cheeks pinked, and she realized she had been holding her breath. She couldn't help it. Being around Sebastian made her forget things, like how to breathe. *No,* she shook her head mentally. *Mustn't think like that.* He wanted nothing to do with her. He made that very clear during the wedding reception. She was just a job, someone he swore to protect because he was being paid handsomely to do so.

"Speaking of which..." Meredith fished out the phone in her pocket. "Jade's phone," she answered. "Fine. Yes, I understand." She turned to Jade. "Mr. Vrost is here. I'm gonna go get him."

"Go ahead," Jade said.

"Are you sure?"

"Yes," she insisted. "Get Mr. Vrost so we can get out of here."

Meredith gave her a concerned look, then strode towards the exit. When she was behind Sebastian, she turned back, slammed her fists together and mouthed *Hulk-smash* to Jade before walking away.

Jade suppressed a giggle and shook her head.

"Jade," Sebastian began as he took a step towards her. "Tell me what happened? Please?"

She shrugged. "Meredith and I were going to this diner on

3rd Avenue for a late supper. Then these guys just came out of nowhere and chased me down. Meredith was able to hold off most of them but one guy found me and put a gun to my head. Zac came and knocked him away..." She choked, and she turned her head away from him. She didn't want him to see her cry and break down.

"Jade," he said softly, putting his hands on her shoulders. His masculine scent tickled her nostrils, making her dizzy. "What's going on? Who is trying to kill you and why?"

She shook her head. Keeping her mouth shut was the smartest thing she could do right now.

"You're hiding something from me," he said through gritted teeth. "Tell me who's trying to hurt you so I can protect you."

Anger bubbled in her. *How dare he pretend to care about her?* She brushed his hands away from her, then hopped off the bed. "I don't need anything from you," she declared, crossing her arms over her chest.

"Jade, if this is about the wedding reception—"

"Shut up!" she shouted. "Just leave me alone."

"What's going on here?" Nick's icy voice broke through the room. He stood by the opening of the curtain partitions, his arms crossed over his chest.

"Mr. Vrost!" Jade exclaimed in relief.

"Dr. Cross, are you ok?"

"Yes, I'm fine," she nodded. "Are we leaving soon?"

"Cady's taking care of it now," he explained.

"She's not leaving until the doctor says she's good and ready," Sebastian said, nodding to the bandages on Jade's knees. "Zac said she was in shock and she couldn't even walk. They might want to keep her overnight."

"And what are you doing here, Mr. Creed?" Nick asked, his eyes zeroing in on the other man.

"I'm protecting her," he stated.

"Meredith," Nick barked. "Take Dr. Cross to the nurses' station. We'll be leaving soon."

With a nod, the blonde took off her jacket and wrapped it around Jade, escorting her out of the ward.

———

"You have some nerve lying to me, Creed," Nick said as soon as Jade and Meredith left.

"Lie to you?" Sebastian asked. "How am I lying to you?"

"Meredith and Dr. Cross seem to be under the impression your man was following them because Creed Security is working for Fenrir. But you know damn well Grant didn't hire you to protect Dr. Cross," the other man stated. "Now, tell me why you were having her followed."

"I didn't lie," Sebastian stated. "I said I was protecting her, and that's what I was doing. And it was a good thing Zac was around, too. Your team obviously wasn't doing a good job keeping her safe."

Nick's eyes flashed with anger, and the air suddenly felt heavy around them. An unfamiliar wave of energy seemed to emanate from the other man and The Beast rumbled. *Kill him.* Sebastian was very tempted, but kept his arms stiff at his sides, his hands curling into tight fists.

"Sweetie," a soft voice called from behind Nick. "Are you done yet? I have Jade's discharge papers."

Sebastian's gaze zeroed in on the source of the voice. At first glance, he thought it was Lara Chatraine, but that didn't make any sense. She and Liam Henney should still be on their honeymoon. As he stared at the woman, he realized that although they looked similar, this woman was not Lara.

"Cady," Nick warned, placing himself directly in front of her. "Stay behind me."

The woman whispered something to Nick and then stepped up from behind him. Another glance at her and he became aware that she had a baby strapped to her chest. The Beast quieted and stilled inside him at the sight of the child.

"You must be Mr. Creed." Dark blue eyes peered up at him and her lips curled into a tired, but warm smile. "I'm Cady Vrost. I'm Grant's Executive Assistant and I take care of HR matters during emergencies."

"Nice to meet you, Mrs. Vrost," he said calmly. He understood why Nick was so protective, seeing as his wife and child were here.

"Meredith told me your guy saved Jade. I just wanted to say thank you. She's very precious to us." A soft cry pierced the room, and Cady immediately began to soothe the baby. "Apologies, Mr. Creed. We don't have a nanny yet, so we had to take Zachary with us." She looked up at Nick. "Ready to leave soon?"

Nick put an arm protectively around Cady. "I'm just wrapping things up, love. You go ahead." His eyes softened for a moment, but as soon as Cady left the room, he glared at Sebastian. "Now, tell me why you were having Jade followed."

Sebastian remained as still as a stone. "I don't have to explain anything to you."

"No? Well then," Nick said in a cold voice. "I'll be speaking to Grant about this as soon as possible. And if you don't stop stalking Dr. Cross, I'll personally make sure you suffer the consequences."

Sebastian didn't reply, but he felt The Beast stir in him again. Nick Vrost gave him one last warning glare before he left. He stood there for a moment, trying to calm the rage inside him, when Zac popped his head from behind the curtain.

"Boss?" The younger man cocked his head. "They're leaving. Do you want me to try and stop them?"

Sebastian shook his head. "No, Zac, it's all good." He let out a gruff. "Good job, by the way," he praised. Zac had saved Jade's life and for that he owed the young man.

"No prob, boss," he grinned.

"I'll drive you home and you can take some time off. But tell me what happened first."

CHAPTER EIGHT

J ade watched from the behind the one-way glass as Nick Vrost interrogated the pale, bald man in front of him. He looked gaunt, with his cheeks sunken in and his skin an ashen gray. If she didn't know any better, she would have thought the man was sick or being treated poorly. But he wasn't. The man was a mage. Marcus was the one who had her kidnapped and drugged. When the New York clan came to rescue her, they were also able to capture him.

While uncooperative at first, Marcus flipped and told them the location of Stefan's last hideout. Jade was also able to perfect the power-dampening bracelet she had been working on. When worn by a witch or warlock, the bracelet rendered their powers useless. The Lycan and witches devised a plan to try and stop the mages. They were able to storm the mage mountain stronghold, but Stefan got away. However, Lara was able to put the bracelet on Daric, Stefan's warlock protégé. Now, both the mage and the warlock were detained deep in Fenrir's basement. Daric, however, refused to talk at all, remaining silent as a stone even though Nick, Alynna, and Grant questioned him for hours.

"Now, Marcus," Nick began. "What else aren't you telling us about Stefan?"

"I've told you everything, dog," Marcus spat. "I don't know where they are now. The Master doesn't reveal all his hideouts to us."

"There was another attempt on one of our own," the Beta said. "He sent more of your puppets to attack Dr. Cross. What do they want with her?"

The mage let out a sardonic laugh. "What else would Stefan want? All of you six feet under, of course."

Nick leaned back and crossed his arms. "Will Stefan come for you? To rescue you?"

"If he does, it's not to rescue me," the mage answered in a serious tone.

"Dr. Cross."

Jade's head whipped to the side. "Primul," she said, greeting Grant Anderson with the traditional honorific for a Lycan's Alpha. "Sorry, I didn't see you come in."

"Are you all right?" he asked, concern marring his face. "I heard about what happened last night."

She shrugged. "I'm fine."

The Alpha's mouth stretched into a grim line. "I'm sorry. If you weren't working for us, then this wouldn't have happened. All of it."

"No." She shook her head. "I knew what this job entailed. I'm proud to serve you, Alpha. And the clan."

"Yes, you have served us well," Grant agreed. "And you've sacrificed a lot. As your Alpha, it's my duty to protect you. And I promise nothing will happen to you."

"I know you will, Primul," she said. She looked back at Nick and Marcus. "I'm ready to face him."

"Marcus?" Grant asked. "You don't have to."

She sighed. "I know. But he's our best resource for finding

out exactly how the mages are controlling the humans. And I can't put it off forever. The best chance we have to stop Stefan is if we can figure out how he's doing it."

"Take your time, then, Doctor." Grant put a hand on her shoulder. "All the time you need. You have all my resources at your disposal."

"Thank you, Primul," she said.

"Now," Grant cleared his throat, "about Sebastian Creed."

Jade froze at the name. "What about him?"

"I don't want to alarm you, but, why was Sebastian having you followed? Does he suspect what we are?"

Her eyes grew wide. "Primul? What do you mean? He said he was protecting me. Under your orders."

"That's what Nick told me," Grant said. "But I didn't ask him to have you followed. His company was hired to do the security at Liam and Lara's wedding reception. That was it. It was a trial run, and I haven't decided if I want to take him on as a full-time contractor. If Stefan is trying to kill you, then you're going to need protection. And with Marcus and Daric here, I simply can't spare the manpower to guard you, too. What do you think?"

"I don't know, Primul," she said. "That's up to you, I guess. Now, if you'll excuse me," she gave him a curt bow, "I'm needed upstairs."

"Of course."

Jade's mind was reeling. Why did Sebastian have his man following her around? Was he suspicious? She wondered if he'd seen anything during their brief encounter. Were her eyes glowing? Could he sense her she-wolf? No, she thought. It was something else.

She took the elevator back to the 33rd floor. Much to her surprise, and delight, two familiar figures were waiting for her inside the lab.

"Jade!" Lara exclaimed as she opened her arms for a hug.

Jade immediately ran to her best friend. "Lara!" she greeted her and looked at Liam. "Alpha! You guys are back from your honeymoon!"

"Just this morning," Liam said. He gave Jade a warm hug. "I'm sorry to run, but I have a meeting with Grant and Alynna in about five minutes."

"Go ahead."

He gave his new wife a kiss on the cheek. "I'll see you at lunch, sweetheart." With that, he left the lab.

"Jade." Lara's voice turned serious. "Meredith told me about what happened last night! Why aren't you at home, resting?" Lara admonished.

"Rat," Jade sneered at Meredith.

The other Lycan was sitting on a chair, not far away, flipping lazily through a magazine. "They would have found out," she answered, not looking at them.

Jade frowned. "I'm fine! Just leave me be, ok?"

"Someone tried to kill you." Lara's voice shook with anger. "Don't you care? What about us? Have you thought about how we would feel if something did happen to you?" The witch's eyes were bright with unshed tears.

With a sigh, Jade sank into the nearest chair. "I'm sorry, Lara. I didn't mean to make light of it and upset you."

"Jade," Meredith stood up and walked over to them. "We need to talk. This is an interfriendtion."

"A what?" Jade's brows knitted.

The blonde Lycan rolled her eyes. "You know, a friendly intervention. I'm your friend, right?"

Jade eyed Lara suspiciously. "Is this why you're here?"

"We're concerned about you," the witch replied.

"Tell her what you told me. About your wolf."

The Lycan scientist turned pale. "I shouldn't have told you."

She stood up and tried to turn away from them, but Meredith grabbed her arm. "Let go of me!"

"Or what, Jade? You're going to hide yourself away? Like you did your she-wolf?"

"Shut up!"

"What happened, Jade? This isn't normal, and you know it! Why can't you shift?"

Lara gasped, her eyes wide. "Jade, I didn't know."

"It's complicated!" Jade reasoned. "Neither of you would understand."

"Then make us!" Meredith shouted, her eyes flashing with anger.

It was the first time Jade had seen the blonde Lycan so serious. "Fine. But don't judge me!"

"We won't, honey," Lara said in a soothing voice, placing an arm on her shoulder. "I promise."

Jade took a deep breath. This was it. She was going to tell them her most shameful secret. "You guys know I was born here, but I moved to England when my parents divorced. Well, I was the reason they divorced..." She took a deep breath. "I hurt some humans when I was eleven years old. Or rather, my she-wolf did."

Meredith's eyes widened in shock, while Lara went pale. The witch reached for Jade's hand. "Oh, hon..."

"I was on the bus, on my way home from school when I suddenly shifted. It was my first time, and too early. Most shifters don't start until they're at least thirteen. I was eleven." Jade said, her eyes somber. "I didn't expect it. No one did. We were on the West Side highway when it just happened. I don't remember exactly...I was just sitting down, talking with some friends when I blacked out. When I woke up, I was in The Enclave Medical Wing."

"What happened to everyone else?" Lara asked.

"When I shifted, everyone on the bus panicked, of course. The driver lost control, and the bus flipped over. The other kids, a lot of them were seriously hurt. I...I was injured badly, too, and my shifter healing hadn't quite kicked in yet. My spine was severed, and I couldn't walk. Dr. Faulkner tried this experimental technique to heal me...basically they had to operate and keep the wound on my back open to make sure it was healing properly." The memory of the pain came back to her. Weeks and weeks of staying on her stomach, the wound on her back sliced over and over again. It was barbaric, but it had saved her life. The surgery scars were so deep and done so often that the scars remained, a reminder of what had happened to her. As soon as she turned eighteen, she got the tattoo to cover it up, though the ink could never cover her shame.

Jade nodded, swallowing the lump in her throat. Tears burned in her eyes, and Lara put an arm around her. She had to continue. Tell them everything. "One of my classmates, Marion Lichtfield, was next to me on the bus. She also sustained similar injuries, but she was human. And so, she was paralyzed."

"That wasn't your fault!" Meredith cried.

"I ruined everyone's lives that day!" The tears began to flow down Jade's cheeks. "They all saw me! The Alpha, Michael Anderson, had the confusion potion administered to all the other kids. They were having nightmares for weeks! He also paid off the parents to keep quiet and if any of them were to say anything, they'd be hauled off to the Lycan Siberian Detention Facility. I not only ruined my classmates' lives, but I almost revealed our secret to the whole world."

"Oh Jade," Lara choked as she hugged her friend tighter. "I'm sorry. I'm so sorry."

"My she-wolf...I couldn't control her. I didn't want to control her. My injuries, the accident, everything put a strain on my parents' marriage." She hid her face in her hands. "It was all my fault! All of it."

"No," Meredith said. "No, Jade, it wasn't your fault. You were a kid. It was an accident."

Jade pulled away from Lara. "I know...but maybe if I were stronger, I could have stopped it."

"You don't know that," Lara said. "You couldn't have predicted what happened."

Meredith looked confused. "What do you do during Blood Moon then, when you don't have a choice but to shift?"

Jade looked mortified and stared at the floor. "I...I take sedatives."

Meredith shot to her feet. "What? How could you, Jade?"

"What's wrong with you, Meredith?" Lara asked, puzzled. "Why are you acting like this?"

"It's okay, Lara," Jade whispered. "Taking sedatives...only those with broken wolves are forced to do that during Blood Moon. Those we can't control. To take it willingly...well, it's taboo among Lycans." Her mother had made it seem normal. Fiona Williams manipulated her daughter into thinking that it was for the best. In fact, she did it herself and told Jade that they simply couldn't risk her turning back into a wolf. So while she was under her mother's care, they would go into the safe room before Blood Moon, lie down, and put the IVs into their wrists and go to sleep. Since then, she'd been too afraid to stop, not knowing if her she-wolf, given the chance, would even give her back her body. And she was too ashamed to tell anyone else.

"I don't understand!" Meredith paced back and forth, and the air around them became thick. Jade could feel Meredith's she-wolf, the barely-contained power from the other Lycan. "How do you even...I mean, how could you do it? Push down your she-wolf so deep inside you that you can't call her?"

"I just...I went to England with my mother after the divorce.

My father fought for me. Even Michael Anderson tried to prevent me from leaving, but my mother went through the human court system and got custody of me." She turned away from them. "I...my mother taught me how to ignore the wolf and keep her down. She's done it all her life. Her husband now doesn't even know she's a Lycan." Fiona was married to a Baron, after all and had gotten used to life as a peerage.

"Jesus Christ!" Meredith shook her head. "Is she one of those self-hating Lycans?"

Jade said nothing, but her face said it all. There were some Lycans who hated what they were and went to great lengths to deny their shifter sides.

"My God!" Meredith exclaimed. "I've never met your mom, but—pardon my French—she sounds like a total bitch."

"Meredith!" Lara admonished.

"She does!" Meredith growled. "What she did...it's like child abuse!" The other Lycan was angry now, her hands balling into fists.

"Jade..." Lara looked at her with somber eyes.

What was she supposed to say? Jade thought her mother was protecting her. Telling her it was for the best and that she'd never learn to control her wolf. And Jade believed her. How could she not? Her mother took her away from her father, from everything she ever knew and locked her up in her grandfather's estate in England. Growing up isolated and alone, she only had her tutors and books for company. When she was fourteen, one of her tutors, Mr. Glendale, had discovered she had an aptitude for science and encouraged her to try to get into the Brighton School for the Talented and Gifted. Her mother didn't want to let her go, but her grandfather insisted. When she tested off the charts, her mother didn't have a choice. She was glad that her grandfather had died after she turned eighteen. The trust her grandfather left her not only allowed her to live comfortably, but that meant Fiona no longer had control over her, nor cared what she did with her life.

Meredith seemed to calm down after pacing back and forth, muttering silently to herself. Taking a deep breath, she walked over to the Lycan scientist. "You can't go on living like this. You can't treat your she-wolf like she's broken. Or she will break."

"What am I supposed to do?" Jade asked, raising her voice.

"I'm not judging you," Meredith said. "Don't be mad at me. I'm saying this because I'm concerned about you. Your relationship with your wolf is a precious thing. I'm surprised you can still use your shifter healing and senses."

"Those don't go away," Jade stated. "I can't call the she-wolf, but I still have the enhanced healing and senses."

"What are you going to do about this?" Lara asked. "I mean, what do you want to do about it?"

Jade shrugged. "I don't know. I'm fine the way I am. This is me. And if you can't accept me as I am..."

"No, Jade," Lara said, shaking her head. "We love you just the way you are. But obviously, the mages are out to get you. Your she-wolf would definitely make things harder for them."

"Or make things worse. What if I hurt someone?"

"Or what if you saved yourself?" Meredith countered. For a brief moment, her eyes glowed, and Jade could feel the power of the other Lycan's wolf. She wondered again about Meredith's mysterious past.

"I don't want to talk about this anymore!" Jade cried. "Please."

Meredith and Lara gave each other pointed looks. "Fine," said the blonde Lycan. "But this isn't over."

Lara embraced her friend. "Whatever you need, hon, just let us know."

Jade sighed with relief. The discussion about her she-wolf was done for now. But there was something else she wanted to ask her friends. Something that had kept her up all night. "Well, there is one thing."

"Anything," Lara said.

"Well..." Her cheeks pinked. "You know what we talked about before...at Blood Moon." Having a gun pointed at her head shook Jade to the core, and she realized what people were talking about when they said their very lives flashed before their eyes. "Like I said, I'm ready to...you know..."

Meredith's face brightened, her anger dissipating. "Wait... do you mean, you want to push through with Operation PTC?"

"Yes. Oh God, am I pathetic or what?" Jade buried her face in her hands. "I just...I don't want to die without knowing...you know..." She couldn't say the last part. It was bad enough she was a virgin, but to have never experienced a real orgasm before? Well, she almost did that one time...She shook her head, trying to forget the memory of being in Sebastian Creed's arms.

"Yes!" Meredith jumped up and did a fist pump. "Operation PTC is a go!" The Lycan grabbed Jade's phone from her bag.

"Hey! What are you doing?"

"I'm downloading Tinder, POF, and some other apps on your phone. Are you just batting for our team, or looking to explore?"

"What?" Jade grabbed the phone from Meredith. "No! I mean...how did you open my phone, anyway? I have a lock code on it."

"Oh please. The first six digits of Pi? Really?" She grabbed the phone back and began typing. "Now, go sit over there next to the light." She raised the phone to take a photo. "Good, now pop open the top buttons of your blouse—"

"Meredith!" Jade exclaimed and looked at Lara pleadingly.

"All right, all right," Lara sighed. "Let's not get too excited, Mer."

"But we want to make sure we're putting our girl's best foot forward!"

"You don't want to show my foot!" Jade protested.

"Give me your glasses," Meredith said. Jade handed them over to her, and the blonde promptly broke them in half and tossed them away.

"Mer!" Lara exclaimed.

"She doesn't need them," Meredith glared at Jade. "Right?"

The brunette bit her lip and shook her head. "I used to wear glasses...before the accident. But with the shifter healing and abilities, I didn't really need them anymore." She remembered that after her spine completely healed, her vision became a perfect 20/20. The glasses were her last link to her past. Before the accident. Before her entire life turned upside-down. She was using them as a crutch, something to hide behind.

"Now there's nothing hiding your gorgeous face," Meredith said, as if reading Jade's mind. "It's time to show the real you."

Jade sighed. This was going to be a long day.

———

Sebastian entered Grant's office not knowing what to expect. The CEO was sitting on his desk, his brows drawn in a frown as he looked at some papers. Nick Vrost was standing to his right, his icy blue eyes zeroing in on Sebastian as soon as he came in. There it was again as if Nick's contempt towards him was something physical. He could feel the wave of negative energy coming from the other man.

Grant's head popped up, and he nodded at Sebastian. "Good, you're here. Take a seat. This won't take long." His voice was cool, even, and didn't give away a hint of emotion.

"In that case, I'd prefer to stand," Sebastian replied.

"Whatever you want," Grant stood up and walked around

his desk. "Now, tell me, why were you having Dr. Cross followed? And don't lie. Nick told me everything."

"I wasn't lying," Sebastian stated. "It was to protect her."

"And you think she needed protection because..."

"Someone wants her dead. Whoever this sick fucker is, he's escalated from just wanting to kidnap her." The look Grant gave him confirmed his suspicions. "Who is it?" Sebastian asked, his voice turning deadly.

"One of our rivals," Grant said. "That's all I can tell you for now."

I'll find out anyway, Sebastian thought. And when he did, that motherfucker wasn't going to be around much longer. *Keep her safe*, The Beast hissed. *Kill him.*

Nick suddenly stepped forward, and the air in the office grew thick.

"Nick, stand down," Grant held his hand up.

"But—"

"Nick," Grant whipped his head towards the other man. "Let me handle this." He turned back to Sebastian. "Look, Dr. Cross isn't just an employee. She's practically family, and I don't want her hurt, but I can't ask her to stop her work, either. So why don't we just make this official? I want to hire Creed security to protect her."

"Grant, you can't be serious!" Nick protested. "He's practically stalking her!"

"Nick, Sebastian obviously has some stake in keeping Dr. Cross safe." Grant eyed Sebastian. "And he's done a great job so far. I can't think of anyone else who would do his best to make sure no harm comes to her."

Nick opened his mouth to protest, then shut it close.

"Great. If you agree, Sebastian, we'll sort it out."

"Yes," Sebastian nodded. "I'll personally see to it that Dr. Cross is safe." *And the bastard trying to kill her won't see the light of day once I find out who he is.* He made a mental note to tell his team to start researching Fenrir's biggest rivals.

They worked out more details of how they would go about protecting Jade. Creed Security would be in charge of Jade's security detail, just in case there were any leaks at Fenrir. Only Sebastian would know who would be watching Jade and when, and would only reveal the details to Grant or Nick if necessary. After sorting out other matters, Grant declared that he had another meeting, signaling the end of their meeting. Sebastian could still feel Nick Vrost's glare on his back as he left, but he paid the other man no mind. All he cared about was that he could protect Jade and keep her close.

He stepped into the private elevators, his mind making a checklist of things to do. The elevator stopped on the 33rd floor, and as the doors opened, feminine laughter and chatter greeted him

"...And he's so hot, too! I don't think Jade could have done better for a first Tinder date!" Lara Chatraine said to her companion.

"I think she should wear that black dress. What do you think?" It was the tall blonde, Jade's bodyguard. "Would it be too much to wear sexy lingerie for a first date? We don't have a lot of—" The woman, Meredith, if he recalled correctly, shut her mouth the moment her whiskey-brown eyes landed on Sebastian. Lara's face, on the other hand, could barely contain her shock and surprise.

"Ladies," he acknowledged.

"Mr. Creed." Lara nodded as they entered the elevator. The two women faced away from him and remained silent.

Sebastian's jaw clenched, the muscles ticking. They were obviously talking about Jade and some hot date she was having. Something ugly reared its head, and it wasn't even The Beast this time. Thinking about Jade and some stranger she met on a dating app going out to dinner, his hands all over her, taking her dress off to reveal whatever sexy lingerie she was wearing...fuck, he was going to go insane. Maybe it was a mistake, agreeing to Grant's offer. He should have taken Lara and Vrost's advice instead and stayed away from her, for his sake. But, he wasn't going to back off now. Instead, he decided he would just have to get someone else on his team to work on this job.

CHAPTER NINE

"So, tell me again what you do, Jade?" Daniel asked.

"I'm a researcher at a food company," Jade replied as she speared some chicken onto her fork and took a delicate bite.

"Sounds interesting," he said.

"It's quite boring actually." She took a sip of her water and looked at the man from over the rim of her glass. Daniel Lane was handsome, with his dark hair and piercing green eyes. He reminded her of a younger Grant Anderson. Though she would never admit to anyone, she might have had a tiny crush on the Alpha when she first met him. When she saw Daniel's profile on Tinder, she immediately swiped right and, much to her (and her friends') delight, was matched with him.

They chatted the whole afternoon over the app, and she learned that Daniel was an engineer at some tech startup. His Tinder profile said he loved reading Proust and Thoreau and enjoyed rock climbing on the weekends. Athletic, hot, and smart. He seemed like the perfect date.

So, they decided to meet at a nice restaurant in the East Village that evening. Daniel was already there waiting for her (which mean he was early, since she arrived at 7 p.m. on the dot). They made some small talk before the hostess led them to their seats.

"It can't be as boring as my job," he said, giving her a smile. "I mostly deal with code the whole day."

Daniel seemed like the perfect guy, and she couldn't believe her luck. She always thought online dating was scary and she'd end up with weirdos. But maybe fate was on her side.

They finished dinner, and Jade felt more at ease. Daniel was charming and polite, and although he complimented her on her dress, his eyes never lingered too long on her cleavage. Meredith had picked out the dress, saying it was tasteful, but with the right amount of sluttiness. Daniel paid for the dinner and asked Jade if she wanted to have a quick drink at this bar around the corner.

As they left the restaurant, Daniel offered his arm, and they walked together, enjoying the late New York summer night. Jade shivered involuntarily, which was strange because it wasn't cool enough to give her a chill. Was someone watching her?

"So, I have a confession to make," Daniel said as they stopped walking.

"What?"

"Here's the place I told you about," he motioned to the bar they stopped in front of. "But, my apartment is also up there." He pointed towards the windows higher up on the building.

"Oh." Jade looked up and then back to Daniel. She took a mental deep breath. This is what she wanted, right? "If you have some wine, maybe we can have a glass or two?"

"Your wish is my command." Daniel motioned for her to follow him, leading her to the door next to the bar. "I have this Italian red you might like."

"Sounds great," she said, trying to sound enthusiastic.

Daniel plucked his keys from his pocket and opened the

door, which led straight to a set of stairs. As they ascended the steps, the door behind them slammed open, making Jade jump and nearly slip down the steps.

"Dr. Cross."

Another shiver rushed down her spine. *Oh no. It couldn't be.*

Daniel twisted his head around and frowned. "Hey, who are you? You're not one of my neighbors."

"No, I'm Dr. Cross' security detail," Sebastian said, his voice gruff. His steely eyes turned hard and seemed to glint in the low light of the hallway.

"No, you're not," Jade protested. "The Al—Mr. Anderson told me the truth."

"Well, whatever he told you, this is the truth now, darlin'," he gave her a smug look. "My company's been tasked to protect you, Dr. Cross. From all kinds of threats." He eyed the other man, his expression grim.

"Jade, what's going on?" Daniel asked.

"I'm sorry, Daniel," Jade said. "I think there was some miscommunication at work. Mr. Creed," she turned to Sebastian, "I don't know what type of protection you're supposed to be giving me, but I'm sure it doesn't extend to my personal life. And aren't you CEO? Why aren't you having one of your goons follow me around?"

"I promised your boss I'd give this job the personal touch," he answered. "He is my best client."

Jade rolled her eyes and then looked up at Daniel. "How about that wine?"

Daniel smiled and took Jade's hand, tugging her up the steps.

"Daniel Lane," Sebastian called. "Or should I say, Daniel Landers?"

Daniel stopped suddenly, and then dropped Jade's hand.

He whipped around, facing Sebastian. "How do you know that name?"

"Oh, I know lots of things, Mr. Landers," Sebastian drawled. "Like how you've got three counts of assault on your record. Are you a man who prefers things a little rough?"

"What's going on, Daniel?" Jade asked as she slowly backed down the stairs.

"I can explain. Jade!" he called, reaching out to her, but she batted his hands away.

"Tell me, Daniel, did you like it when those girls said no to you?"

"Don't listen to him, Jade," Daniel said, his face suddenly turning serious.

"What's wrong? Couldn't get it up unless they were fighting you?"

"Shut the fuck up!" Daniel lunged towards Sebastian, but he was too fast. For a large guy, Sebastian moved quickly, stepping aside and letting gravity do its work. Daniel ended up sprawled on the ground.

Jade gasped. What the hell was going on? She quickly hopped down the stairs, stepping over Daniel's prone figure as she burst out of the apartment building. She heard Sebastian call her, but ignored him. That asshole! He was still following her around! What the hell did he want with her?

She walked away faster, not caring which way she was going. But her short legs were no match for him, and Sebastian quickly caught up to her.

"Let me bring you home," he said as he stepped in front of her.

Jade collided into him, and she braced herself by planting her palms on his broad chest. Fudgesicles. The man was built like a rock. "I can take a cab home by myself, thank you very much."

"No, you won't." He clutched her arm as she tried to get around him.

"What?!" she exclaimed, wrenching herself away from his grasp. "What do you want?"

"How about a thank you?" he yelled. He took his phone out of his pocket and showed her a picture of a pretty young girl whose face was marred with a black eye and split lip. "Daniel Landers' high school girlfriend. And this wasn't even the worst one! I can't believe you were going to go up to that asshole's apartment."

Jade turned red. "Thank you!" she screamed at him sarcastically. "Now, leave me alone!" God, she had to get away from him. The humiliation and shame were creeping in, making her cringe. He must think she was terribly desperate for sex if she'd go to bed with someone who liked to hit women. But she didn't know. Couldn't have known. Sebastian's eyes were cold and unfeeling, making her wince.

"I'm here to protect you, Jade," he explained in a soft voice.

"Daniel wasn't...I mean..." Why did she want to tell him that she didn't want to sleep with Daniel? The moment Sebastian showed up, she wanted absolutely nothing to do with Daniel or anyone else. Sebastian Creed was making her all turned around and crazy, and she couldn't do anything about it because he'd already rejected her. Apparently, she didn't affect him as much as he did her since the paycheck Fenrir offered was enough to make him forget he couldn't stand to be around her.

"Jade!" he called again. "Where are you going?"

"Anywhere but here with you!" God, she despised him. She waved a passing cab and pulled the door angrily, slamming it behind her. "Just go," she barked at the driver before he could ask where she wanted to go. The cab quickly sped away, and Jade take a backward glance.

———

"That two-faced son-of-a-bitch!" Meredith exclaimed. It was the day after the Daniel disaster, and the three women were sitting in the Fenrir employee cafeteria having lunch. "I bet he's never even read Proust!"

"Wait, back up a moment," Lara said. "You said Sebastian Creed just showed up?"

"Yes," Jade gritted her teeth. God, it was like anytime something embarrassing was about to happen to her, he was there.

"Sounds like he got there just in time," the witch commented. "But what was he doing, following you around?"

"The Alpha hired his company," Jade explained. The first thing she did that morning was go to Grant's office and ask if it was true. He confirmed he just signed the contract the day before. The Alpha had ordered around-the-clock protection for her whenever she left Fenrir. There would be guys following her when she left the building and outside watching her apartment. They would stay out of her radar, of course, to give her privacy, but any time she was out in public, she would never be alone. Jade wanted to protest, but as her Alpha, she had no choice but to accept Grant's decision.

"Well, I'm glad you didn't sleep with that bastard," Meredith sneered. "Now, let's see who else we can find." She made a grab for Jade's phone, but the other Lycan snatched it away.

"Oh no, no more!" Jade shook her head. "I'm not doing that again. I told you, there are psychos out there! And I found the Norman Bates to trump all Norman Bateses!"

Meredith rolled her eyes. "Well, then where else are we going to find the next candidate for Operation PTC?"

Lara nudged Jade and motioned across the cafeteria. The brunette's eyes lit up and then lowered to her lap.

"Jade?" Meredith turned around and saw who they were looking at. The man standing in line at the coffee bar was tall, handsome, and well-dressed. He had longish blonde hair and a designer scruff that made him look dangerous and exciting. Feeling eyes on him, the man turned his head towards them, his face opening up into a smile.

"Who. Is. That?" Meredith asked, her eyes glued to the man as he approached them.

"That's Gabriel. From Marketing," Lara whispered.

"*Bonjour,* ladies," the man greeted. "Jade." He fixed his deep blue eyes at the Lycan scientist.

Meredith looked like she was going to have a seizure as she turned to Lara and Jade and mouthed *Oh my God.*

"*Bonjour,* Gabriel," Jade greeted.

"May I join you for a bit?" he asked.

The three of them nodded, and Meredith scooted over to make room for the Frenchman.

"How about those lemon curd muffins?" the blonde quipped and Jade gave her a swift kick to the shins.

"Are you new here?" he asked, turning to Meredith.

"This is Meredith," Lara introduced. "She works with Alynna Westbrooke and Nick Vrost."

"Ah," he took Meredith hand and kissed it. "*Enchanté.*"

"Uh...nice to meet you, too," Meredith babbled.

"So, I haven't seen either of you around much," Gabriel said to Jade and Lara.

"Yeah, we've been busy," Jade said.

"It's too bad, I do miss speaking in French. No one else here speaks my mother tongue."

Jade sent Meredith a warning glare before the other woman

could make a comment about tongues. "We can't ignore my friends, though."

"Oh of course, but they won't mind if we sometimes slip, *non*?"

The four of them continued to chat, with Jade and Gabriel switching between French and English. After twenty minutes or so, Gabriel bid them goodbye, saying he had to get back to his office.

"Oh. My. God," Meredith fanned herself as she watched the Frenchman leave. "Jade, he is gorgeous! And he's employed by Fenrir, so you know he can't be a psycho!"

"See, I told you he was totally flirting with you!" Lara said. "C'mon, go after him! Ask him out before he gets away!"

Before Jade could protest, the witch shoved her off her chair and pointed towards the doors leading out of the cafeteria. "Go!"

Jade grumbled but followed Lara's orders. She chased after Gabriel, just as he was going up the stairs. "Gabriel, wait!" she called.

He turned around and flashed Jade a smile. "*Oui?*"

"Um, I was wondering...would you like to go out to dinner? Like tomorrow or something?" Jade said in a breathy voice.

Gabriel's blue eyes lit up in pleasure. "Well, this is a surprise. I was thinking maybe you were not receptive to my advances?"

"Well, you know...I just wasn't ready," Jade said quickly.

"Tomorrow is perfect," Gabriel said. "Shall I pick you up at 7?"

"Sounds good!" Jade nodded. "I'll see you then."

"I look forward to it, *cher*," he replied with a wink.

Jade walked back to the cafeteria with a spring in her step.

"Well?" Meredith asked. "Are you going on a date with him?"

"Yes."

The Lycan gave an unladylike squeal, prompting the people next to them to stare.

"Good for you, Jade," Lara said. "Just get back in the saddle."

Jade smiled at her friends. "You're right. I'm glad you made me do that. I have a good feeling about this." She would go out and have a good time with Gabriel. And Sebastian Creed could go jump off a cliff.

———

Sebastian liked to think he was a reasonable and level-headed man. Some even described him as cold, like the women he often sent on their way after they'd had their fun. But ever since he met Jade Cross, years of building that cool exterior and reputation were headed down the shitter.

What the fuck was he thinking last night? Jade had every right to date and go out and sleep with whomever she wanted. The thought of that, though, had The Beast clawing and screaming at him and he forced the animal to shut the fuck up. When he heard her two friends discussing the date, he called Zac to tell him to start following Jade as soon as she left Fenrir, despite the fact that the ink on the contract hadn't even dried.

He went back to his office downtown and tried to concentrate on his work. But, he couldn't. Not when all he could think about was Jade's date. By seven p.m. he was crawling out of his skin and after confirming Jade's location with Zac. He went to the restaurant where he tailed Jade. Sebastian ordered full surveillance, and when he got a picture of Jade's date, he sent it to his best computer guys and had them do a search on all law enforcement databases. After seeing the records, he went into a rage. Even worse was when he watched

Jade and Daniel leave the restaurant and head towards his apartment. It took all of Sebastian's strength not to tear the man's head off.

Sebastian told himself he was doing the right thing. He couldn't let Jade fall for that asshole. She hated him even more now. No, that was good. That was the point. Jade should stay away from him. But still, he had a job to do—protect Jade and find out who was trying to kill her. And today, he found himself back at Fenrir Corporation. He needed to ask Grant for more information and more access to Jade so he could do his job. Then, maybe, he could put Fenrir and Jade behind him, and get on with his miserable life.

"Mr. Creed," Jared greeted him. The younger man was leaving his desk, a stack of folders in his arms. "Mr. Anderson is running a bit late. He's stuck in an HR meeting, but said you should go ahead and wait for him inside his office."

"Thank you, Jared," Sebastian said.

"I need to drop these off at Mrs. Westbrook's office, but I can get you some coffee or tea as soon as I'm back."

"Just water, please."

"Of course, Mr. Creed," Jared said with a nod as he left.

Sebastian let himself into the office, taking the seat opposite Grant's large desk. He sat there, looking around the room, trying to put pieces of the puzzle together. The CEO's desk was neat and held no personal items, or other things that might give a hint to Grant's personality outside of Fenrir Corporation.

The sound of the door opening caught his attention. Expecting to see Grant stride in, he stood to greet his client. He was surprised, however, as a petite woman in a yellow floral dress walked into the room.

"Oh, excuse me," she said, realizing there was someone else in the room. "Jared wasn't at his desk, and I just assumed Grant was in here."

Sebastian eyed the woman. She was pretty and he couldn't help but appreciate the sight before him. Lush curves filled the dress in the right places, and her thick, jet-black hair was piled on top of her head. Her most startling feature was her eyes—one green and one blue. And they were staring right back at him.

The woman crossed her arms over her chest. "Can I help you, Mr..."

"Sebastian Creed," he said, walking towards her and extending his hand.

"Oh." Her lips parted, then spread into a smile. "So, you're Sebastian Creed."

"And you are?"

"Frankie," she supplied.

"Grant's not here," Sebastian explained. "Sorry to disappoint you."

Frankie let out a chuckle, her eyes sparkling. "Oh, I'm not *that* disappointed. You certainly live up to your reputation, at least from what I hear from the women around Fenrir."

It was Sebastian's turn to laugh. "I do my best."

"Get your own wife, Creed, and stop trying to steal mine," Grant interrupted as he entered his office. He strode towards them, putting a possessive arm around Frankie's waist.

"I didn't know who she was," Sebastian said with an apologetic nod.

"I think you can forgive Mr. Creed, can't you Grant?" Frankie traced a finger on Grant's chest.

"My wife is gorgeous," Grant said, leaning down to press a kiss on her forehead. "I understand if men flirt with her. Not that I have to like it."

Frankie rolled her eyes. "Oh please. Like I never have to fight off women falling over themselves to get your attention."

Grant pulled her closer. "You never have to worry about me, sweetheart."

Sebastian cleared his throat, and the two lovers pulled apart, Frankie's cheeks growing pink.

"All right, Creed," Grant began. "Your assistant said you wanted to meet with me and that it was an urgent matter. I only have ten minutes to spare. I promised Frankie I'd take her to lunch."

"We get very hangry," Frankie stated, smiling at him and rubbing her belly. Sebastian didn't notice the slight bump there, but now he could see it. "I'll give you a few minutes, though. I have to answer some emails." She walked over to the couches and sat down, taking out her tablet.

"I just need five minutes," Sebastian stated as he sat down.

"Good. Now, what is it you wanted to talk about?' Grant asked as he stepped behind his desk.

"I need access to your lab. I mean, Dr. Cross' lab."

"Request denied," Grant said flatly. "Is there anything else?"

"What do you mean denied?" Sebastian's brows furrowed.

"I mean, no. You can't have access to her lab. It's restricted."

"I'll sign any NDA you want. Or I can give you a bond for whatever you think is the value of her work if there's a leak. But, if you want me to find whoever is trying to hurt Jade, then I need to be around her...work," he added.

"There's no reason for you to access her lab," Grant said. "The work she's doing there is of the utmost importance to me, and I can't risk it. Besides, that lab is stronger than Fort Knox. We have the most advanced security in there, and we just upgraded after the last breach."

"Last breach?" Sebastian asked incredulously. "And how many breaches have you had? Why does this keep happening?"

"Sebastian," Grant said in a deadly voice, his green eyes going dark. "Dr. Cross' work is of no consequence to you or the job I hired you for. Protect her. Keep her safe while she's outside of Fenrir. That's all you need to do."

Sebastian felt the anger rising in him. What was Grant hiding in that lab? All he wanted to do was protect Jade, and the best way to do that was to stop the threats on her life. "Grant. I—"

"*Madre de dio!*" Frankie exclaimed as she got up from her seat and walked over to the two men. "Mr. Creed, if you want to spend time with Jade, just man up and ask her out already!"

"That's not why I want access to her lab," Sebastian replied defensively.

"Sure, it isn't," Frankie said, her mismatched eyes sparkling.

Grant eyed Sebastian suspiciously. "My answer is still no."

Sebastian gritted his teeth, but nodded. "All right."

"Should I hire another company to do this job?" Grant asked. "Or can I trust you to be professional?"

The warning in the other man's voice was clear. "It's fine, Grant," Sebastian said, getting up from his seat. "Sorry for intruding on your time with your wife." He gave Frankie a last nod and then left the office.

CHAPTER TEN

The restaurant Gabriel picked was much classier than her previous date's choice. While Daniel took her to some hipster East Village restaurant, Gabriel seemed to pull out all the stops. It was French, of course, and according to Gabriel, it was very hard to secure a reservation. Luckily, the chef was a former client from his last job and agreed to give them a table on very short notice.

"Are you enjoying your *Matelote, cher*?" Gabriel asked.

"Yes, it's excellent." Jade took a spoonful of the fish stew. "Thank you for recommending it."

"*De rien, ma petite*," he replied, giving her another one of his charming smiles.

"My French is rusty," she said, putting her spoon down. "I hope you don't mind if we switch back to English for a bit."

"Not at all," he said. "But we can always practice your French later."

"So, tell me why you decided to work for Fenrir?" Jade asked, changing the subject. She caught the meaning in his voice, not that Gabriel was hiding it. The Frenchman was obviously trying to seduce her, giving small touches here and there, telling her she was beautiful. And she did feel beautiful. Tonight, Lara picked out her dress. It was a vintage red cocktail dress with a full skirt. Since it covered her back, she let the witch sweep her hair up in a fashionable updo. With the dress and the hair, Gabriel declared she looked like Audrey Hepburn.

"...And so when the opportunity came up, I thought, why not?" Gabriel finished his story of how Fenrir recruited him. Jade caught only half of it, but nodded anyway. "And how about you?" he asked. "You're quite young to be a Doctor, *non*?"

"Uh, yes, well, I finished school quite early," she explained. She gave Gabriel the details of her study and work history, a carefully crafted cover she and Mr. Vrost worked on—one that wasn't too different from her real background but didn't give away any details of her research.

"Ah, beautiful and smart," Gabriel declared, grabbing her hand from across the table. His hands were smooth and warm, and his fingertips were tracing lazy circles on her palms.

Jade couldn't help but frown. Here was a gorgeous and sexy man, paying her compliments and attention, but still she felt...nothing.

"Jade?" Gabriel asked, his brows drawing together. "Are you all right, *cher*?"

She pasted a bright smile on her face. "Yes, of course," she said, giving a small laugh. "I was thinking of something I forgot back at the office."

"Ah, well, sometimes it's hard to leave work, right?" he laughed. "How about some dessert? I was thinking we can have it to go and head back to my place? I have this lovely digestif that would go well with the apple tart."

———

"C'mon, Smith, I need something."

"Sorry, boss, I'm workin' as fast as I can." The voice from the comm unit in his ear sounded agitated, but Sebastian didn't care. That stupid Frenchman was probably charming the pants off Jade right now. He needed some dirt on him, like that idiot Daniel the other night. Smith was a genius, head of Creed Security's tech department and there wasn't anything on the planet he couldn't find.

"Um, boss," Zac whispered. "You ok?"

"Yeah," he said gruffly. "I'm fine."

"Don't break the steering wheel, though, yeah, boss?"

Sebastian looked at his hands as they gripped the wheel. His knuckles were white, and he could almost hear the plastic creaking under his fingers. Releasing his grip, he relaxed back into his seat and scowled.

He wasn't planning on being here tonight. The conversation yesterday with Grant and his perceptive little wife had rattled him. No, he didn't want to spend more time with Jade. Just the opposite. So, he decided to rotate Jade's protection detail among his best guys and have them log hourly reports. Last night, he didn't get anything unusual, just Jade going home after work, so he didn't pay much attention to what was happening.

Tonight, however, he was sitting at home, ready to head out to Luxe when he saw the latest report. Jade left her apartment at 7:06 p.m. with an unknown male subject and got into a cab headed uptown. Sebastian ignored it at first, but all the time he was sitting at Luxe, he kept waiting for the next report. When it arrived, saying that Jade and the unknown man were sitting inside some fancy restaurant with a name he couldn't even pronounce, Sebastian lost his cool. Leaving Luxe in a huff, he drove downtown as fast as he could, calling Smith on the way to have him find out who this man was.

He found the car tailing Jade tonight parked across from the restaurant. Sebastian must have scared the shit out of Zac when he pulled open the door and ordered the younger man to move to the passenger seat. By the time Sebastian had turned on his in-ear comm unit to call Smith, he already had a name. Gabriel Marchand, an employee at Fenrir Corporation, but nothing else.

"What's going on, boss?"

"None of your business," he growled.

"I mean, with the Doc and her date?" the younger man clarified. "They still in there? How long does it take to eat French food? Don't they have those tiny servings of leaves and sauce an' shit?"

"I wouldn't know, Zac," Sebastian replied. This place was fancy, for sure, and someplace you'd take a hot date to impress her. He wished he could get a visual of what was happening inside, but he couldn't see from the street, and he damn well couldn't just walk in there and tip them off before he found something incriminating on Marchand.

"Anything, Smith?" he called again.

"Workin' on it, boss," came the gruff voice in his ear. "No criminal records, no immigration flags, not even a parking ticket. But, I'm working an angle, I just need some time."

"Do what you can," he ordered and then switched the comm unit to mute.

"Boss," Zac nodded his head towards the restaurant.

Jade was leaving the restaurant with her date. Some blonde, male model-type Sebastian had never seen before. *So that was Gabriel Marchand*, he huffed. He didn't understand why women fell for men like Marchand. Too pretty and dressed way too fancy.

They were chatting as they stood on the street, and the way Jade looked up at Gabriel with a smile on her face set

Sebastian's teeth on edge. He wanted to punch something right now, preferably that Frenchman's jaw.

Gabriel waved down a passing cab, opened the door, and ushered Jade in. He then joined her in the back seat, and the cab sped away.

"I'm gonna need your car, Zac," he said as he turned the key in the ignition of the younger man's ancient Toyota. "Why aren't you driving one of the company cars, by the way? We have tons of new cars in the garage for you to use for stakeouts, you know that, right?"

"This seemed more authentic, boss," the younger man explained. "But, what about your ride?" he asked, tipping his chin towards the black Tesla Roadster parked behind them.

Sebastian didn't even glance at the car, but instead, tossed a set of keys to the other man. "Here," he said. "Take my car back to my apartment. I'll take it from here."

Zac looked at the keys like they were the Holy Grail. "Um... you sure, boss?"

"Yeah, go ahead. The key to my apartment's in there, too. You can crash at my place or get yourself a cab home." He nodded towards the passenger side door.

"Thanks, boss!" Zac said as he quickly exited the car.

It didn't take long for Sebastian to catch up with the cab. He memorized the plate number, and soon was following them discretely, staying at least two cars behind. They went all the way to the Upper West Side where the cab deposited the couple in front of a brownstone apartment building.

"Shit!" Sebastian cursed as he watched them walk up the stoop. He parked the car a few houses down, slamming the door shut as he exited the vehicle.

"Hey!" a voice called out to him. "You can't park there, buddy!"

He ignored the voice and instead turned on the comm unit as he strode towards the brownstone. "Smith," he barked. "Whatever you have on Marchand, I need it, now."

"Just sent it to you, boss," Smith said, relief in his voice.

"Thanks." Sebastian fished his phone from his pocket, opening the secure message from Smith. His eyes widened as he opened the link. "That fucking bastard!"

Luck must have been on his side because as soon as he reached the brownstone, one of Marchand's neighbors was leaving. He quickly slipped his hand into the door before it shut completely, glancing at the list of tenants to find Marchand's apartment. It was on the third floor, and he took the steps two at a time to get there.

Sebastian stalked down the hallway, all the way to the end. When he reached the door to Marchand's apartment, he stopped suddenly. *Shit. Fuck.* What exactly was his plan? Break in there? The Beast was howling. *Yes*, it said. *Get her. Kill him.*

With a growl, he pivoted away from the door. No. He couldn't. This obsession with Jade had to stop. Before she got hurt.

He must die. He touched her. Mine. Ours.

"Shut. The Fuck. Up!" he yelled as he slammed his hand into the wall. His fist went right through the plaster. Damn these old buildings. Practically made of paper.

"Sebastian?"

He turned around, following the voice, though it was no mistaking who it was. The sweet scent of cherries and vanilla filled his senses. "Jade," he whispered.

She blinked up at him. Once. Twice. There was a look of shock on her pretty face, which quickly scrunched in anger.

"What are you doing here?" she cried, marching up to him. "Are you foll—"

"Jade?" A voice interrupted her. "Everything all right?"

Sebastian swung his head towards the door behind them. Gabriel Marchand stood in the hallway, casually leaning against the wall. He wasn't wearing his suit jacket and tie, and his shirt was opened halfway down his chest. Jade backed away from Sebastian, running back towards Gabriel.

"I changed my mind again, Gabriel," she said. "Let's go back inside."

Gabriel flashed Sebastian a smug smile and put his hand on Jade's back. "Whatever you want, *cher*."

"You!" Sebastian stalked towards the other man, slamming his hand on the door.

"Do I know you?" he asked in heavily-accented English. "Are you one of my neighbors?"

"No," he replied and took his phone out of his pocket. He dialed the number that Smith had sent him. "But I bet you know who this is."

Gabriel frowned, looking at the screen. Then, his eyes widened in shock when the screen flickered to life.

"Gabriel?" The blonde woman on the tiny display had a confused look on her face.

"Sylvie!" he exclaimed. He tried to grab the phone, but Sebastian kept it out of his reach.

"Gabriel, who is that?" Jade asked as she peered up at the screen.

"Gabriel!" The woman on the phone screamed and let out a string of French. Both Gabriel and Jade flinched, and Sebastian didn't need to understand the language to know what she was saying. He tapped the red button on the screen and put his phone away.

"You asshole!" Jade shoved at Gabriel. "You're married? That was your *wife*?"

"Listen to me, Jade, *cher*," the Frenchman pleaded. "Yes, I'm married, but I thought you knew! You were the one who asked me to dinner!"

"Because you've been flirting with me for months!" Jade put her hands up. "And why didn't you say no when I asked you out."

Gabriel gave a shrug.

"That's what I thought, wanker!" She hit him on the shoulder with her bag. Turning around, she stormed past Sebastian, stomping angrily towards the elevators.

"*Merde!*" Gabriel cursed. "How dare you come in here and —" The Frenchman's head reeled back as a large fist connected with his jaw. He went straight down, his eyes rolling back and then closing.

"Fuck you, asshole," Sebastian said, as he rubbed his fist. It barely even hurt. Giving Gabriel one last disgusted look, Sebastian barreled down the stairs and out the door, chasing Jade down the street. "Stop!"

"What do you want?" Jade whipped around, raising her clutch at him. "Why won't you leave me alone!"

"I'm trying to keep you safe!"

"You're only supposed to guard me against the m—" She stopped short, putting her hand over her mouth.

"From who, Jade?" he asked, gripping her by her upper arms "Tell me who's trying to kill you!"

"Stay away from me!" she hissed, wrenching away from him.

"I'm taking you home," he said, taking Zac's keys out of his pocket. He pointed the key fob towards the direction of where he parked the car. "Fuck!" he cursed. A tow truck was pulling away, the Toyota hooked to its back. An old woman stood where the car was, her arms crossed over her chest. She gave Sebastian a dirty look, then flashed him the finger before disappearing into the nearest apartment building.

"Fucking New Yorkers," he muttered under his breath. He looked back and saw Jade climbing into a cab. "Shit. Jade!" It was too late. For the second time in a week, Jade Cross had once again run away from him.

CHAPTER ELEVEN

"Gabriel has a wife?" Meredith exclaimed.

Jade nodded. "She was on vacation, visiting her parents back in France." She couldn't help it. With a little bit of Facebook sleuthing, she found Sylvie Marchand's profile and confirmed she was, indeed, Gabriel's wife.

"Oh, Jade." Lara shook her head.

"I think I must be cursed or something," Jade sat down at her desk, placing her chin in her hands and staring at her computer screen. "First, a wife beater and then an adulterer. Let's forget the whole thing. I'm obviously going to be a virgin forever."

But it wasn't just that she kept ending up with the wrong men. Something was holding her back. Last night, she could have easily slept with Gabriel, but she couldn't do it. While they were at his apartment, all signs were pointing to them ending up in his bed. While having their dessert wine and apple tart, they sat on his couch, talking and chatting. He was charming, saying all the right things, making her feel good. Finally, Gabriel put their glasses away and moved in for a kiss. She should have let him, but something didn't feel right. Pushing him away, she got up and apologized, saying she had an early day, and quickly left his apartment. To her surprise, Sebastian was right outside Gabriel's door. But he wasn't waiting or even about to burst through the door. He looked like he was about to leave. Then the whole blowup happened, and, while she was angry, she was also relieved nothing had happened between her and Gabriel.

"You'll never get some with that attitude," Meredith said, trying to cheer Jade up. "We'll vet the guys you go out with. All I need is a computer, and I can run all kinds of background checks."

"The legal or illegal kind?"

"Which one do you want?"

Jade rolled her eyes. "Well, that takes care of one problem, but how about the other one?"

"And what is that?" Lara asked.

"Not what. Who," Jade said, scowling. "As long as I have my bodyguards, I'll never have any privacy."

"Sounds to me like someone wants to invade your lady cave," Meredith said casually.

"What are you talking about?"

"Well, it's obvious," Meredith said matter-of-factly. "Sebastian Creed is staking his claim. He's driving away all his rivals and making sure he's the only one sniffing around. He might as well pee all over you to mark his territory."

"Gross!" Lara tossed a balled-up piece of paper at the Lycan.

Jade shook her head. "Nuh uh. No way."

"Why is that so impossible to believe, Jade?" Meredith sat on the scientist's desk, dragging her hands away from the keyboard. "He's following you around, finding ways to get rid of all those guys. He wants you for himself, obviously."

"He does not!" Jade stood up so quickly she nearly knocked Meredith down.

"Yes, he does!"

"Then why didn't he have sex with me at the reception?" Jade suddenly shut her mouth when she realized what she said. *Oh, Merlin's pants.*

"Jade!" Lara exclaimed.

"So that's where you were when you disappeared? You naughty girl," Meredith said, her eyes going as big as saucers.

"I...I..." Jade sank back down into her chair.

Walking over to Jade, Lara put a hand on her friend's shoulder. "Jade, hon, what happened?"

Jade took a deep breath and told them everything. All the humiliating events of the night of the wedding reception and how she offered herself to Sebastian, but he rejected her.

"And then he just left?" Meredith asked.

"Yes," Jade answered, her eyes dropping to the floor.

"That asshole!" This time, it was Lara who got mad. "How dare he! He should be proud you were going to give him your virginity."

"I don't want to talk about that night anymore," Jade said somberly. Even though she completely trusted her two friends, the memory of the mortification was crushing her. Sebastian's rejection was making something in her middle ache. "I just want to get on with my life. And get him to stop cock-blocking me!"

"I believe the term, in this case, would be beaver damming." Meredith corrected.

"Or clam jamming," Lara offered.

"Or running clitorference?"

"Whatever," Jade shrugged. "While he's around, my cave won't be seeing any invaders."

"So," Meredith began as she stood up and paced back and

forth. "We need to get Creed to back off so you can get down to the business of getting some!"

"Oh my God, Mer," Lara said. "What have you got planned?"

The Lycan's eyes glinted. "Just leave it up to me. Jade, I need your phone."

CHAPTER TWELVE

"This is stupid."

"Shut up. It'll work."

"No, I mean this outfit is stupid!" Enzo Moretti whipped the bow tie from his neck and threw it on the ground. He was wearing khaki pants, a checkered shirt, and suspenders. "Matt does not dress up like some hipster douche!" He also tossed the fake glasses aside. "And he only wears glasses when he's working."

"Fine!" Meredith said. "But you better start acting like your brother."

Enzo rolled his eyes. "I don't even know why you think Matt is a better candidate for this. Besides, if you wanted him, why ask me?"

"Because Matt is too honest," Jade said from across the room. "He would never pretend to date me." And she didn't want the other man's feelings hurt, either. It was much easier to ask Enzo to play Matt.

"And what's wrong with being Enzo Moretti?" he asked indignantly.

"Aside from the fact that Creed has met you," Meredith

began. "You've got at least three arrests on your record. We need someone who Creed can't object to."

"Oh yeah," Enzo said, shaking his head. "I forgot about those. Alright, then, let's get this show on the road."

Meredith's grand plan was for Jade to pretend she was dating someone so perfect and boring, Sebastian couldn't possibly object. If Jade had a fake boyfriend, she could get Creed to back off enough so she could find an actual boyfriend (or one night stand, as Jade continued to protest that she didn't need or want a relationship). Jade and Lara thought it was a half-baked plan, but went along with it anyway because Meredith had the personality of a steamroller. They called up Enzo Moretti, explained they needed his help, and told him to meet them at Lara and Liam's suite at The Plaza Hotel. The young man was intrigued by their plan and was happy to help.

Meredith handed Enzo a small black device. "Here's your comm unit."

"What the fuck is this for?" Enzo eyed the small earpiece.

"It's so I can communicate with you," Meredith said matter-of-factly.

"Are you supposed to be using the comms this way?" Lara asked. "How did you get this, anyway?"

"Pshaw, details, details," the blonde said. "Okay, let's review Operation: Unjam the Clam. First, you guys will be center stage, and Lara and I will be in the booth across the room." She looked at Enzo. "Did you remember to book the right tables?"

"It's my restaurant, of course I did." The plan also involved staging the date at Muccino's, which had an extra layer of security so they could control most of the variables. And Meredith believed in having control of as many variables as possible to reduce risk in any plan.

"Good, good," Meredith cackled, rubbing her hands together like a movie villain. "Now you're ready. Go and get your car from the garage and pretend to pick Jade up here, okay? She's got a tail on her, the black Tesla Roadster. It's been following us since we left Fenrir."

"Yeah, yeah," Enzo said, putting the comm unit in his ear. "Hey babe, I got you in my ear!"

Meredith rolled her eyes. "Yeah, whatevs. Just make sure you listen to me, okay?"

"Aye, aye, Captain!" he said with a jaunty salute as he left the suite.

"Now," she turned to Jade and Lara. "How's it going on your end?"

"Just great, I'm almost done!" the witch said. She brushed some powder on Jade's face and then made the Lycan stand up.

"Perfect!" she said.

"Do I really need to be this dressed up?" Jade asked as she twirled around. Lara had picked out a beautiful tulle dress in a light powder blue color. It had a bustier top and a short skirt that ended just above the knee. Lara had pulled back her long brown locks into a high ponytail. It covered her back tattoo, but one swish of her head and the artwork was exposed. She felt self-conscious, having never shown her ink and scars before, but Lara and Meredith assured her it was beautiful.

"It's a special night, you need to look your best," Meredith said. "Now, Lara and I will go ahead to Muccino's. You give us a fifteen-minute head start, and then go down and meet Enzo in the lobby. Got it?"

"Yes, yes, I know," Jade assured them. "Go ahead."

The two women bid her goodbye before leaving the suite. Jade flopped down on the couch, counting the minutes until she had to go downstairs.

This was insane. But she knew one thing for sure: her friends loved her. They loved her so much that they would do anything for her, even come up with harebrained plans just to get her laid. God, she hoped this would work. She had to drive Sebastian away before she became a complete nutter.

After the fifteen minutes had passed, she stood up, left the suite, and headed down to the lobby.

"My lady," Enzo said as he stepped out of the bright yellow Dodge Challenger. He walked to the passenger side and opened the door for her.

"Enzo, why didn't you switch cars with Matt?" Jade asked. "This isn't going to work. Sebastian will run the plates and figure out who you are."

"Oh, ye of little faith," Enzo said in an exasperated voice. "This *is* Matt's car. On paper anyway." He helped Jade in and then walked over to the driver's side, sliding into the leather seat. "You think I can get a car like this with my record? Shit, no. Matt had to put his name on the deed, and well, we're twins and all, so it's not that hard to pretend to be each other. We've been doing it for years."

"What does Matt drive?" she asked.

"A Kia," Enzo said as he jammed his foot on the gas, making the engine roar to life. He looked in the rearview mirror. "Now, since I'm not getting paid for this, how about we have some fun? Let's see if we can lose that glorified Prius your bodyguard is driving."

"Enzo!" Jade exclaimed as the car lurched forward. She clung onto the grab handles and seriously began to question her life choices.

———

"Looks like Operation: Unjam the Clam has begun," Meredith whispered into the comms.

Jade and Enzo strode into Muccino's, her arm on his. To his credit, Enzo did seem to transform into Matt, putting on the quieter persona of his twin. It was a big change from the time they were inside the car, as he gleefully wove in and out of New York traffic, trying to lose Sebastian. For a while, they thought they got away, though Enzo slowed down enough so the other man could catch up. Losing him wasn't the point of the plan, after all.

"Jade? Enzo? What the hell are you doing, dressed up like that?" Frankie Anderson exclaimed as she approached the couple.

"Shhh!" Enzo whispered to his sister. "I'm Matt, not Enzo!"

"No, you're not!" Frankie said, which made Enzo reach over and cover her mouth. She brushed him off. "What is going on?"

"Lupa!" Meredith said as she approached the trio. "Sorry, I didn't know you were working tonight or I would have explained. This is a secret op. We're calling it Unjam the Clam." The younger Lycan quickly told Frankie about their plan.

The Lupa let out a rich laugh. "You think Jade pretending to date Matt will drive away Sebastian Creed?"

"It's a perfectly reasonable assumption," Jade added.

Frankie shook her head. "Oh no, you're going to achieve the exact opposite. He's gonna go insane with jealousy, and then he'll never leave you alone. But, then, that might not be a bad thing?" The Lupa's blue-green eyes sparkled.

"Trust me, Lupa," Jade said. "That man won't be jealous." He probably didn't even feel any emotion, she thought bitterly.

"And they roped you into this hair-brained plan?" Frankie eyed her brother.

"Just go with it, Sis," Enzo urged.

"Alright, but don't say I didn't warn you," Frankie said as she walked away.

Enzo led Jade to the table in the middle of the dining room, taking her seat out and then sitting across from her. Lara and

Meredith were in a booth in the corner where they could see the couple, as well as most of the dining area.

Their waiter came to their table, and Enzo ordered for them since he already knew the menu forward and backward. He wasn't just part owner of Muccino's after all, but also the head host.

"The clam has entered the building!" Meredith whispered into their ears.

"The what?" Jade asked. "What are you talking about?"

"Wait, isn't Jade the clam?" Enzo quipped. "I mean...you know..."

Jade turned red as Enzo motioned to her lap.

"Fine. The jam is here. On your six, Jade."

Jade swung around. Her heart thudded as she saw Sebastian enter Muccino's, a scowl on his face as he lumbered towards them. God, he looked handsome, like he had stepped out of a magazine ad. He was dressed casually tonight, wearing a leather jacket and jeans, his hair spiked up into a faux hawk. His employee, Zac, was right behind him.

"You must think you're some kind of smart ass," Sebastian said as they stopped in front of their table. "Dr. Cross, kindly tell Mr. Moretti we're supposed to be keeping you safe, and he will not pull a stunt like that again."

"I—"

Before Jade could protest, Frankie came and put on her best surprised face. "Mr. Creed! How nice to see you again!" She looked meaningfully at Zac. "Will you and your...er...date be having dinner here? I'm sure I could find you a free table, especially if it's a special occasion. We're very inclusive here, I assure you."

Meredith laughed so hard Jade nearly went deaf, though she herself could barely contain her own giggles. She was glad the Lupa was on her side.

"I'm not...he's not my...wait, what are you doing here, Mrs. Anderson?" Sebastian looked genuinely confused.

"This is my restaurant, of course. I mean, it's the newest branch of my family's original restaurant. Muccino is my maiden name," she explained. "And how do you know my brother, Matt?" Frankie emphasized the name.

"Wait...your restaurant? Your brother?" Now he looked really confused.

"Yes, Matt is my half-brother. He's one of the geniuses of my family, you know?" Frankie eyed Enzo. "The first of our family to graduate college, and he works at a tech startup that's going to go big. Pure smarts. Unlike my other good-for-nothing brothers."

"Frankie," Enzo warned. "You shouldn't talk that away about...our other brothers."

Frankie's teasing eyes sparkled. "Well, we do have that one brother who's practically a convict."

"He was never charged," Enzo said as he gritted his teeth. "Only arrested."

"Anyway, Jade," she said, giving the younger woman a pat on the shoulder. "You're in good hands with Matt, and if he doesn't treat you right, he'll answer to me." Frankie looked back at Sebastian. "So, a table for you two?"

Zac swallowed a gulp. "I'll go wait in the car, boss," he said as he walked away.

"Just one," Sebastian said gruffly. "That one," he said, pointing to the table directly behind Jade.

"Of course. Just a moment," Frankie signaled to one of the waiters. "All right, Mr. Creed. Go ahead and sit down. One of my servers will bring you a menu."

Sebastian gave Enzo one last glare and then walked to his table.

Frankie placed her hands on her hips and leaned down to

stare at Jade straight in the eyes. "The way that man looks at you, Jade..." She sighed and shook her head. "You are in big trouble. Remember what they say about apex predators: don't show him your back and for God's sake, don't run." She whipped around and headed to the host's station, where a group was waiting for their table.

Jade's hands curled into fists. How dare he? How could he just walk in here and think he could interrupt her fake date?

"Careful, Jade, I can see the steam rising out of your ears," Meredith said into the comm.

"Is he really sitting behind us?"

"Oh yeah," Enzo answered, glancing behind Jade. "And it looks could kill...well, let's say I'd be dead ten times over by now."

"I think this isn't working out the way we wanted," Lara whispered.

"Shush...it's all going exactly as planned," Meredith said.

"How?" Jade grumbled. "He's supposed to back off and leave me alone. Now he's practically sitting in our laps."

"The night isn't over yet, Jade," the other Lycan assured her.

"Don't remind me," Jade said wryly.

Thankfully, their antipasti arrived, and Jade dug into the delicious cheese and *proscuitto* plate, trying to ignore the fact that Sebastian's eyes were boring a hole into her head.

"Enzo," Meredith whispered. "You have to make it look more convincing. You should hold her hand or kiss her or something."

"What? Are you crazy?" Enzo exclaimed. "This guy looks like he could tear me in half right now. I don't want to die yet."

"Pussy," Meredith huffed. "Jade, start flirting! You guys look like you're attending a funeral, not a hot, romantic date."

Flirting? How was she supposed to do that? "Um, so, Matt... tell me about the company you work for." Enzo looked like he was a deer in headlights. *Oh, shoot a monkey!* That's right, she couldn't ask him about his job! He probably didn't even know the first thing about computers. "I mean, tell me about the restaurant! Your family owns it, right?"

Enzo looked relieved. "Uh, yeah...my grandparents moved to America from Italy and started it. The first one's in Jersey and my Nonna Gianna, that's my grandma's cousin, runs the kitchen there while my brother Dante works the one here."

"Sounds great," Jade said nonchalantly, taking a sip of the Chianti their server just poured into her glass. The cool liquid went down her throat and a warm feeling pooled in her belly. "How does your family manage to run both restaurants?"

"Well, Frankie still is general manager of both restaurants. She splits her time between the two. I run...I mean, my brother Enzo runs things here when she's gone. Rafe, my youngest brother and I help out on the weekends when it's packed," Enzo explained.

"Blah blah blah," Meredith interjected. "Are you guys gonna get it on or what?"

"We are not making out!" Jade hissed and downed the rest of her wine. "He's still there, right?"

"Oh yeah," Enzo said, tugging at his shirt's collar. "And it looks like he's done just watching."

"What?" Jade felt the shadow looming over her. Slowly, she looked up and saw Sebastian standing by their table. He had his arms crossed and a scowl directed right at her.

"Care to tell me what game you're playing?"

She gave him a venomous stare, poured herself another glass of Chianti, and chugged it down as delicately as she could. "I don't know what you're talking about."

Sebastian grabbed the comm unit from her ear, and threw it on the table then gave her a pointed look.

"Well, I'm done poking this bear," Enzo shrugged as he

stood up. "Good luck, buddy," he said to Sebastian as he walked away.

"Abort! Abort!" Meredith shouted from across the room as she and Lara stood up from the booth and scampered towards the rear exit.

"Traitors," Jade said to no one in particular. She made a grab for the bottle of wine, but Sebastian snatched it away.

"I think we're done here," he said. "Get up. I'm taking you home."

"But we haven't paid," she replied.

"I'm sure Enzo can put it on his tab. Let's go."

Jade shot him an annoyed look. *How the fudge did he figure out that was Enzo and not Matt?* She huffed and pushed back on her chair, the wood scraping loudly against the floor. "I'm perfectly fine getting home on my own."

A large hand wrapped around her arm. "You're not getting away from me this time, darlin'." Sebastian tugged her towards the exit.

"Have a good evening, Mr. Creed. Jade," Frankie said as they left Muccino's. Pleading eyes sent to the Lupa did nothing, and Jade found herself being dragged out the door.

"Will you please stop manhandling me?" Jade demanded as soon as they were outside.

"Only if you promise you won't run away again."

"Fine. I won't."

Sebastian released her arm, sending her a warning glare. "Don't move from that spot." He took his phone out of his pocket and dialed.

She considered making a run for it, but the Lupa's warning rang in her head. Still, the nerve of this man! And where were her friends? Shouldn't they be coming to her rescue? Maybe they didn't love her, after all. She'd give them a piece of her mind tomorrow.

A sleek black car pulled up in front of them, and Zac got out of the driver's seat. "Here you go, boss."

"Thanks, Zac," Sebastian said. "Open the door for the lady, would you?"

"No prob." The young man walked over to the other side and pulled the passenger side seat open.

Jade stomped over to the car and glared at Zac. "I hope you're happy with yourself."

"Just followin' the boss' orders, Doc," he shrugged.

With a huff, Jade got into the passenger side seat and angrily clicked her seatbelt into place. Sebastian spoke to Zac and then slid into the seat beside her. Without a word or glance at her, he drove away from Muccino's.

"Where are we going?" she finally asked.

"I'm taking you home, where you can stay out of trouble," he said gruffly.

"I wasn't in any kind of trouble!" Jade protested.

"Then what was that all about? You never go out, not even to dinner or with your girlfriends, and now you've had three dates in a row?"

"Who I go out with is none of your business!" she sneered.

"You're a virgin. You can't possibly know what those men want from you," he said through gritted teeth.

"And what if I told you I wasn't a virgin anymore?"

The car suddenly stopped with a loud screech. His hands gripped the steering wheel, and then his head slowly swung towards her. "Who the fuck is he?" Sebastian bellowed, his gray eyes turning to stone. "Who touched you?"

The interior of the two-seater sports car was already compact, yet Jade felt the air inside constrict. The anger from Sebastian was palpable, making it hard to breathe. "I haven't...I didn't..." She shook her head.

Sebastian visibly relaxed and Jade felt the tension ease.

"Not that anything's going to happen anytime soon with you always around," she grumbled, sinking back into her seat.

"What are you talking about?"

"Nothing!" she said petulantly.

Sebastian continued driving and, after a few minutes, they stopped in front of her apartment building. Jade unbuckled her seatbelt and stormed out of the car, heading straight through the doors.

The doorman greeted her good evening, but she ignored him. She thought she had gotten rid of Sebastian, but he quickly caught up with her as she entered the elevator.

She seethed, pressing herself against the wall, trying to get as far away from him as possible. Why the hell was he following her?

As soon as the doors opened, she marched out, ignoring Sebastian as he called her name.

"Just wait, Jade!" Sebastian's boots stomped on the hardwood floors as he overtook her, blocking her front door.

"I'm here at home where no one can harm me! I'd say your job is done for the day!" She pushed against him, not that it did anything.

"Stop, Jade. Stop!" he bellowed. "Now, tell me what's going on with you. What was tonight all about? Why was your friend coaching you on the comm?"

"Coaching me?"

"That's what they were doing, right? I could hear them, you know. Your friends weren't being subtle, and I know when I'm being watched."

She frowned. Did he hear the comm unit from that far away? "If you must know, they were helping me."

"Helping you get laid?" he said, his jaw tensing.

"Helping me get rid of you!" She looked up at him, her eyes blazing with anger. "You've been interfering with my dates—"

"You mean saving you from those losers?" he retorted. "Really, Jade? That asshole Daniel and then that slimy French guy?"

Jade felt the mortification course through her veins, her cheeks flaming. "So, I've made some questionable choices! That doesn't give you the right to judge me or make me feel small or worthless, just because I can't get a guy to..." She fought the tears threatening to spill, swallowing down the great big lump forming in her throat.

Sebastian's face changed from anger to shock. "No," he shook his head, running his fingers through his hair. "Fuck! Jade, that's not...you're not worthless!" He pushed her against the door, trapping her with his arms. "You're not, Jade. Absolutely. Not. Worthless. You're worth more than any treasure in this world."

"Then why did you..." No, she couldn't take it anymore. He was too much, too overpowering. His scent seemed to envelop her, clinging to her, and it was making her dizzy. She tried to wiggle away from him, but he was too big, too strong. "You didn't want to be my first, but I can't have anyone else?" Anger bubbled up inside her. What was his game? Did he get some sick enjoyment from humiliating her? "What kind of thinking is that? That you get to screw whoever you want but I can't—"

"I haven't been with anyone else!" he roared. "Not since you."

"Well, good for you. I'm sure this job's been keeping you busy, but don't worry, I won't be inconveniencing you for much longer!"

"I mean I haven't even looked at another woman since Liam Henney showed me your picture the night before we rescued you!"

Jade's jaw dropped, the shock from his confession making

her freeze. That was weeks ago! Had he really not been with anyone else? "Then why?"

"Why what?"

"Why did you run away from me in the greenhouse? When you found out I was a virgin? Were you repulsed by the thought of touching me—"

Sebastian pushed his body against her, and something hard and warm poked at her stomach. "Does this feel like I'm repulsed? Goddammit, woman, I've had a near permanent hard-on since I met you, and I can't get it to go away."

Jade didn't think she could be more shocked. Or aroused. Sebastian's rock hard body pinning her against the wall, his cock pressing insistently at her, it was too much. Desire pooled in her belly, making her nipples hard and wetness gush between her legs. "Sebastian," she said in a low voice, her eyes dropping.

"Don't say my name like that, darlin'," he whispered as he bent his head. "Or I won't be able to hold myself back."

His lips were close to her ear she could feel his hot breath. She looked up at him, first into his steely eyes and then to his mouth.

With groan, he bent his head down and pressed his mouth against hers. She eagerly accepted his kiss, opening up to him so he could dip his tongue into her mouth. He tasted even more delicious than she remembered, and oh so warm and masculine. Teeth nipped at her bottom lips, sucking back. He was devouring her, consuming her, and Lord knows she wanted it.

He pulled away, and she whimpered at the loss. He groaned, thumping his forehead against the door.

"Sebastian...please..." She slid her hands up his hard chest. "I want you to be my first," she confessed. "It doesn't have to mean anything afterwards. I swear I don't need a relationship."

———

The Beast roared inside him, and he pulled away from her.

Jade was offering herself to him, no strings attached. Wasn't that the perfect arrangement for a man like him? Have his fill, get what he wanted, and then leave without any consequences.

Sebastian looked down at her, ready to walk away. The blush on her cheeks made her look even more beautiful and innocent. If only it were someone else. But not her. He shouldn't be anyone's first. He was too rough, too jaded. He should say no.

"Yes," he said against his better judgement. He brushed a strand of hair away from her forehead, running his fingers down her smooth cheek to her jaw and down to her collarbones.

"Do you want to come in?" she asked, looking up at him with expectant eyes.

He nodded, unable to say another word. Jade twisted around, grabbed her keys from her purse and opened the door. She walked in, taking his hand.

Sebastian looked around Jade's apartment, taking in everything at once. It was neat, not overly feminine, but not too cold either. The decor was very homey, with a large central living and dining area and an open kitchen in one corner. An entire wall was lined with bookshelves, filled with probably close to a hundred books. On the opposite wall was a door that probably led to the bedroom.

Jade stepped out of her shoes, then padded to the living room, placing her purse on the coffee table. She turned around, looking up at him with her light green eyes.

He closed the distance between them in a few strides. Gently, he gathered Jade into his arms, lifting her up and wrapping her legs around him. Fuck, he could feel the heat of her core through their layers of clothing. Her sweet scent shot desire straight to his crotch, making his cock strain even harder against his jeans. With a grunt, he settled them down on her couch, making Jade straddle him.

"Are we going to have sex on the couch?" she asked, her brows wrinkling.

"No," he said with a small smile. "Not yet. Not tonight."

"But I thought—"

Sebastian silenced her with a kiss, his beard scratching at her delicate skin as his lips sipped from hers. "Your first time will be special," he said, staring deep into her eyes. "I don't want you to think about what happened tonight or any other night before this. I'm going to make you forget about what I did and how I made you feel like nothing."

"Then what are you...oh!" Her eyes rolled back as Sebastian spread her knees and shifted her hips, so the bulge under his jeans hit her in the right spot. Her scent was mixed with something else, something he couldn't identify but was probably all her, and it went straight to his brain.

"Tonight's just a little preview, darlin'," he drawled. "Just so you know what you're getting into and to give you a chance to change your mind."

"I won't," she said, frowning at him.

"Still..." He buried his hand in her hair and pulled her to him for another kiss. Her sweet, lush mouth opened up to him, warm and delicious. She sighed against him, pressing her curves against him. His hand crawled up her ribcage, pulling her dress down to release her breasts. He palmed one soft tit, the hard nipple pressing against his palm.

"Sebastian," she cried out, her hands planting on his shoulders as she arched into him. He shoved his other hand under her skirt. His fingers slipped between then, tracing the seam of her pussy through the damp, silky panties. "Please, please," she moaned. Glittering green eyes looked at him, pleading. "I've never...had an orgasm."

"Fuck," he groaned. "Never?"

She shook her head, her cheeks heating.

"Don't be embarrassed, darlin'," he cooed. "That's nothing to be ashamed of." She was completely untouched, innocent, and he would be the one to give her the first taste of pleasure. He wanted to make sure it was memorable. Picking her up like she weighed nothing, he laid her back down on the couch cushions, then took off his leather jacket. It was getting way too hot in here.

Her eyes looked at him appreciatively as he sat there in his white t-shirt. Her gaze moved across his broad shoulders, over his muscled arms, lingering on the tattoos that covered his left arm.

"Just lay back and relax, Jade," he said, flashing her a wicked smile. He positioned himself between her legs, spreading her knees and pushing the skirt up around her waist. Her white silk panties were soaked through, the wet spot in front growing. She smelled delicious, and it took all his energy not to rip her panties away. Sebastian hooked his fingers over the waistband and pulled the fabric down, exposing her perfect, pink cunt.

"Sebastian!" she cried out as he pressed his lips against her. She squirmed under him as he made a meal out of her, kissing and licking her wet nether lips. Her scent filled his nostrils, and her taste on his tongue and in his mouth were driving him crazy. He rubbed his cock against the couch cushions, trying to relieve the ache.

She dug her hands into his hair, raking her fingers through the strands as she pushed her hips up to get closer to his mouth. Sebastian thrust a tongue inside her tight little hole, making her squirm and thrust her hips. His finger found her hard clit, and he rolled it between his thumb and forefinger, teasing her in a slow, torturous dance. He was relentless, keeping the rhythm of his tongue and fingers on her. He didn't stop, not even when her pussy walls clenched around his tongue and her honey flooded his mouth.

Jade screamed, lifting her hips up off the couch, her pussy squeezing around his tongue. Sebastian reveled in her first orgasm, pride surging in him knowing he had given it to her. Fuck, he could come right then and there, surrounded by her scent and her soft thighs around his head. He took a deep breath, scrambling for the control that seemed to be on the verge of shattering.

She fell back on the couch, her breathing ragged. Sebastian took his shirt off and tossed it aside, then moved up over her. His eyes devoured the sight of the rise and fall of her breasts, her skin flushed and covered in a light sheen of sweat. Bending his head down, he kissed her, letting her taste herself on his lips.

"That was..." she sighed when he pulled away. She closed her eyes and let out a short breath.

"It's not over yet," he teased.

Her eyes flew open. "It's not?"

"Oh no...that was your first orgasm, but not your last." He pulled her panties back up, then hooked his arms under her and pulled them both up on the couch, in the same position they started, with her knees on either side of his thighs, straddling him. Pushing the frothy fabric of her skirt up, he slipped one hand between them.

"I thought you said we weren't going to have sex tonight?" she asked, cocking her head to the side.

"That's why we're keeping these on," he said, stroking the fabric of her panties with his knuckles. He lifted her hips so he could unbutton his jeans. His cock was hard as steel, and he needed some relief. Wrapping a fist around his cock, he pressed up against the silky, wet fabric of her panties.

Jade gasped, and she rocked her hips forward. Her eyes grew wide, and she moved her own hand between their bodies.

A soft, delicate palm wrapped around his dick and he nearly came right then and there.

"Jade?" he asked in a ragged voice. "What's wrong?"

She was frowning. "Er...I'm a doctor, and I know biology, but are you sure this will work?"

He let out a pained laugh. "Don't worry, darlin', it'll work. I...ugh!" She gave his cock a gentle squeeze, and it took every ounce of what was left of his control to stop from cumming all over her dainty fingers.

"But I can't even wrap my hand all the way—"

"Sorry, darlin'. You need to stop," he said, quickly pulling her hand away. He gave her soft kiss, then repositioned her over him. He pressed his cock up between her smooth thighs, the underside sliding against her heat.

"Sebastian..." she sighed, arching her breasts up against him. He bent his head down and captured a nipple, drawing it deep into his mouth.

He moved his hips, sliding his cock between her thighs. She cried out his name, and ground her hips down, the fabric of her panties getting even wetter. Jade moved faster and faster, pushing against him harder as her body tensed, her second orgasm fast approaching. He could feel her hard clit through the soaked fabric, bumping against the length of his cock.

"Fuck!" he cried out, unable to stop himself as he spilled his cum all over her thighs and belly, the sticky liquid shooting out so hard he thought he would pass out. He popped the nipple back into his mouth, giving it a gentle nip. That seemed to send her over the edge as she screamed, clutching onto him, her fingernails digging into his shoulders as her body shook with her orgasm.

She collapsed against him, her sweaty body trembling with small aftershocks. He wrapped his arms tight around her, holding her close. Hanging his head back over the couch, he took a deep breath, remembering to suck air into his lungs.

Her breathing slowed down, and she slowly pushed herself back, planting her hands on his chest. "That was...uh..." Her cheeks were flushed, her eyes glazed over, and tendrils of hair were sticking to her face. She was magnificent.

"I told you, darlin'," he said, tipping her chin up to meet his gaze. "You never have to feel ashamed or embarrassed with me. I won't ever let you feel like that again."

"I'm just...this is...sorry, I don't know what to say." She planted her face in her hands.

He pulled her hands away and drew her down for another kiss. This time, he was gentle, pressing his lips against her softly.

She started to move her hips again, then gasped and pulled away. "I'm sorry...I should...uh...get you a towel." She scampered away, disappearing into the bedroom.

Sebastian leaned back, stretching his arms out. He looked down at his cock, which, for some reason, was already half hard, despite having just shot a load all over Jade's sweet thighs. Fuck, he needed to be inside her, but he calmed himself. He meant what he said. When he took her for the first time, she would only remember him. Jade looked beautiful tonight, as she did every night, but she didn't dress up for him. And damn if that didn't make him want to destroy something. He craved her, all of her. Wanted to see her get all nice and pretty just for him, thinking of him when she picked her outfit or put on her lipstick. He was a selfish, possessive bastard for sure, but he couldn't help it.

Her words suddenly rang back in her mind. *It doesn't have to mean anything afterwards.* She didn't want a relationship. She just wanted some stud to help her get rid of her cherry and then what? His hands clawed at the couch cushions.

"Sebastian?" Jade called softly. She had changed into a terry cloth robe, and held a towel in her hand.

"Thanks," he nodded, then stood up and took the towel from her. He entered the bathroom and wiped himself down. Tossing the towel and his ruined underwear into the hamper, he washed his hands quickly, pulled on his jeans, and went back to the living room.

Jade sat on the couch, her arms wrapped around her legs. Her face didn't have a trace of makeup, and her hair flowed down in waves around her shoulders. God, she looked exquisite.

"Everything all right?" she asked in a small voice.

Sebastian sat down next to her, gathering her into his arms. He kissed the top of her head. "Yes. And you?"

She sighed. "It was...more than I could hope for."

"Good," he said, stifling a yawn.

"Well, um, I guess if you're tired...you can head home. I've got an early day, too and I'm sure—"

"You kickin' me out?" He frowned. Something squeezed around his chest, making it hard to breathe.

"No, I mean...you don't have to stay...if you don't want to," she said, her eyes lowering away from him. "But you don't have to go, either."

"It's a long way downtown," he said. "And I am tired." He didn't wait for her to say anything but instead picked her up, carrying her back towards the bedroom. Pulling the covers aside, he placed her on the bed and then took his jeans off. He slipped into the bed, gently pushing her towards the other side to make room for him.

"Take off your robe." He wanted to feel her skin against his.

With a nod, she untied the belt and shrugged the material off her shoulders. She stiffened at first, as he wrapped his arms around her, but then relaxed against him.

They lay there in silence, and soon Jade's breathing became

even, and her body grew heavier against him. Sebastian brushed her hair aside, exposing her neck and back to him. On impulse, he kissed the whorls of ink on her back, his breath hitching when he felt the faint scar against his lips. He blinked, staring at her tattoo in the scant moonlight, trying to discern the raised tissue. It was long and straight, starting from the middle of her back and went straight down along the spine. It seemed the more he thought he knew Jade Cross, the more she became wrapped up in mystery.

There was one thing he knew for sure. He felt something he had never felt before. Calmness. The Beast inside him snorted in contentment and lay still.

CHAPTER THIRTEEN

J ade stared intently at her screen, trying to make sense of what she was reading. The text was fascinating, and she'd been devouring the old books, trying to find some clue as to how the mages figured out how to control humans. As far as she could tell, there were at least six separate sources from all over the world that talked about this kind of magic.

The knowledge itself didn't seem to come from one single source, and she wondered how Stefan was able to gather all the information. It must have taken the mage years, traveling thousands of miles to find the right people and encantations. One of the books was translated from old Norwegian and talked about the runes, while another book in Swahili had at least the first part of the necessary spell. But, finding out how he got the spell was only a minor part. How it worked, and more importantly, how to stop it, were the more crucial tasks at hand.

In the beginning, she put off having to interview Marcus. Fear and apprehension prevented her from even looking at the mage. He had, after all, orchestrated her kidnapping and detention. The Alpha had been generous, giving her as much time as she needed before confronting Marcus. However, the clan needed her. She was the only person who could figure out how the mages were controlling the humans and how to stop them. Now, she was ready to face Marcus.

"Jade!" Meredith called from the main lab downstairs. The other Lycan was late. Usually, Meredith arrived at the lab at the same time or just before Jade arrived, escorted by one of the Lycan security people. Jade was surprised to find the lab empty that morning, but it meant she could work in peace.

"Good morning," Jade replied as she descended the staircase.

"Sorry, I'm late," Meredith said, plopping herself on her favorite office chair. The blonde Lycan had declared it her princess chair, and covered it in pink and purple glitter stickers, writing "Princess Meredith" all over the back. Jade had warned her that was vandalism, to which she replied, "Awesome. Put it on my tab."

"What happened?"

"There was some excitement with my roommates." She rolled her eyes. Her "roommates" were Marcus and Daric, who were detained on the same floor as her, deep in Fenrir Corporation's super secret, secure bunker. Meredith had never actually seen either of them during her time there nor shared a room with them, but said roommates sounded much better than fellow prisoners. "Anyway, the security guys were tied up, not literally—but damn, have you seen that Tate Miller? Anyway, they were all busy, so there was no one to bring me here."

"Well, I was just working, so no worries," she turned to walk back up the stairs, but Meredith used her cat-like reflexes to bounce from her chair and catch her arm, spinning her around.

"Hold on, young lady! Aren't you going to tell me what happened last night?"

Jade clamped her mouth shut, her face going red all the way

to the tips of her ears. Oh, God. Last night. She still couldn't believe it. Had it really happened? Waking up, alone in bed this morning, she wasn't sure it was real. But the beard burns on her neck and between her thighs told her otherwise. She and Sebastian...on the couch. And then he slept over, right next to her on the bed. He held her all night, his rock hard body pressed up against her. It was still dark out this morning when she felt his lips on her cheek, murmuring an apology. There was some emergency at work, and he had to leave right away. She was half asleep, and she remembered reaching out to him—

"Hello? Earth to Jade?" Meredith waved a hand in front of her. "Oh. My. God. Was it that good that he literally fucked your brains out? Jade, you slut! High five!" The other Lycan raised a palm at her.

"Meredith!" she exclaimed, swatting the palm away "He didn't...we didn't..."

"You're telling me nothing happened?"

"Well, *not* nothing." God, she wished Lara were here. It was too bad she and Liam had to fly to San Francisco and wouldn't be back until next week.

"So you guys..." Meredith wiggled her eyebrows.

"I'm not telling you anything about my private life!"

Meredith, of course, took that as an invitation to cajole her further. "I don't need to know everything! Just the juicy bits! Although I should have known you didn't serve him your cherry pie since you can still walk straight."

Jade let out a pained groan. "Look, it's not what you think. And by the way, your grand plan was a failure. We didn't drive him away."

"Well, that was the genius of my plan!" Meredith cackled. "I knew Sebastian would either leave you alone or pull his head out of his ass and finally admit he wanted you himself."

"What?"

"Well, it worked, didn't it? Jealousy on a man is so hot and Sebastian was off the charts last night! And while you may still be v*irgo intacta,* you won't be for long, will you?"

"I—"

"You're welcome!" Meredith preened, giving her an exaggerated curtsey.

"Ugh!" Jade threw up her hands. "I don't know—" A vibration from her pocket startled her, and she quickly fished her phone out. She frowned when she saw the unknown number on the screen. "Hello?"

"Jade, it's Sebastian."

Her stomach did flip-flops, hearing his rough voice. "Um, hi," she said, feeling her face go hot. How could the bloody man make her blush over the phone? She quickly ran up the stairs to her inner office, locking the door behind her before Meredith could guess who it was.

"I'm sorry about this morning. We had an emergency with one of our jobs over in the Middle East," he explained. "Are you okay? How are you feeling?"

"I'm fine. Dandy. Just great," she said. God, did she sound like a dork? "How did you get my number?"

"I called my number from your phone before I left," he explained. "Listen, I don't have a lot of time to chat right now— I'm still putting out fires here—but I should be done here in a couple of hours. I'm taking you out tonight."

"Where are we going?"

"It's a surprise," he said cryptically. "But wear something nice. A dress. Like you had on last night." His voice was thick and warm like honey, and Jade wondered if he was thinking of the same thing she was. Could she go through with it? Maybe she should think about it first. Yes, she should step back and re-examine this whole thing.

"I'm not sure—"

"Great, I'll pick you up at seven, darlin'," he said, hanging up before she had a chance to protest.

Jade leaned back against her table, her brows knitting in confusion. He was taking her out? Like on a date? Honestly, she thought they could just go back to her apartment. It was a perfectly good place for sex, and she changed the sheets on her bed regularly. They didn't need to go somewhere fancy. Maybe some takeout at her favorite Chinese place beforehand.

"Was that him?" Meredith asked as she burst into the room, the supposedly locked door flying open.

"That door was locked," Jade said wryly.

"Did you forget who I am?" the other Lycan asked, waving a small metal tool in her hand. "You need a better lock."

Jade sighed and shook her head.

"Soooooo," Meredith said, sauntering over to her. "Are you going to see him?"

"I guess? I mean, yes. He's taking me out tonight. He said I should wear something nice."

"Woohoo! Shopping time!"

Jade groaned. It was a wonder she got any work done, spending half her days shopping. Looking at Meredith, dancing happily at the prospect of being able to get out of Fenrir, she sighed. *I'm such a pushover.*

———

"You look gorgeous," Sebastian said, his eyes roaming over her. He was standing outside Jade's door, looking handsome himself in a dark suit.

"Thank you," Jade replied, her skin heating from his perusal. As much as she hated shopping, she was glad Meredith convinced her to pick this dress. She thought the white color was a bit much, but it was sexy. The lacy sheath dress skimmed her slim figure, ending in an asymmetrical hemline. The deep V neckline flattered her cleavage without being vulgar, and the peekaboo ladder-stitch insets under and between the bust line gave just a tiny hint of what was underneath. It was the back that made the dress show-stopping. Thin straps crisscrossed over her naked skin, intersecting over the lines of her Tree of Life tattoo. Her hair covered the back part, so she felt confident enough to wear the dress.

"Now go change," he said gruffly.

"What?" she exclaimed.

"I can't stand anyone else seeing you in that dress," he said. "I'd end up spending half this date beating up anyone who looks at you and the other half trying not to tear it off. Go change, darlin'."

Jade stomped back into her apartment and grabbed the white shawl hanging from her coat rack. With an exaggerated flourish, she draped it over her shoulders. "Better?" she asked sarcastically.

Sebastian gave her a quick kiss on the lips, a gesture that sent zings of electricity straight to her core. "It'll do," he said, tying the shawl around her. "I can unwrap you later."

He offered his arm, and with a wry smile, she took it. They went downstairs, where his car was parked. He opened the door and helped her inside, then slipped into the driver's side.

"Where are we going?" she asked.

He flashed her a grin. "Like, I said, it's a surprise."

Sebastian drove expertly along the streets of Manhattan, heading downtown. They turned on 23rd Street and then slowed down as they approached 10th Avenue. He parked the car right underneath some old above-ground railroad tracks.

"We're at The High Line," Jade said, looking up at the old freight train line that was turned into a public park.

He said nothing, but exited the car and opened her door,

helping her out. He led her to one of the metal staircase, holding her hand as they ascended.

When they finally reached the top, Jade took a sharp breath of air. They were in the middle part of the park where a table and two chairs were set up on the lawn, surrounded by hanging lantern lights. Two people dressed in white shirts and black pants were waiting next to the table. A champagne bucket was standing by the side, chilling a green and gold bottle.

"Sebastian, how did you..." Her eyes darted around her, still wondering how he pulled this off. The High Line was a public park, after all, and tonight, they seemed to be the only ones there.

"You like plants, right?" he said, leading her towards the table. He pulled out her chair and helped her sit. "I thought you'd like it here. Have you been here before?"

She nodded. It was one of the few times she ventured out of midtown. "I love the concept of using only local flora. Do you know that all the plants here were sourced from local growers, no more than a hundred miles from Manhattan? The landscaping was actually built to create different microclimates so that's there's less—" She stopped short and blushed. "Sorry. I must be boring you. Meredith calls it my 'science word vomit' and I've been trying my best not to do it."

Sebastian chuckled. "You're not boring me," he said. "Not at all. I've never been here. Maybe you can show me the different plants later."

"I'd like that," she said.

Sebastian nodded to the two servers, and they quickly went to work. One opened the champagne bottle, and the other scurried to a small tent set up in the corner.

"Thank you," she nodded and smiled at the young man who filled her glass. "What should we drink to?"

"How about...to the High Line?" he said.

"Yes, to the High Line." They clinked glasses, and Jade took a delicate sip of the bubbly liquid.

"So, Doctor," he teased. "What else can you tell me about this park?"

As the waiters brought them their food, Jade began to spout off facts she had read about the park. Being a biologist and bioengineer, she loved everything about the concept of not only re-using the old freight car tracks but also planting species endemic to the area, which meant less waste and fewer plants dying. Sebastian listened to her attentively, asking questions every now and then, which meant he was actually listening to her. She felt a little self-conscious though, as his steel gray eyes stared at her intently, lingering on her lips or between her breasts when he thought she wouldn't notice. Or maybe he did want her to notice.

"I've talked your ear off, I'm afraid," Jade said as she took a spoonful of the caramel cheesecake. "Why don't you tell me about yourself? Where did you grow up? Do you have brothers and sisters?"

Sebastian's eyes suddenly turned a dark, stormy gray, and his body tensed. "I'd rather not."

"Oh," Jade said lowering her eyes. The tension in the air was tangible, and Jade felt herself shrinking away from him. She turned her head towards the view of the Manhattan skyline, closed her eyes, enjoying the feel of the cool air on her skin.

"Jade?"

She nearly jumped out of her chair, as Sebastian was suddenly beside her, his shadow looming overhead. "You move so quietly," she said, putting a hand over her galloping heart. That masculine scent that seemed to cling to him wafted through the air, making her dizzy.

"I got you something," he said, placing a robin's egg blue box with a white ribbon on the table.

"I..." She touched the box with her finger. "Th—thank you." No one had ever given her jewelry before nor did she see the point of buying some for herself, which is why she never wore any.

"You haven't even opened it."

Jade undid the white ribbon and opened the box. Inside, nestled in tissue paper, was a thin, delicate gold chain necklace. Lifting it up with her fingers, she realized it was actually three strands of chains linked together, each a different color of gold.

"May I?" he asked, offering his hand.

She nodded, and he helped her up, then made her turn around. His callused fingers brushed her hair aside, lingering a little longer on her skin. Taking the necklace from her, he draped it over her neck, letting the strands fall between her breasts.

"It suits you," he proclaimed, leaning down and pressing a kiss on her shoulders. His lips seemed to brand her skin, and she suddenly felt dizzy and feverish. "You should wear jewelry more often."

"Thank you," she managed to say.

Sebastian twisted her around to face him, snaked an arm around her, and pulled her up, slamming his lips down on hers. The kiss was wild and passionate, and she thought her knees would buckle if he weren't holding her up against him.

"Sebastian," she moaned, her hands moving into his jacket to get as close to him as possible. The hard muscles underneath his shirt tensed and flexed under her touch and he moved in again for a rough kiss.

"Jade," he rasped as he pulled away. "I can't wait. Do you want to leave now?"

She nodded, not sure if she could speak.

"I got us a room, not far from here. Just give me a sec."

Sebastian walked over to the two servers, giving them curt instructions.

A hotel room. There was a small part of Jade that was disappointed. She thought that well, maybe he would take her to his home. Her curiosity was burning with all the secrets Sebastian Creed kept hidden. No, she told herself. Better not to know. There was no point, not when there would be nothing between them after tonight. A stab of pain gutted her, but she pushed it down.

Sebastian walked back to her, placing an arm around her shoulders. "Are you all right?"

Jade tugged her shawl around her tighter. "I'm fine."

"Let's go."

Jade followed him down the metal steps and back into the car. The drive was short, less than five minutes, and they pulled up next to the tall, sleek building. A uniformed man waiting outside opened Jade's door and helped her out, and then took the keys from Sebastian.

He guided her into the doors of the Gansevoort Chelsea Hotel, walking past the luxurious lobby and straight into the elevators. Jade felt her heart beat staccato rhythm against her chest. A few people got on the elevator with them, and she pressed herself back against the cold metal wall.

After a few minutes, they arrived on the top floor. They stepped out, and Sebastian led them to the door on the right, opening it swiftly with his keycard.

The first thing Jade noticed about the suite was the view— an entire wall was made of glass, giving them an incredible view of the Hudson River. The room itself was massive, decorated in a modern style in dark gray and black tones. There was a large sofa in the middle facing the window, a bar in the corner and a kitchen/dining area to the left.

"I hope you like the room," Sebastian said, walking up

behind her, removing his coat and loosening his tie. His arms came around her waist, pulling her to him. She gasped when she felt the bulge poking against her lower back. "Change your mind yet?"

She shook her head and then turned around in his arms. "No. I want this. I want you."

With a low growl, Sebastian picked her up and walked them towards the bedroom, lying her down on the soft mattress. He removed the loosened tie and began to unbutton his shirt.

Her eyes devoured him. As he removed the shirt, she watched the muscles on his arms and chest ripple with contained power. She also found out the answer to her question that night at Blood Moon. The tattoos went from his left wrist all the way across his chest, a mix of various designs from tribal to classic to modern lines. There were a few military ones, too, and some she didn't recognize. But she thought they were all beautiful and suited him so well. God, he was massive, and she felt a twinge of fear that he would crush her. But she knew he wouldn't. Not Sebastian.

"Hmmm..." Jade mewled, throwing her head back. Suddenly, Sebastian grabbed her by her legs and pulled, hauling her up on his lap. She could feel his erection pushed up against her nakedness, and she grabbed onto his shoulders to get some leverage as she ground against him.

"Slow down, cowgirl," he teased. "This won't be like last night. This time, it's gonna be the real thing. Are you ready?" His gray eyes searched hers, waiting on her, giving her one last chance to turn back.

Jade nodded. "Yes. Sebastian."

He let out a growl from deep within his chest, and she thought she saw a flash of gold in his eyes. That was probably her imagination, her brain heady with pleasure. His hands reached behind her, finding the zipper of her dress and pulling it down. Jade eased down the straps on her shoulders, exposing her breasts to his heated gaze.

Sebastian bent his head, kissing her between her breasts, then capturing a nipple with his mouth. The sensation of his warm tongue on her sensitive nipples sent pleasure straight between her thighs.

"God, you're so perfect," he murmured against her skin.

Suddenly, her eyes flew open as she felt something against her thighs. Something...vibrating? "Sebastian!" she called.

"Yes, darlin'..." he soothed, his hand stroking her back and his mouth drawing in the other nipple.

"Sebastian...no..."

His head popped up, a confused look marring his face. "No?"

"I mean yes, but...there's uhm...something vibrating in your, er...pants?"

Sebastian let out a cuss and released her. He shoved his hand into his pocket and retrieved his phone. "Shit!" he cursed, looking at the screen. With a sigh, he gave Jade an apologetic look. "I told the office to contact me for absolute emergencies only. Sorry, darlin'."

"It's fine," she replied in a breathy tone. "Go ahead."

With a nod, he answered the phone with a gruff hello, and then slid away from the bed. Jade watched as his ripped back muscles tensed. He slowly turned to face her.

The look on his face made Jade's blood run cold. He put a hand over the receiver. "Where's your phone?"

"It's in my purse," she answered.

"Go check it," he urged.

Her heart thumped, and she knew something was going on. She slunk off the bed, pulling the straps of her dress up to cover herself. Walking out into the main suite, she snatched her purse and pulled her phone out. Eight missed calls. All from Fenrir.

Dread gripped her chest like a vice, and she quickly tapped on the green button to call the number back.

"Dr. Cross," Nick Vrost answered, his voice tight. "Where are you?"

"I'm...I'm out," she said nervously.

"Are you safe? Do you have your protection detail with you?"

"Yes." *I supposed this counted*, she thought to herself.

The Beta let out a sigh of relief. "Good. Stick to your security team. Whatever you do, don't come to Fenrir. Go home."

"Mr. Vrost, what's going on?" She chewed on her lip, anxiously waiting for Nick to give her good news.

There was a pause, and finally, Nick spoke. "I'm afraid the mages tried to break into Fenrir. Marcus is dead."

She let out a soft cry. "I'm sorry. I mean..." Oh God, she would never get to talk to Marcus now. They would never find out how the mages were controlling humans. It was all her fault for being so weak.

"Jade," Sebastian called as he stood in the doorway. "Did they tell you?"

She nodded, the lump in her throat preventing her from speaking.

He padded over to her, gathering her in his arms. "I'll keep you safe. I promise, nothing will happen to you."

God, she wanted to break down. He was so big and warm, and she felt so safe. She wanted his comfort and his solace.

"You know who's out to get you, don't you?" he asked, his voice growing cold. "Tell me, Jade. Tell me so I can put him away."

She tried to speak, but all that came out was a choked sob. "I...I don't know."

"You're lying," he growled, his hands going to her shoulders. "Tell me now."

What was she supposed to say? Should she make something up? She shouldn't have done this, shouldn't have gotten so close to him. Now she not only lost the opportunity to deal a major blow to the mages, but their secret could be exposed. "I'm sorry, Sebastian," she pulled away from him. "Take me home now, please."

The anger seemed to roll off Sebastian, and she nearly shrank under the heaviness of the air around them. He turned as silent as a stone and stalked back to the bedroom. Jade stood there, rooted to the spot until he came out again, buttoning his shirt.

"Let's get out of here," he said, not looking at her.

She followed him meekly, keeping her distance. It all seemed like a blur to her, the events whirling in her mind. Soon, she found herself in his car, and then they were right outside her apartment building. Her door clicked open and she stared at the short, stocky man waiting patiently for her.

"Dr. Cross, I'm Aiden James," he said, holding out his hand, friendly blue eyes looking at her curiously.

She took it, and let him help her out of the car. When she heard the car door slam shut, she flinched visibly.

"Aiden is my right-hand man, Dr. Cross," Sebastian explained as he walked around the car. "He'll stay with you tonight."

"Where are you going?" she asked, unable to help herself.

"Out," he said brusquely. "I have work to do."

"I'll make sure she's safe," Aiden said.

Sebastian said nothing but gave his friend a curt nod. He walked back to the driver's side, slipped into the sleek car, and then started the engine.

Jade watched the car speed away. She felt an ache in her

heart, clawing at her, and it wouldn't stop until she sent it a plea. "No," she choked.

"Did you say something, Dr. Cross?" Aiden asked.

"I didn't...I mean, I'm just tired," she sighed.

"No worries. Sebastian wants to make sure you're safe for tonight. I hope you don't mind, but I'll be crashing on your couch, but I won't be sleeping," Aiden explained. He nodded to the car parked across the street. "Additionally, we have two guys watching your building."

"Uhm, thank you," she mumbled.

"No worries, Dr. Cross. Sebastian had this on top priority. Anything you need or want, just tell us, okay?"

"Thank you, Mr. James," she replied.

Aiden nodded. "Of course. Let's head back to your place and make sure you're settled in. Don't worry about anything. You can sleep soundly tonight."

Jade very much doubted that.

CHAPTER FOURTEEN

After tossing and turning the entire night, Jade couldn't take it anymore. She marched into her bathroom, took the coldest shower she could manage ,and dressed for the day. It was six o'clock by the time she was ready to go to work.

"Good morning, Dr. Cross," Aiden greeted her, his expression turning from surprise to concern as he looked at her face.

She knew she looked awful. She'd seen it in the mirror this morning. There were bags under her eyes, and her skin was sallow. Her hair was still wet, too. She didn't have the patience or time to dry it this morning, so she left it hanging over her shoulders.

"I'm going to work," she said, slinging her purse over her shoulder.

Aiden got up from the couch and rubbed his face. "Sure thing. Just give me a second."

She eyed the gun on her coffee table as he grabbed it and placed it into his shoulder holster, then put on his jacket. "Let's go."

Aiden opened the door, taking the lead as he escorted her downstairs and into the waiting car. She squeezed into the back with one of the Creed Security guys as Aiden slipped into the front seat. The traffic was light, and her apartment wasn't far from Fenrir. When they got to Fenrir Corp's headquarters, Aiden exited the vehicle, helped her out, and then walked her into the building. He hung back, though his eyes trained on her as she entered the private elevators. As soon as she got into her lab, she ran up to her inner lab and got to work, booting up her computer and reading through the texts, pouring over them in case there was something she missed. There was absolutely no time to waste.

Jade became engrossed in the readings, and she was glad because they were the only thing that kept her mind from drifting off. She had to stay focused. Study the texts. Stop thinking about last night.

"Jade!" A familiar voice exclaimed, jolting her out of her trance. "Are you okay?"

She turned around saw Meredith entering the lab, Nick right behind her.

"Dr. Cross," he began.

"Mr. Vrost," she said, swinging her chair around to face them.

"They told me you came in early."

"Yes, I needed to get some work done," she explained. "Please, tell me what happened last night."

Nick and Meredith sat down on the chairs in front of her desk. The Beta took a deep breath. "There was a break-in in the building. Six armed men and two mages. They caught us just as we were changing shifts. They forced their way in and made it all the way to the basement levels."

Jade gasped. "How far did they get?"

Meredith frowned. "All the way to the detention levels. I

don't know how, but they knew where to go. They went right past my cell and straight to Marcus'. They used Ognevaia to blow down the doors." Ognevaia was a magically-powered explosive that had ten times the power of a molotov cocktail. The mages would have only needed a small amount to create a massive explosion.

"Marcus died instantly," Nick explained. "They didn't want to take him alive. And then they went to find Daric."

"Did they get him?" Jade asked.

"No, our security forces came just in time. There was a fight, and we were able to take down two of their guys, but the mages and the rest got away," he said, his jaw tensing.

Jade sighed in relief. It was a good thing they didn't free Daric. "What now?"

"First, we keep you safe," Nick said. "Creed seems to be doing a good job, so we'll stick with that plan. No one in Fenrir or any of the Lycans know any details about your security plan, and we want to keep it that way, in case there are any leaks."

"I'm going to be assigned downstairs for now," Meredith said. "They're putting me close to Daric, just in case. Sorry, Jade, you'll be alone up here for a while," her friend said sadly.

"Meredith..." She thought about her not seeing her friend and her chest tightened. The other Lycan didn't seem too happy either. "I can come by and see her, right?"

Nick frowned, and Jade shot him a pleading look. He shrugged. "Meredith needs her downtime too, so, of course, you're free to visit her and socialize."

"Good," Jade said, breathing a smile of relief and giving Meredith a reassuring smile. "I'll come by when I can. I do have to get to work." She shook her head. "I'm sorry. Please tell the Alpha. I shouldn't have waited so long to talk to Marcus." She took a deep breath.

"We still have Daric," Meredith reminded her.

"Has he started talking?" Jade asked.

Nick's jaw tightened, his ice blue eyes going steely. "Not yet. But we'll make him talk."

"He might be the only chance we have to figure out how the mages are doing all this," Jade reasoned. "I should talk to him too. Find out what he knows."

"I'm not sure—"

"Please," Jade said. "We'll take every precaution. Maybe I can try and talk to him? Convince him to help us. Besides, I should really check on the bracelet. I've made a few improvements on the design and Lara was able to help me test it." She got up from her desk and walked over to her 3D printer. She took out a large, metal band. The latest version of her bracelet. "This one is thicker and harder to take off. I've also added tracking capabilities, though I haven't tested them yet."

"Fine," Nick said. "Let's go now."

———

Jade didn't spend a lot of time in Fenrir's basement levels. In fact, she'd only been there once, when Meredith broke into her lab, and she and Lara watched the interrogation. The security on the sub levels was already tight, but now they were even stricter. They had added extra guards and Nick had talked about having Vivianne Chatraine, head of the New York witch coven, come down and add protection spells.

She followed Nick and Meredith to the end of the long hallway. They passed the first door on the right, which Meredith explained was where she was staying. A few doors down, they passed another cell that looked like it had its door blown off, which Jade guessed had been Marcus' cell. She shivered, thinking about the way the mage died. Despite what he did to her, he didn't deserve such a gruesome death.

Finally, they reached the end of the hallway, where a burly Lycan guard was standing outside a metal door. He moved aside as Nick approached them.

Nick opened the door and entered first. "Daric," he called.

The man sitting on the narrow bed in the corner of the room didn't move. Jade stifled a gasp. She didn't almost recognize the warlock, though she'd only seen him once, when she checked to make sure the bracelet was secure. She remembered glancing at him, thinking he was extraordinarily handsome. The man in the cell was unrecognizable. He had a thick beard that covered half his face and his long blonde hair hung down in limp strands. He was dressed in a dark gray jumpsuit that hung loosely from his body. His shoulders hunched over, making him look smaller than his over 6'5" frame. Thick shackles wrapped around his ankle connected to large chains bolted to the wall.

"Daric," Nick called again.

Daric's head turned, looking over at them. "What do you want?"

"You know what we want."

He let out a huff. "And what makes you think I will tell you anything?"

"We have ways of making you talk," the Beta said, crossing his arms over his chest.

"Do your best," the warlock challenged. "It can't be worse than what happened to Marcus. Or what awaits me if I betray Stefan and he finds me."

"How did they know about this place?" Nick said, walking over to him. "Are you communicating with them?"

"Would I tell you if I did?" The warlock's blue-green eyes narrowed up at the Lycan.

"Like I said, we will find ways to make you." Nick sounded like he almost relished the idea of torturing Daric for information. On the outside, cool and collected Nick Vrost seemed like he was in control, but Jade could feel the contained maelstrom inside the Beta.

"And who do we have here?" Daric turned to Jade and Meredith. His eyes flickered over Meredith first, then zeroed in on Jade. "Ah, the good doctor." He raised his hand, showing off the bracelet. "I suppose I should thank you for this piece of jewelry."

Jade said nothing, her fingers growing tight on the new bracelet in her hands.

"Don't be shy, doctor. Come here and show me your new toy," Daric mocked.

She swallowed a gulp and walked closer, Meredith following behind her. This was her chance. Maybe she could trick Daric into telling her how the mages were controlling the Lycans. "I'm going to put this on you and remove the old one," she explained. "It's a new version. You won't be able to remove it, and if you try...well, let's just say you don't want to know what happens if you do." A lie, but he didn't know that. There was no way he could remove it anyway. This version used nanotechnology to keep the bracelet sealed, and was powered by a supercharged battery that could last up to a year. The only way to remove it was by using a key fob, plus a password authorization from her computer.

Daric was silent as he held out his left hand. Jade placed the new bracelet on his wrist, securing it tightly. She took his other hand, and removed the old bracelet. This older version only required the key fob to remove.

"Will you tell us how the mages are controlling humans? And how to stop them?" she asked, looking him straight in the eyes. "It might save you a lot of pain. Perhaps we can even give you something in exchange."

Daric gave her a sardonic smile. "And what would that be... sweet doctor?" He asked, touching his fingertip to her chin.

"Don't touch her!" Meredith hissed, stalking closer. Nick gave Jade a warning glare.

Jade waved her friend away, her eyes never leaving Daric. "We could...offer you some freedom. Like Meredith. She's a prisoner here, too, but she's allowed to roam and leave."

"So, you would hand out treats to me, like a good little puppy?" He glanced at Meredith.

"Why you—"

"Meredith!" Nick warned.

The other Lycan let out a growl but lowered her fists to her sides.

"You'd prefer to stay down here forever?" Jade asked.

"There could be worst things," Daric said mysteriously, his eyes going cold.

"You should think about it," Jade said.

Daric gave her a menacing smile and leaned down to whisper in her ear. "I won't be thinking about your offer, but let me give you some advice. Watch your back and stop playing with fire. You don't want to awaken the beast."

Jade felt her blood run cold at his warning. "What...what are you talking about?"

"You need to be careful who you give your heart to," Daric warned.

"I don't—" Jade let out a cry as Daric's large hands grabbed her by the shoulders and slammed her against the bed.

Meredith shouted, jumping into action. Her arms wound around Daric's neck, using her body weight and Lycan strength to pull the giant away from Jade. They both ended up on the ground, with Daric rolling over Meredith and pinning her hands over her head.

With a loud growl, Nick grabbed the chain connected to Daric's ankle and yanked it, sending the warlock flying back against the wall.

Jade ran to Meredith's side, helping her friend stand. "Are you all right?"

Pure shock registered on her friend's face. "Yeah..." Her eyes seemed glazed over, and she rubbed her hands over her arms as if she was cold. "That guy...he gives me the heebie-jeebies!" Jade looked down and saw the goosebumps forming over the other Lycan's pale arms.

"Let's get out of here then," Jade said, putting an arm around her friend. "Mr. Vrost?"

Nick gave the unconscious Daric one last disgusted look. "Yes, let's get out of here."

CHAPTER FIFTEEN

S ebastian stared down at the reports on his desk. Aiden
sat across from him, watching him silently.

"This is all we got?"

Aiden nodded. "Yeah. We have three possible suspects. Or
rather, three companies who would benefit if Fenrir's Food R
and D division were to shut down. But without knowing what
she's working on, we can't pinpoint who would directly benefit
from Dr. Cross' death."

"I'm working on finding out."

"Is that the angle you're working with her?"

Sebastian's fists slammed down on the arms of the table.
"Watch your mouth," he growled.

"Hey, hey." Aiden raised his hands in surrender. "Jesus,
Sebastian, calm down! What's the matter with you? Sleeping
with a client, really? Why does she have your fucking panties in
a twist?"

Sebastian let out a breath and fell back down in his chair.
He rubbed his face with his hands. "Damn if I know, Aiden."
He looked out the large windows behind his desk, staring at the
view of midtown Manhattan from his office. He could see the

tall, black tower that was Fenrir Corporation's headquarters spiraling high into the sky and wondered what Jade was doing now.

"Sebastian," Aiden said in a serious voice, shaking Sebastian out of his reverie. "Look, I'm your friend. Do you need to talk? Have you been having nightmares about Afghanistan again?"

Sebastian shook his head. "I'm fine. I just need sleep." He was tempted to grab the bottle locked in his liquor cabinet, but knew he couldn't. Jade's life depended on him, and he had to keep his head clear.

"Well, what do you want us to do?"

"Grant said to just keep to the same security plan," Sebastian instructed.

"Are you going to be with her tonight?" Aiden asked. "I just need to know so I can fix the rotation schedule."

"I don't...no," he decided. "But I want hourly reports on Jade's movements."

"And what about finding out who's trying to kill her? Anderson still not budging?"

He shook his head. "He keeps evading the question, but he knows something. I don't want to push him too much or we might lose this contract."

"We don't need it," Aiden pointed out. "As is, we already need to expand to meet demand."

Sebastian huffed. Yes, there was always demand for war somewhere in the world. "Still, Fenrir's a big client and local, too."

"Fine," Aiden shrugged. "You're the boss." The other man got up from the chair. "See you later, Sebastian."

He gave Aiden a nod and then turned back to his window. Late summer storm clouds were rolling from the distance, painting the sky a dark gray. He sat there for what seemed like hours, watching the clouds come closer and closer.

Jade. Last night, they had been so close. He had her in his arms, ready to lose himself in her. And then the threat came back. Aiden had called him, saying Grant Anderson was looking for Jade. There was a breach at Fenrir and one of their employees was killed in the break-in. Anger and fear replaced lust, and The Beast was roaring at him to protect Jade and destroy anything and anyone who wanted her dead.

Even now, the rage was there, simmering under the surface. Working all night trying to find out who was trying to harm her was the only thing that kept the animal at bay. After dropping Jade off at her place, he went straight to the office. He summoned his most trusted employees, putting them to task. He also called in as many favors as he could, trying to find out as much information about Fenrir Corporation, but came up with nothing, at least nothing they didn't know already. Short of hacking into their personnel files, he couldn't find the answers, and it was driving him crazy.

Sebastian stood up from the desk and took off his suit jacket. He needed to do something to blow off some steam. He changed into his gym clothes and headed to the basement level of Creed Security Headquarters.

He spent the rest of the day in Creed Security's basement training rooms. He lifted weights, sparred with his employees, and even emptied a few rounds in the target range. It was a good distraction, and his muscles were sore and aching by the time he hit the showers, but it didn't help calm the fury building up inside him. He needed Jade. Needed to know where she was and that she was safe. He glanced at his phone several times throughout the day, but according to the hourly reports he was getting, she stayed put at work.

He went back up to his office to use his private shower, blasting the water up as high as he could take it. It felt good on his tired muscles, soothing and relaxing him. He shut off the tap as the steam hung thick around him, the white clouds quickly sucking out of the tiny stall when he opened the shower door. He put on a fresh white shirt from his closet, shrugged his jeans on and towel-dried his hair.

Sebastian picked up his phone then opened latest message. Still no movement and it was already 7 p.m. A strange ache gnawed at him and the questions blasted into his brain. Why wasn't Jade on the way home? What did she do all day? Has she eaten? The thought of Jade hungry and alone set off his protective instincts. Fucking hell, he was acting like some mother hen.

He sat down at his computer, trying to get some work done. But he couldn't help but glance at his phone, waiting for the next report to come in. Finally, an hour later, the message came. Jade just left Fenrir and got into a cab.

"Where the hell was she going?" he muttered to himself. He tapped the phone, calling Zac.

"Boss," the young man answered. "We're on her tail."

"She's not going home?"

"Negative, boss. She's heading downtown."

"Text me as soon as she gets to wherever she's going."

"Sure thing."

Sebastian got up and paced around. Jade was deviating from her routine. Where was she going? Was she meeting someone? Jealousy gripped at him, and he had to sit down to calm himself. When his phone rang minutes later, he quickly answered.

"She got out in the Lower East Side. A club called White Elephant."

"Send me the address," he ordered. What was Jade up to?

———

The White Elephant was an unassuming music club off

Houston Street on the Lower East Side. The outside looked like any typical New York bar, sandwiched between a bodega and a dry cleaner. Zac was waiting outside by the time Sebastian pulled in.

"She's still in there, boss," Zac said, jerking his thumb towards the door.

"Anyone follow her?"

"Just us."

"Good," he said, tossing him his keys.

Sebastian entered the club, his eyes scanning the area. The inside was dark, and the low ceilings made it feel even smaller than it looked. Various concert posters, pictures, and albums hung on the exposed brick walls. The bar took up a third of the room, and there were several tables and chairs set up around the stage. After noting all the exits, he turned his attention to the stage. A band was playing classic rock songs, and the crowd seemed to be enjoying the music. He spied Jade, sitting up front, her eyes fixed on the band as she swung her head side to side in rhythm with the song.

Seeing that she was safe, Sebastian relaxed. He walked over to the bar and ordered a beer, his eyes leaving Jade for only a second. What was she doing here?

As the band went straight into the next song, and Sebastian continued to nurse his beer, watching Jade, her attention focused solely on the stage. Did she know them? He shook his head. No one in the band looked younger than fifty. They were all older musicians, and based on the type of music they played, had been playing for a long time. Classic rock tunes, some bluegrass, a little country and southern rock. He actually enjoyed their music.

The set wound down, and the band leader announced their break. Jade got up from her chair and then walked up to the guitarist. The older man gave her a warm smile, removed his instrument, and then Jade launched herself into his arms.

"What the fuck?" Sebastian slammed the bottle down so hard the woman next to him jumped in surprise. She flashed him a dirty look, but he ignored her. Who the fuck was that man? He seethed, watching as Jade seemed to hold on to the older man tighter as he ruffled her hair affectionately. When they pulled away from each other, he sat down on one of the amps, and Jade planted herself beside him. They bent their heads together, chatting and laughing as the rest of the band came over to greet Jade.

Sebastian saw red. Who was this man? He didn't like the way he sat so close or looked at Jade with familiarity.

Jade was in the middle of a conversation when she suddenly frowned, and then swung her head in his direction. Her mouth opened into a perfect "O," her face a mask of shock.

The older man followed her gaze, his intense green eyes landing on Sebastian. Jade whispered something into the man's ear, stood up, and strode over to him.

"Sebastian," she said, her eyes wide with surprise. "What are you doing here?"

"I'm here to keep an eye on you," he stated. Her shoulders sank at his answer. Disappointment?

"Right." She straightened her shoulders. "You didn't have to come in here and check on me," she said in a cool tone.

"Blue Sky," a voice behind Jade called. "Everything okay?"

It was the old man, the guitarist. Sebastian took a closer look at the man. He was short, a couple of inches under 6 feet, but had a compact and stocky build. The man was maybe in his mid-fifties but looked good for his age, so he could have been older. His long, salt-and-pepper hair was pulled back in a ponytail and tattoos curled out from under the neckline and sleeves of his shirt.

"Who is this man, Blue Sky?" he asked, frowning at Sebastian.

"He's my—"

"Sebastian," he introduced himself.

"Your Sebastian?" His eyebrow raised at Jade.

"No!" Jade denied. "I mean, he's not my...this is Sebastian. Fenrir hired him...his firm, I mean, to be my bodyguard."

"Bodyguards?" The older man's voice raised a notch. "Young lady, what's going on?"

"Nothing!" Jade raised her hands defensively. "Nothing you have to worry about!"

"Nothing to worry about? Why wouldn't I worry, I'm your father!"

"You're her father?" Sebastian couldn't stop himself. He looked at the man again, scanning his face. Now, he saw the similarities. The eyes were a shade darker, but it was the same shape as Jade's, as were the nose and chin.

"Eric. Eric Cross," he introduced himself. His voice was smooth, and the accent was definitely all New York. "So you're protecting my daughter? From what, exactly?"

Sebastian crossed his arms over his chest. "I'd like to know that, too," he said, his eyes training on Jade.

"It's a long story, Dad," she sighed. "I'll explain later."

A look passed between father and daughter, then Eric Cross scowled at Jade. "You bet you will, young lady."

"Yo, Eric!" Someone called. "We're on in 5!"

He gave Jade a kiss on the cheek and then stared at Sebastian, pinning him with his gaze. "Stay a while, Sebastian. And let's have a drink after this set."

"He doesn't have to stay," Jade protested.

"Thank you, sir," he said, his palms suddenly sweaty like some teenage boy. The last time he called someone "sir" was when he was in the Marines.

"Blue Sky, get him another beer and put it on my tab," Eric said before heading back to the stage.

"Blue Sky?" Sebastian asked.

"It's my middle name," Jade said in an exasperated voice. "And yes, I'm very well aware of the irony. All the ironies."

He chuckled and she sent him a glare. "Don't say it—"

"Jade Blue Sky Cross."

"That's Dr. Jade Blue Sky Cross," she corrected, a smile tugging at the corner of her mouth. "He named me after his favorite song. Jade was my mother's contribution. Apparently, she was in her Eastern Philosophy phase when I was born."

"So, your dad's a musician?"

"Yes, he's been with his band since before I was born," Jade explained as she signaled the bartender for two more beers.

"Are they famous?"

"They had one hit a couple of years ago, but I'm sure you've never heard of it. But they still tour," she said. "What are you doing here?"

He looked down at her. What was he doing here? His mind raced back to the events of that 24 hours. Everything was going great, until that call. Before he could open his mouth, though, the band started their first song. Jade cocked her head, motioning for him to follow her to the table in front of the stage.

Sebastian took the seat next to her, relaxing as soon as they sat down. He listened to the band, but mostly he watched Jade. She seemed to be engrossed in the performance, her head bopping along with the music, mouthing along with the lyrics now and then.

A couple songs later, the band wrapped up, playing one last song before taking their bows.

"Great set, Dad," Jade said, wrapping her arms around Eric.

"Thanks, baby," he replied and sat down on the stool next to her. "So, Sebastian. You're a personal bodyguard?"

"Yes, sir," he said.

"Dad, he's the CEO of the company," Jade explained.

"How nice of you to give my daughter the personal touch."

Jade choked on her beer, the liquid sputtering out her nose and mouth. With a quick apology, she wiped her face with a napkin from the dispenser on the table.

Eric gave her a curious look, but didn't say anything. He took a sip of his beer and turned back to Sebastian. "Tell me more about your company, Sebastian."

They chatted for a few more minutes, and Sebastian learned that Eric was from New York, but he toured with his band around the country year-round and sometimes outside of the US. Jade went to see them play every time they were in New York, though with the summer concert season winding down, he was going to be in town for a couple of weeks.

"Well, it's time for this old timer to pack up and get some rest," Eric said, getting up from his chair and extending his hand. "Sebastian, nice to meet you. Thank you for taking care of my daughter."

"I'll keep her safe, sir," he replied, shaking the older man's hand with a firm grip.

"You do that." That one seemed to be a warning. "We'll talk later," he said to his daughter. She nodded and gave him a last hug before he rejoined his bandmates.

"I'm going to powder my nose," Jade announced and stood up, then scurried to the bathrooms.

Sebastian sat there for a moment, wondering what he was going to do. He could wait for Jade, take her home, and just leave her be. Then spend more time trying to find out who was intent on killing her. He was still frustrated and angry she wouldn't tell him who was out to get her.

The other option was to continue what they had started.

Making his decision, he chugged the last of the beer and

followed Jade to the bathroom. The door to the ladies' room opened, and before she could protest, Sebastian pushed Jade back inside the stall, trapped her against the sink and caught her lips with his.

She let out a small protesting shriek, which turned into a sensual moan. Soon, she was responding to his kiss. Sebastian perched her up on the sink and settled between her legs, his lips never leaving hers.

She pushed him away gently, her breathing heavy. "Sebastian," she said. "As exciting as this is, I don't want to lose my virginity in a dirty public toilet."

He laughed, picked her up, and then set her down. "Don't worry, darlin'. I told you your first time would be special, and I meant it."

CHAPTER SIXTEEN

"**W**here are we?" Jade asked as the car stopped in front a nondescript building in Tribeca. The large metal doors in front slid open as they moved closer, and Sebastian maneuvered the car inside. Overhead lights flickered on after the doors shut behind them.

"You'll see." Sebastian cut the engine, walked to her side, and let her out.

The inside of the warehouse was a garage and housed several cars, as well as three motorcycles parked side-by-side. Sebastian led her to a wide door in the far right corner. He punched a code on the keypad beside the door and pulled it open, revealing an old freight elevator. After a few seconds, it stopped, and Sebastian pushed on the door. The elevator opened into a small hallway with a single door. He punched in another code and pressed his thumb against a sensor before the door swung open.

"Sebastian?" she asked, looking at the room. It was one of those converted factories, a wide open space turned into a loft apartment. It was massive, and the ceilings were tall and cavernous. The open plan had the kitchen in the far corner, the dining room beside it, another room closed off with a partition, while the rest was the living space. Stairs led up to what she assumed was the bedroom.

"This is my home," he said. "It used to be an old canning factory, I believe. I bought half the warehouse and had it renovated. There's a garage on the bottom floor, and I haven't decided what to do with the two other floors yet."

"It's...big," she said.

He chuckled. "What can I say, I like having space, especially in New York." He took her hand, and they crossed the vast living area to the stairs. "Still sure?"

She nodded. "Most definitely. But," she looked at her outfit. She was wearing a khaki skirt, a matching jacket, and a blue, long-sleeved shirt. "I'm not...you know, dressed up or anything. I'm even not wearing lingerie."

Sebastian pulled her close, digging his hands into her hair to loosen it from the ponytail she wore. "That doesn't matter. You're beautiful, whatever you're wearing."

With a sigh, she tipped up her head, letting him swoop down for a kiss. Sebastian seemed different tonight. There was an intensity she couldn't quite place.

"You taste amazing," he said, nipping at her lips and making her whimper.

"Please, Sebastian. No more teasing," she cried, arching her body against his.

With a soft grunt, he picked her up and carried her all the way up to the bedroom. He planted her down on the hardwood floor so they stood next to his bed. He removed her jacket and tossed it on the floor. His fingers fumbled at the front of her shirt, and, with a grunt of frustration, he simply ripped the buttons off. He unclasped the front hook of her bra, exposing her breasts to his gaze.

"Jade," he rasped, his eyes going wide when he saw the

delicate chains around her neck and between her breasts.

"I didn't want to take it off," she confessed.

With a satisfied roar, he bent down, taking a nipple into his mouth. Hands moved to her waist, unzipping her skirt and letting it fall to the ground. His fingers brushed over the front of her white cotton panties, which were already soaked. He let out a growl, taking a deep breath as if he could smell her arousal, then pushed her down on his bed.

Sebastian stepped back, his hands grabbing the hem of his shirt. Her eyes devoured him as he undressed, excitement making her heart hammer against her ribcage. He slipped the white shirt over his chest, his muscles rippling as he tossed it aside. God, how could one man be so sexy? The ink on his skin moved as he stalked towards her. Broad shoulders and chest, his muscled torso tapering down to the small V of his waist. And... oh my Lord, the man had the most defined set of eight-pack abs she'd ever seen.

"Like what you see?' he teased.

She blushed, turning her head away.

"Don't be shy, Jade," he said, popping the buttons of his fly open. He hooked his thumbs into the waistband of his jeans and pulled them down. His fully erect cock bobbed up against his stomach, the tip shiny with his precum. Her breath caught, and again she wondered how this would work.

Sebastian kneeled on the bed, stalking towards her like a predator, reaching for her. "Are you on birth control?"

She nodded.

"Good," he said. "Because I don't want anything between us. I want to feel all of you around me, squeezing me."

Jade gasped as he yanked her panties down, ripping them off her legs and tossing them aside. "Sebastian," she cried out when his fingers found her clit, stroking the hard little nub until she was clawing at his shoulders.

"So tight and hot," he whispered against her neck. "Sweet, innocent Jade," he rasped, his fingers slipping inside her. "That's it, darlin'," he encouraged as her hips began to thrust up at him. "Do it. Make yourself cum on my fingers."

Her cheeks pinked at his words, but she couldn't stop herself. She pumped her hips up, enjoying the feeling of his fingers inside her. He pushed another finger in and then twisted his hand so the heel ground up against her clit.

"Sebastian!" she screamed, her body tensing as she came hard, convulsing around his fingers. As she came down from her orgasm, Sebastian pushed her down on the bed and settled himself between her thighs.

"I'll take it slow, darlin'," he whispered, his hand caressing the side of her face. "Just tell me if it's too much."

Jade nodded and held her breath. He braced himself on one elbow, then reached down with his other hand. She felt the wide tip of his cock at her entrance, pushing slowly into her, stretching her. Looking up at him, she could see his face was tense as if he was barely holding onto his control.

"I need you, Sebastian," she said, reaching up to touch his cheek. "Please. Take me."

With a soft moan, he pushed in, the tight barrier giving way. Jade let out a soft cry, the pain was unbearable, but only for a moment. It slowly dulled down to a mild ache.

"Are you..." He looked down at her, concern marring his handsome face.

"I'm fine," she said reassuringly.

He let out a relieved sigh and then shifted his hips, making Jade moan.

"Feels...good." She arched up at him, making him groan.

"Fuck...Jade. You're so fucking tight around me..." He gasped and began to move.

Sebastian felt amazing inside her, and she wanted to tell

him that but lost the ability to speak. He started slow, pulling out about halfway and then pushing all the way in. She craved the delicious friction, and despite her inexperience she knew there was more. Greed and lust took over, and she pushed at him, urging him to go faster. And he did, thrusting in and out of her, dragging his length along her tight, slick walls. He changed the angle and brought one of her legs up over his shoulder. The pleasure hit her so fast she nearly howled, and each thrust pushed her closer and closer to the edge.

"Please...please..." she begged. Sebastian must have been getting close too. His thrusts became shorter, his breathing erratic. Ripples of pleasure spread out from her body, propelling her towards her orgasm.

"That's it, darlin'," he rumbled. His hips pummeled harder and his mouth came down on hers. With one last thrust, she felt his cock twitch and then spill his seed inside her. It was the last straw, and a guttural cry ripped from her mouth as her orgasm flooded through her, her entire body bursting with earth shattering pleasure.

Jade blinked. The next few minutes seemed surreal as she came back down. Sebastian withdrew from her, rolling away quickly. She wasn't sure where he went, but he was back in a flash, and a warm, damp towel was pressed up against her. The air tasted slightly metallic. She must have been bleeding. Not that she needed the towel. Her Lycan healing would quickly take care of that, but it was a sweet gesture. Tossing the towel aside, Sebastian lay next to her, pulling her to his muscled chest and then settling her against him. He was murmuring against her neck. Soon, his breathing became even and he settled. Jade felt her eyelids become heavy and she drifted off to sleep.

The thrashing woke her up.

Strong legs kicked at her, arms waved around. Jade's eyes flew open, and she knew something was wrong.

Sebastian's eyes were shut close, but his body struggled to move. He opened his mouth, and a growl escaped, sending chills up her arms.

"No...stay...bea..." He was slurring his words, and Jade couldn't understand what he was trying to say. *He must be having a nightmare.* She reached out, her fingers barely touching his arm. The skin was hot to the touch like he had a hundred degree fever.

She tried shaking him awake. "Sebastian!" She yelped when he suddenly grabbed her and rolled her around, pinning her to the mattress. His fingers were like talons, digging into her arms.

Sebastian's eyes flew open, and the gray pools shone in the darkness of the bedroom. For a second, she didn't recognize him. He stared down at her, his pupils blown, his teeth bared. The wild look on his face frightened her. After a few seconds, the warmth in his eyes returned. "Jade?"

"Shhh..." she soothed, running her hands over his arms. As her fingers ran down his left arm, she suddenly felt the raised scars there. A question rose up inside her, but she tamped it down. Sebastian needed her. "I'm here. You're here."

He let out a soft groan and rolled onto his back, letting out a pained cry. "Fuck." He wiped his face with his hands. "Jade... did I hurt you?"

She cuddled up next him, laying her head on his chest and throwing an arm over him. "I'm fine. You didn't hurt me. Did you have a bad dream?"

Sebastian remained silent, but she could feel the tension in his body. Her enhanced hearing picked up his heartbeat, which was thumping erratically. *It must have been an intense dream.* She ran her hands over his chest, trying to soothe him. After a few minutes, his heart rate slowed down and she felt him relax. He traced a hand lazily over her back. "Tell me about your tattoo," he murmured. "And your scars."

Jade stiffened, but then took a deep breath. "I was in an accident when I was a child, and the surgeries to fix my back left me with those scars," she began.

"I'm sorry. But you survived."

"I hated those scars, hated what they represented and what they reminded me of. My parents divorced right after the last surgery. Their marriage couldn't take the strain." Her voice broke, and Sebastian held her tighter. "So, when I turned eighteen, my dad was touring in London. We were having dinner one night and talking about old times. He asked me how I felt about the scars. I told him the truth. I hated seeing it every day. It reminded me that I broke our family apart."

"No, Jade," He pulled her closer. "It's not your fault."

"That's what he said. That their relationship had fractured long before my accident. Anyway," she took another deep breath, "he asked what I wanted for my birthday and I told him I wanted a tattoo to cover my scar. Turned out he knew a great artist in London, had gotten one from him a few years back. We both got tattoos. He has my initials, done in the same style, along his rib cage."

"Why did you choose your design?"

"I loved the symbolism of the tree, that it represented nourishment from nature and transformation," she explained.

"It suits you," he said, leaning down to kiss her forehead.

"How about you?" she asked, tracing the scars running along his arm. She realized that they extended all the way up to his chest. "Will you tell me about these?"

"Another time," he pleaded. "Not now."

She nodded and snuggled closer to him.

CHAPTER SEVENTEEN

The warm, naked body pressed up against him startled Sebastian. Unused to waking up with someone next to him in bed, he was confused. The memories came back, and his chest constricted at the sight of Jade cuddled beside him, looking so achingly beautiful.

Jade stirred, throwing her arm back, and he used the opportunity to slip away from her. Planting his feet on the ground, he rubbed his face with his hand. Christ, he couldn't do this. He was supposed to protect her, not take advantage of her like this. Her confession last night, it hit too close to home. She had enough baggage. He came with an entire moving truck of issues from his own childhood, not to mention PTSD.

"Sebastian," she called out, her voice raspy with sleep. "Everything all right?"

He straightened his spine. "I'm fine, Jade."

The sheets rustled behind him and a warm hand touched his shoulder. He flinched away from her, then stood up and stalked to the bathroom. Turning the tap on, he splashed water on his face.

He was no good for her; he knew that from the beginning,

but he took her anyway. And, now, she would pay for it. He would eventually show his true colors, and she would get hurt.

Wrapping a towel around his waist, he walked back into the bedroom where Jade was still lounging on the bed. Fuck, she looked so beautiful with her long, dark hair spread over the pillows, the sheet wrapped around her body, and the chain necklace he had given her glinting in the morning sun.

"Sebastian," she purred, reaching out to him. "Come back to bed."

It took all his strength not to say fuck it, and just jump back into bed with her. Bury himself inside her and just forget the outside world. "Uh sorry, darlin'," he said, clearing his throat. "I have an early meeting. I need to get ready."

She gave a pout. "Really?" She sat up, exposing her breasts, toying with the necklace.

Fuck.

"Really," he said curtly. He grabbed her shirt and jacket and tossed it to her on the bed. "You should get dressed too. Don't you have to go to work? My guys'll be waiting outside for you if you need a lift. I'm gonna go shower." He was a fucking bastard. And a coward, too, because he turned around before he could see her reaction. It was better this way.

He got under the shower. Cold this time, as cold as he could stand it, but it did nothing to ease the pit growing in his stomach.

No. Go back.

Fucking Beast. "Shut up. Go away. You're not satisfied ruining my life, so you have to do it to hers too?"

Ours.

Ignoring The Beast, he turned off the tap and grabbed the towel hanging from the rack, drying himself off violently. When he got out of the shower, she wasn't in the bedroom, but he heard her angry footsteps across the hardwood floor and then the door slamming. *Good*, he thought. She should run away. Far away from him and the monster.

————

Sebastian's eyes scanned the room. Luxe was in full swing tonight—more beautiful women than he'd ever seen at one time. Redhead, blonde, brunette, heck, there was even one chick with rainbow-colored hair. A lot the women had thrown interested glances at him (and some more than just looks). He could have his pick of women tonight. Lose himself in them, forget about her. That's why he ran away, right? Because he wanted her too damn much, wanted to keep her for himself when he wasn't good enough for her.

Fuck. Damn it all to hell.

He was a complete bastard. And The Beast made no bones about its anger at him. It was uncontrollable today, roaring in his ear, scratching at his insides. He was so distracted he couldn't get any work done. He also screamed at his assistant for no good reason. Even now, The Beast was there, stalking him in his own head.

He wanted her so bad, to touch her again, to feel her around him, and to hear her whisper his name. Why couldn't he stay away from her? She opened up to him about her past, leaving herself vulnerable. And what did he do? He pulled away from her. Hurt her.

The Beast. The nightmares. No, that was just an excuse. He had been scared at first, afraid he'd hurt her physically, but Jade was fine. She didn't even have any bruises this morning. He couldn't blame it on The Beast. The damn animal actually wanted Jade *for him*. Wanted him to protect her and keep her. That's why The Beast was fucking furious at him the whole day.

No, it was his own goddamn fucked up brain that made him push her away. Scared of her. Afraid of what she made him feel. And that was just one more reason why he wasn't the man for her.

Slamming the glass on the bar, he stood up and left. He'd go home and sleep it off.

CHAPTER EIGHTEEN

Jade snorted and laughed at the video on her laptop, popping another piece of General Tso's chicken into her mouth. She reached for the can of soda on her coffee table, washing down the chicken and rice. God, she could always count on these hilarious cat videos to cheer her up. Her favorite was a song by an Internet comedienne about how she loved cats.

Oh yeah yeah I love cats
I want all the cats
Let's get some more cats
There's no such thing as having too many cats!

She loved singing along to that one. It was hilarious. When the video ended, she hit the reload button, but the screen froze.

"Boo!" she jeered at the screen. She grabbed another egg roll from the bag and ate it in two bites. She let out a loud belch. "Excuse me," she said to no one in particular, and then blew out a deep sigh.

She was pathetic. Finally free of her virginity and what does she do? Buy a ton of Chinese takeout, put on her favorite pajamas, and watch cat videos all night.

Memories of last night flooded back, and she slammed her head down on one of her couch pillows, letting out a frustrated groan. *Stupid brain. Stop it.*

This was what she wanted, right? Get rid of her virginity, no strings, no distractions, no boyfriends. That's what she had told Sebastian. *It didn't have to mean anything afterwards.* Those were her own words. Sure, she was angry when he started acting like a wanker this morning, but she couldn't blame him. He made no promises, and she really should have known. Sebastian was an experienced player, probably in it for the thrill of the hunt, and he was done, already moving on to his next conquest. Pain slashed through her, and she quickly pushed the feeling aside.

Lord, she was so confused. He had been so sweet and affectionate to her this whole time. Sweeping her off her feet with that date and then coming to listen to her dad play. What was that about?

"Ugh!" She reached for the box of fried rice, stuffing her face as fast as she could. If Meredith were here, she'd probably say something like, "Move on, girlfriend! The world is your oyster now!" Right. *Now, where was the last eggroll?* She snatched it from the other bag, taking a bite out of one end.

The loud knocking on her door made her jump in surprise, the remains of the egg roll falling from her mouth, onto her couch, and then to the floor with a splat. *Great.* Who could be knocking on her door at this hour? She picked up the half-eaten egg roll and wondered if the five-second rule applied in this case.

The knocks turned into loud bangs. She opened her mouth to tell them she was coming, but quickly clamped it shut when she heard the voice on the other side of her door.

"Jade! Open up!"

Sebastian? What was he doing here? Oh sugar iced tea, her

place was a disaster area. The coffee table was littered with open boxes of Chinese food, soda cans, chopsticks and sauce packets. Also, her hair was a mess and she was wearing a shirt that said "Future Cat Lady" on the front, and her favorite pair of pajamas with cute baby sloths. Maybe if she stayed real quiet, he would go away.

"I can hear you in there!" he called.

"No, you can't!" she answered, then covered her mouth. *Fudgsicles.*

"Open up, Jade! I know you're in there."

"Oh yeah?" she challenged. "What if I'm not alone in here right now?"

Silence. Did he leave?

Jade had a wicked idea. She started to moan. "Oh yeah... baby...that's it, do it like that. Oh!" That'll teach him.

Another five seconds of silence passed. Then there was a loud, rhythmic thumping sound. "Open this door, Jade, or I swear to God, I'm gonna break it down!"

The nerve! She stood up, stomped to the door and threw it open. Unfortunately, Sebastian had been in the middle of his impersonation of a battering ram at that exact moment and he barreled into her, sending them both to the ground.

"Oomph!" She groaned when she hit the carpet. Her braced himself on the floor, to avoid crushing her, but he kept her pinned down.

He swung his head around, his eyes scanning the room. "There's no one here. Why did you lie to me?"

"To make you go away!"

"Pretending there's a man here is the last thing that would get me to go away."

"Well, it doesn't matter, you need to leave anyway," she stated.

"Why?"

"I'm busy."

"Busy with what?"

Ugh. Obstinate man. "With important things. I can't be disturbed, can't you see?"

At that moment, the video that froze earlier decided to play.

Oh yeah yeah I love cats

I want all the cats

Let's get some more cats

There's no such thing as having too many cats!

Sebastian looked down at her with a raised brow, and she grew red. She pushed him with all her might, but he didn't move.

"Get off me!" she said, shoving at him again. With a long sigh, he got up, pulling her up to her feet with him. As the video droned on and on about cats and how great cats were, he began to laugh.

Jade dove for her laptop and slammed it shut. "Fine!" She marched back to him. "Make fun of me if you want! But just get out!" She pushed at him again, not that it did any good, except make him chuckle harder. Anger flowed through her. "I said get out!"

Sebastian stopped laughing, his face turning serious. "I'm sorry, darlin'," he said, drawing her into his arms. "I'm not making fun of you. You're too adorable, that's all."

She sank into him and sighed. "What are you doing here?"

"I came to say I'm sorry."

Jade froze, and then disentangled herself from his arms. "Look, I understand. I said no strings, and it didn't have to mean anything afterwards, so it's okay. I'm a big girl." She turned away from him, hoping he wouldn't notice the way she trembled or how her face betrayed her words.

"No, it's not okay," he sighed and put a hand on her shoulder. "I hurt you. And I did it on purpose."

She whipped around. "What? You said those things on purpose?"

His shoulders sank. "I'm no good for you. I'm a bastard, and I fucked up. I'm sorry."

He was apologizing for that morning. Should she believe him? Or would he rip her to shreds again come morning?

Sebastian stalked towards her. "I mean it. I'm sorry I pushed you away. Again. Like that first night. Back then, I told myself you were innocent and inexperienced, that I should stay the hell away from you. Now I know I was afraid of how big this thing between us was and I thought I could stop myself from feeling this. But every time I saw you with some asshole, all I wanted to do was beat the living daylights out of him and take you for myself."

She stood there, speechless. "Sebastian, I don't know what to say."

"Tell me you forgive me."

"I..." Could she risk it? She followed her gut. "I forgive you."

Sebastian swept her into his arms and carried her straight into the bedroom. He didn't even give her time to breathe, depositing her on the bed and shucking his clothes off as fast as he could. She whipped off her shirt, tossing it aside.

"Jade." He whispered her name reverently, like a prayer. He crawled over her, making her lie back on the bed. The heat of his body burned her as his chest touched down over her breasts. His lips moved over hers in a soft caress, the gentleness surprising her. Hands brushed her hair aside, spreading it over the pillows.

Sebastian relaxed against her carefully so as not to crush her with his weight. He dragged his lips lower, tracing a path from her jaw to her neck and lower still. His tongue darted out to lick her skin and the delicate chain nestled between her breasts.

She moaned, clutching the sheets underneath her. Sebastian

continued to lave attention to her cleavage, then grabbed her wrists. Lifting his head up, he pinned her hands over her head, leaning down to give her another kiss. He settled between her legs, his erection pressing up against her core.

Jade struggled underneath him, not to get free but to try and get closer to him. He released her wrists, and then his hand reached down under her pajamas. As his fingertips brushed her lace panties, he let out a groan.

"What are you wearing?" he asked.

"My favorite pajamas," she replied.

He looked down and saw the print on the pajamas and let out a chuckle. She frowned at him, but he kissed her forehead. "Not those," he emphasized. His hands tugged at her lace thong panties. "Hmmm...naughty Jade," he said, giving her a smile. He tugged off her pajamas and positioned himself between her legs. Grabbing scrap of fabric, he pulled it tighter against her, pushing the lace up between her dripping cunt lips.

"Sebastian!" she cried as she thrashed on the bed.

With a menacing smile, he ripped the scrap of lace off her. "I need to taste you again, Jade. Your gorgeous pussy has been on my mind the whole day."

Jade cried out as his mouth landed on her. He held down her hips, steadying her as his tongue lashed against her wet entrance. His lips found her hard little bud, and he drew it deep into his mouth, sucking back.

"Sebastian!" she yelled out, teetering on the edge of her orgasm. It came fast, ripping through her and making her body shake with pleasure. He was relentless, his mouth and tongue working her into such a frenzy that she barely finished the orgasm when the next one came in a wave, washing over her. She almost cried as she came down, her mind reeling.

"Fuck, you're incredible," he murmured. "And you smell so

good." He nuzzled his nose up her thighs to her knees. "I wanna fuck you. Do you want that?"

She nodded. "Yes..."

"Say it," he said.

"I..." She blushed. Could she really?

"I want to hear you say it. What do you want me to do to you?"

"Sebastian...I want you to fuck me," she blushed, her cheeks heating at the words coming out of her mouth.

He let out a growl and spread her legs, pulling her to him so he could press the tip of his dick against her pussy. The thick head nudged up against her, and this time, he slid in all the way in one smooth motion.

"Sebastian!" she gasped at the sensation of being filled. It was too much and her mind reeling.

"Sweet Jade. Not so innocent, but still as sweet," he whispered as he began to move inside her.

She grasped at him, her nails raking down his back. He moved slowly, deliberately, coaxing the pleasure from her. Letting out a deep cry, she pushed at him, squeezing her muscles around him, making him groan.

"Jade," he whispered, then stopped moving. She whimpered, but let out a soft yelp as he grabbed her hips. He rolled them over so she was on top. "Go ahead, darlin'," he teased. "Do what you want. Make yourself cum."

Bracing herself on his chest, she began to move, grinding down on him, lifting her hips slightly so she could feel him drag inside her. Sebastian seemed to like that. His head tossed back and he gritted his teeth. She did it again, getting on her knees for leverage so she could slide up and down his cock.

"You're so fucking hot," he cried out, his hand snaking down between them. His fingers found her clit and began to play with the little nub.

She continued to bounce on him, angling her hips until she found the sweet spot, the tip of his cock hitting her just right to send powerful shockwaves through her body. He continued to play with her clit, while his other hand reached up to cup her breasts and roll her nipples between his fingers.

"Fuck!" Sebastian moaned, his body spasming "Darlin', I can't...."

Jade felt him flood her, and that sent her over the edge too, exploding from her core and spreading through her body. Her body shook, and as the pleasure ebbed away, she collapsed on top of him.

Sebastian rolled her to the side, and his arms wrapped tight around her. As he softened and slipped out of her, she sighed, reaching up to touch the sides of his face.

"You're mine," he growled, nipping her lips. "And I'm not going to push you away again."

Jade sighed contentedly, laying her head on his chest.

———

"C'mon, just say it."

"No!"

"You can do it," Sebastian teased.

Jade gave him a naughty grin. "I don't know...I don't want you to think I'm some foul-mouthed hussy."

"Why not?" He rolled their bodies over, pinning her to the mattress. "What's wrong with having a dirty mouth?"

It was early morning, the sun barely peeking around the New York skyline. They were both exhausted, having woken up twice in the night, seeking each other out. Jade had orgasmed so many times she stopped counting somewhere after thirteen. Sebastian's stamina and refractory period were amazing, and she was deliciously sore all over.

"Say it for me," he coaxed.

"How about I say...manhood."

"Uh uh," He pushed his hips against her. "You know the word."

"Maleness?" she offered.

He shook his head.

"Your turgid...instrument?"

He bit his lip, trying not to laugh, and then hid his face against her neck.

"Oh, I know..." She raked her fingers through his hair. "Your hot...hard...spear!" She giggled as fingers found her ribs, tickling her until she begged him to stop.

"You know what I want to hear." His fingers lay still over her stomach, ready to tickle her.

"All right," she said, her lips curling into a naughty smile. "Cock. Dick."

"You drive me wild when you say dirty things in that accent of yours."

"I don't have an accent, you do," she pointed out. "It comes out, you know, when you're trying to charm someone into doing something. Or when you're aroused."

"Is that so, darlin'?" he drawled. "Like this?" His hand parted her legs wider, and she felt the tip of his cock sliding up and down her entrance. "Hmmm...wet already? I think someone likes to talk dirty."

"I do not...ugh!" She moaned as he slipped into her, filling her. "Sebastian! Fuck me, please."

The sex was hard, fast, and wild, and they soon panting and sweating as he collapsed on top of her. Jade couldn't figure out which way she liked it—quick and hard, slow and steady, or everything in between. It was all amazing, and she couldn't get enough.

Sebastian rolled onto his back, stretching his massive body

across the bed, taking up more than half the space. "Where the hell did you learn those other words for penis anyway?" he asked, his brows furrowing. "Sounds like you got them from some damn romance novel."

Jade's mouth opened and then slammed shut, her cheeks going red. Sebastian gave her a curious look. "Are you..." He sat up and looked around the room.

"Sebastian?" she asked. "What are you—no, don't look down there!"

She was too late. Sebastian was already hanging off the mattress, the upper half of his body disappearing under the bed. She tried to pull him off, but it was no use. He popped back up to the bed, several well-worn paperbacks in his hand.

"*The Pirate's Booty?*" he read. "*Lord of my Manor? Surrender to the Earl?*"

"Oh no!" She buried her head in the pillow. "Please, stop."

He chuckled and tossed the books away. "I'm not making fun of you, okay?" he assured Jade, taking her into his arms. "I just like to tease you and see you blush."

Jade peeked up at him. "You don't mind...that I'm not experienced? That I don't know a lot about sex?"

A growl rumbled through his chest. "Mind? I'm fucking over the moon you chose me to be your first. And I don't know how I would deal with it, thinking about you and other men." His expression soured.

"Oh yeah?" she huffed. "How about when I imagine all the women you've—"

A loud ring interrupted Jade, and Sebastian's face turned serious. "I'm sorry, I should get that." He gave her a quick kiss and rolled off the bed, reaching for his discarded pants on the floor. "Hello?" he said in a gruff voice.

Jade used the opportunity to go to the bathroom and freshen herself up. When she walked back into the bedroom, Sebastian was sitting on the bed, his back to her. His shoulders sagged, and she could feel the tension in the air.

"Sebastian?" she called softly.

He turned his head to look at her, his eyes hard as steel. "I have to go home."

Her heart sank. "Of course," she nodded. God, she was a fool for believing him again!

"No, Jade." Sebastian lumbered towards her. "I have to go back to Tennessee. My dad died."

"Oh no, Sebastian!" She wrapped her arms around his waist, pressing her cheek to his chest. "I'm so sorry. What can I do?"

"Come with me," he rasped. "Please."

She nodded. "Of course."

CHAPTER NINETEEN

T he private jet landed at a small airstrip outside
Knoxville. As they descended the steps to the tarmac,
an older man in a dark suit approached them, handing
Sebastian a set of keys and taking Jade's suitcase. Sebastian led
them to the black Ford pickup truck waiting next to the stairs,
and then opened the door for her before getting into the driver's
side. Sebastian told her it was another hour's drive to his
hometown, Maysville, which was right at the foot of the Smokey
Mountains. She sat in the front seat next to him, watching the
lights on the highway as they drove by, the scenery changing
from city to more rural country landscapes.

They hadn't spoken more than a handful of words since that
morning. Sebastian was like a rock, silent and betraying no
emotion. She felt a little impulsive, agreeing to drop everything
to go with him to Tennessee, but she couldn't say no.

Sebastian had to do some work before they left, so she went
to the lab for a few hours. She also checked in with Nick and
Alynna, telling them she was going away for a day or two to see
her dad perform and that Creed Security already had a plan in
place for her protection. She also consulted with Cady Vrost,

making sure she wasn't about to venture into some other clan's territory. Thank God, the nearest clan was in Nashville, and Eastern Tennessee was not under their jurisdiction. Sebastian had Zac pick her up after work and bring her to the private airport where the jet was fueled and ready to leave.

After 45 minutes in the car, they took a turnoff and the roads became smaller. Soon, they were on a back-country road that ended at an imposing metal gate. Sebastian pressed the small box clipped on the driver's side visor and the gates swung open.

They drove slowly up a long gravel road, and Jade could see a house not too far in the distance. It was dark, so all the lights in the house were lit, as well as the surrounding perimeter lights. Well, it was more like a mansion built with giant logs. Sebastian stopped the car, walked to her side, and helped her out. Two men came out of the house, and Sebastian gave them brief instructions. As the men scurried to get their things, he took her hand and led her up to the main door.

A woman was standing in the open doorway waiting for them. Her long, bleach-blonde hair was tied back in a ponytail, and she was wearing a tank top and cutoff jean shorts, showing off tanned legs. Jade wasn't sure how old the woman was, but if she guessed, maybe in her 40s. Familiar gray eyes flickered at her curiously, then moved to Sebastian.

"Momma," he greeted, taking the woman into his arms.

"Sebastian, thank the Lord you're back," she said, her voice thick with emotion. She pulled away and looked at Jade.

"Momma, this is Jade," he introduced.

"How do you do?" Jade extended her hand.

"I'm Connie Creed, Sebastian's mother." She took Jade's hand, giving it a soft squeeze. "Are you his—"

"I'm here to offer my support," Jade said quickly. "I'm so sorry about your husband."

"Ex-husband," Sebastian corrected. "They're divorced."

Connie's face fell, and she withdrew her hand from Jade's. "Are you hungry? I can make some fried chicken. I have biscuits—"

"It's okay, Momma," Sebastian pulled Connie in for another hug. "I'm not hungry. Jade?"

She shook her head. "I'm good." Jade had eaten the meal the flight steward on the jet had prepared, but Sebastian barely touched his.

"A—alright then," Connie said. "The funeral's at 10 a.m., so we need to be at the church by 9."

Sebastian gave an acknowledging grunt. "Goodnight, Momma."

Connie gave Jade a sad smile, and then turned around, disappearing down one of the hallways. Jade followed Sebastian as he led her to another part of the huge house. It really was beautiful, but she didn't have the inclination to admire it at the moment.

It was understandable that Sebastian had became withdrawn upon hearing the news. Though she had never lost a parent, she could imagine what it was like. But there was something not right. Sebastian had been quiet the whole day, but the moment they landed, it was like he had erected this wall around himself. He had always been a little standoffish, but now he was downright cold and emotionless.

They walked to another wing of the house, and Sebastian opened the door to a bedroom. Much like his loft in Tribeca, the room was enormous and had high ceilings. An entire wall was glass with a view of a lake behind them. The moon was full and large, hanging in the distance, the light casting an eerie glow over the water. It was amazing, and she knew it would probably be even more beautiful in the sunlight.

As Sebastian began to strip down, Jade walked over to her

suitcase, which was on a stand right next to his. She grabbed her toiletries and her pajamas and went into the bathroom. Much like the rest of the house, the bathroom was huge with a large jacuzzi tub in the corner and an enclosed shower area. Soft, fluffy towels were hanging on the rack, and there was an assortment of bath gels, salts, shampoos, and soaps neatly displayed in one of the shelves.

When she strode out of the bathroom, Sebastian was already on the huge bed, lying on his side, his back to her.

She hated his silence, but she had to give him time to grieve properly. Slipping into the bed, she moved closer to him. She wrapped an arm around him, and he shifted, but didn't move. Pressing her cheek against the warm skin of his back, she listened to his heartbeat, letting the soft, rhythmic thumping lull her to sleep.

———

"Are you sure I can't get you anything, Mrs. Creed?" Jade asked as the took the plate from the other woman's hand.

"Jade, sugar, you're fine," the other woman gave her a tired smile. "And please, I told you to call me Connie."

She nodded. "Of course, Connie." She gave the plate to a passing waiter and then sat down next to Connie as people came over to chat with her and offer their condolences.

The whole morning went by in a blur. Jade had been by Connie's side the entire time. At the church, she sat to Connie's left, while Sebastian planted himself on the right. They rode together in the limo to the cemetery, and she held Connie's hand as she watched them lower her ex-husband's coffin into the ground.

Despite having attended the service, she had learned very little about Sebastian's father, Ethan. Connie explained over coffee that morning that Ethan was driving home and smashed his car into a tree. The coroner said he had died on impact, and that he lost control of the vehicle, which was not surprising since his blood alcohol level had been three times over the legal limit.

The entire town came out for the funeral, and now, Connie was hosting a reception at their house. Most of the people gave Jade curious glances, but said nothing nor asked who she was or why she was there. Connie simply introduced her as a family friend and Jade was grateful that seemed to be explanation enough. She was already having trouble trying to define her relationship with Sebastian herself. Speaking of which…

"Connie, have you seen Sebastian?"

The older woman shook her head. "No, sugar, I haven't."

"Hmmm…" They had all traveled back to the house together for the reception. Sebastian had helped greet people when they came in, and the last time she spotted him, he was talking to a group of guys who looked to be about his age, probably his old friends.

"I'm worried," Jade said, her brows furrowing. "He's just… he's been acting strangely."

"Has he…said anything to you? About his daddy?"

Jade shook her head. "He hasn't said more than two words since he received the news. I know he's grieving, but I can't help feel something is off."

Connie sighed and got up. "Come with me."

She followed the older woman outside, to the large porch that wrapped around the house. "How long have you known my son?"

"Not very long," she confessed. "Sebastian doesn't talk much about his past."

"His relationship with Ethan is…complicated," Connie began. "We weren't rich. In fact, we were dirt poor. This is the first house I ever lived in that didn't have wheels underneath it." She paused and took a deep breath. "I had Sebastian when I was seventeen. Ethan Creed was the town charmer, and he got me pregnant after one night in the back of his truck." She turned away and stared out into the lush greenery surrounding the house. "He married me, of course. My daddy made him. And then we had Sebastian. He was a wonderful child, so smart and so beautiful, my boy. But Ethan, he had anger issues." She choked, and tears pooled in her eyes. "He beat me when he was drunk. And I couldn't stop him. But I couldn't leave him, either. I was trapped."

Jade sucked in a breath. "Connie...I'm sure you did what you could."

"I had no job, no money, not even a high school diploma. When Sebastian was thirteen, he started beating on him, too." The tears spilled down her cheeks. "I...I was pregnant the summer Sebastian turned seventeen. He had grown too, and he was taller and bigger than his daddy. I was in the kitchen and Ethan came in a rage, smelling of whiskey. He pushed me on the floor and...and...I lost the baby."

"Connie, I'm so sorry," Jade said, feeling the lump in her throat grow.

"When Sebastian found out, he was furious. He hunted Ethan down at his favorite bar and beat the shit out of him. Put him in the hospital for weeks. That was the last time they saw each other. Sebastian ran away, and a few months later, I got a call from him, telling me he had enlisted." Connie wiped the tears from her face with the back of her hand. "He sent me every penny he made. Told me to divorce Ethan and leave him, but I wouldn't. I just..."

Jade put an arm around Connie. God, what it must have been like for her. And for Sebastian, knowing his mother was living with her abuser. She couldn't even begin to know what that felt like. She too had been trapped under her mother's thumb, but Fiona never hit her.

"When he was captured in Afghanistan...well, I finally opened my eyes. I thought I had lost my boy. I left Ethan and served him divorce papers. Sebastian had been begging me to do it for years, and it was his death that finally pushed me over the edge."

Captured in Afghanistan? Jade's mind was reeling. She and Sebastian never talked about his past. And it wasn't like she could tell him about being a Lycan.

"When I got the news he'd been found," Connie continued. "Well, I was so happy and shocked I fainted right in the middle of my shift at the diner. I never thought I'd see him again and weeks later, here he was walking into my arms. My boy is a survivor." She sniffed. "I'm sorry, sugar, for unloadin' on you like this."

"No, please." Jade shook her head. "I'm here for you."

"He built that company from scratch, you know. And once he made it big, he built this house and had me move into it. Now, I don't have to worry about working or anything. Sebastian bought me the diner I worked at, and I run it now, but only so I have something to do."

"And Ethan?"

"Well, you know how they say people can't be all bad? Well, I think deep down Sebastian knew his daddy was a good man. He was just angry over his circumstances. When he wasn't drunk or angry, well...he and Sebastian actually had some good times. Sebastian doesn't know that I know, but he's been paying for Ethan's rent all this time and even paying off any debts he's run up. He still took care of his daddy, even after everything."

Jade felt all the air rush out of her lungs. Sebastian. How he must be hurting. A pain slashed through her.

Go...to...him.

"What?" Jade asked. "Did you say something, Connie?"

"No, sugar, I didn't." Connie frowned. "You okay? Maybe you should lie down. Don't worry, I know everyone here, and they'll all be leaving soon."

"No, I'm good. I just need to find Sebastian." The urge to be with him, comfort him, was great. "He's gone." Deep inside, she knew it. He wasn't in the house or anywhere near here.

Connie sighed. "I might know where he is."

"Tell me, please."

The older woman nodded. "Alright. Go and find him. Be with him."

———

Sebastian swore to himself he would never, ever get drunk. He enjoyed bourbon, maybe a glass of wine or two with dinner, but he always stopped himself before the buzz came. But now, here he was, staring down a half-empty bottle of whiskey.

Fuck.

He looked around at the tiny trailer where he was currently holed up. It had already been ancient when they lived in it, and now it was just a fucking disaster area. There was a hole in the roof that must have caved in a few years ago. Someone had probably broken into it and trashed all the furniture. All kinds of critters had turned it into their home over the years, judging from the smell. Why he bought the fucking thing and the land around it, he didn't know. He should have sold it years ago or never bothered with it at all.

But he did keep it, and now he was sitting on the floor of the dilapidated trailer, trying to drown himself in whiskey. How much liquor did a man need to get drunk, anyway? It was like the alcohol was burning off his system faster than he could drink it.

The news of Ethan's death hit him with the force of a Mack truck. He hated the man, and his first thought was that he was glad he was dead. He remembered the first time the back of Ethan's hand met his cheek when Sebastian came home late after hanging out with his friends. Or how his head was slammed down on the kitchen table after talking back to Ethan that Christmas when he was fourteen. He could go on and on. The memories of his younger years, however, muddled up the emotions. A younger and more sober Ethan took him out for a drive in his ancient, beat-up Chevy truck, singing along to country songs on the radio. Or when Ethan took him to the diner for lunch and to see Momma while she was working. Or how he scooped him up and ran all the way to the hospital when he fell off the old tire swing and broke his arm.

"Goddamn motherfucker!" He threw the bottle across the narrow room. It smashed against the wall, the glass shattering into a million pieces. Screw it. Those good memories didn't make up for the bad ones he created later. The world was better off without Ethan Creed in it.

"Sebastian?" came a voice from the outside.

Jade? What was she doing here?

The rusty door swung open, and Jade entered. Stepping over the various bits of trash and debris, she stood in front of him, then knelt down, placing her hands on his knees. Fuck, she didn't belong in her. She shouldn't be tainted by the memories that haunted this place.

"How did you find me?" he asked.

"Your mother told me you might be here."

He said nothing, but hung his head, staring at the rotting floor boards.

She bent her head, trying to look at his face. "Why are you here?"

He wished he knew the answer. Looking up at Jade, he

stared into her light green eyes, trying to get lost in them. "She told you."

Jade nodded. "I'm sorry. So sorry," she choked. "Sebastian..."

"Ethan was a fucking bastard," he began. "He beat me, yes, but I didn't care. Because as long as he took out his anger on me, he didn't touch Momma. Then, I grew up, got big, and he beat up on me less and less, as if he knew I was gonna snap one day. And I did. When I saw my momma lying on the floor over there," he motioned towards the kitchen. "She was bleedin'. Losing the baby. My sister..." His throat closed from all the emotion, and he couldn't continue.

Tears streamed down Jade's cheeks, and she sobbed as she wrapped her arms around him.

"I almost killed him that day," he said when he finally found his voice. "I ran away because I would have finished the job another day. So, I joined the Marines. And..." No, he couldn't talk about his capture. That was pain for another day. "Why the hell are you with me, Jade?" he asked. "I'm fucking broken. I've hurt you twice. And I'm a bastard, like my father."

"No," she protested. "Listen to me. You are nothing like that man. Not the bad parts of him. You protected your mother and saved her from more beatings, something no child should ever have to do. And yet, you still cared for your father, in your own way." He tried to protest, but she silenced him by placing a finger over his lips. "Connie knew, and she told me. And it's okay," she tipped up his chin. "It's okay if you love someone, even if they were a terrible person. Because people are not all black or white or good or evil. Sometimes we're in-between."

Emotions he'd never felt before bubbled up in him, fighting and clawing at him. Hate. Love. Despair. Confusion. Amazement. How could Jade still be here? How could she want to be here, knowing how fucked up he was? "You followed me here," he whispered.

"Why wouldn't I?"

With a throaty groan, he grabbed her by the shoulders and bent his head towards hers, his mouth seeking hers in a desperate kiss. Jade opened up to him eagerly, their lips, teeth, and tongues clashing together. He pulled her closer, seeking the warmth and comfort of her body.

Jade's hands clawed down his shirt, fingers fumbling with the buttons. *No, not here.* He got to his feet, hauling her up with him. Slipping his hands underneath her, he lifted her up, the skirt of her black dress riding up her thighs as her legs wrapped around his waist.

Sebastian walked them out to his truck, pinning her against the side. "I'm sorry, darlin'," he rasped. He unbuckled his belt and unzipped his pants, taking his already rock hard cock in his hand. "I can't wait." Pulling her panties to the side, he entered her in one stroke.

"Sebastian!" she cried, her arms winding around his neck.

"Sweet Jade," he whispered in her ear as he fucked her against the side of his truck. "God, you're incredible." He thrust in deep, seeking comfort in her, the pain slowly ebbing away from him until there was only pleasure and Jade.

"Harder," she begged. "More."

He grabbed her neck and pressed her forehead to his as he pumped deeper into her moist heat. Jade's cherry vanilla scent surrounded him, making him feel dizzy and buzzed. Making him forget.

"Jade!" he cried out as she flexed her inner muscles, grasping at his cock. She bit into his shoulder, the little hell cat, letting out a moan of pleasure against his skin. It didn't hurt, didn't even pierce his skin, but the sensation of her teeth marking him made him lose control. His cock twitched and shot his load deep into her just as her pussy clasped at him, signaling her own orgasm. He shuddered uncontrollably as he filled her, emptying himself into her until he was spent.

Jade peppered soft kisses on the side of his neck and shoulders. With a deep sigh, he let go of her, slipping out of her and placing her on her feet. She braced herself against the SUV, her breathing ragged. Her hair had come undone from its neat bun, her lipstick was smeared, and her pale skin was painted with a pretty blush. Fuck, he wanted her again.

Seemingly getting back to her senses, Jade pulled her skirt down and tried to put some semblance of order to her hair and makeup. Sebastian tucked his cock back into his pants, zipped up, and straightened his shirt.

With a rough growl, he grabbed her by the waist and pulled her to him, planting a firm kiss on her lips. "Let's go back home," he said.

CHAPTER TWENTY

They stayed another night in Maysville, much to Connie's delight. Jade thought she was a warm and wonderful woman, and she obviously loved her son very much. Sebastian was incredibly lucky to have a strong and loving mother. He, of course, adored her and she was happy to see this other side of him. The three of them had a quiet dinner at home, then went to bed early.

The next morning, they flew back to New York. Connie promised to visit them soon, hinting that she'd love to see Jade again. The older woman didn't prod either of them about their relationship, and for that, Jade was grateful. She wasn't sure herself what they were, and Sebastian made no indication if he thought they were in a relationship or not. She supposed they were lovers or friends-with-benefits, but whatever was between them seemed much more than that. It frustrated her keen, scientific mind, as its instinct was to put labels on things, arrange them neatly in little boxes. But her emotions refused to be categorized or organized. The cyclical arguments led nowhere, so she just decided to ignore them for now.

After they touched down, Sebastian brought her home. She

thought he was dropping her off, but he marched her up to her apartment, unloaded all her dirty clothes from her carry-on, and ordered her to pack—they were going to spend the night at his place. Normally, the caveman act would have turned her off, but on him it was sexy. And she spent the rest of the night showing him exactly how turned on she was.

Jade showed up to work the next day, feeling surprisingly refreshed. The lab on the 33rd floor was much quieter without Meredith and Lara, not that there was much activity in there these days. She had hit a wall in her research. She'd read all the texts twice, backwards and forwards, and even ran various translation programs to try and decipher what they meant. There was only way to discover how the mages were controlling humans, and that was to talk to someone with direct knowledge on the subject. That meant she had to talk to Daric.

She decided to go and see the warlock and try to get him to help her with the texts. The warlock was probably not going to cooperate, but she could try. She took a printout of the text she needed to ask him about and headed to the basement level under the pretense of checking on the newer version of the power dampening bracelet.

"Hi Meredith," she greeted the Lycan, who was standing outside the metal door that led to Daric's cell.

"Jade!" the other woman cried. "Have you come here to save me?"

"What's wrong?" Jade frowned. "Did Daric hurt you?"

"You mean Hobo Jesus?"

Jade laughed at her descriptive moniker for Daric. He did very much look like a hobo with his long hair and beard.

"I mean," Meredith continued. "Save me from boredom! Do you think you can bring me my princess chair here?"

Jade laughed and patted her friend on the shoulder. "I'll see what I can do."

Meredith's brows drew together. "Say...did you do something different?" She grabbed a lock of her hair and sniffed it. "New shampoo? Or face cream? Girl, you're seriously glowing."

She swatted her off. "I'm not...I mean..." God, what should she say? "I'll tell you later, okay?"

"Fine," Meredith said. "Now, what are you doing here?"

"I have to check on the bracelet, make sure it's working. I cleared it with the Beta," she lied, mentally crossed her fingers.

"All righty." Meredith punched a code into the door and pressed her palm on the sensor.

"Has he said anything at all?"

The blonde Lycan shook her head. "Hasn't said a word since the last time you were here."

Jade waited for the door to open and then stepped inside, Meredith standing just behind her. Nothing much had changed since her last visit. Daric sat in the same spot on his bed, his eyes fixed on the wall.

"Daric," she called softly.

He gave her an acknowledging nod. "Doctor. To what do I owe this pleasure?"

"I want to make sure the bracelet is working."

"Oh, it's working," he sneered, raising his hand. "I'm still here, aren't I? But what else?" Haunted blue-green eyes stared at her.

It was as if he saw through her, and it sent chills down Jade's spine. "I want to ask you something."

"You can ask. Doesn't mean I will answer."

She took a deep breath and came closer to him, unfolding the piece of paper she had tucked away in the back pocket of her jeans. "Here. This text. It refers to a source."

He looked at the text and made a motion to grab the paper, but instead, brushed his hands over hers.

Jade quickly jerked away from him, but his large hands held on to hers. His touch was like a hot poker, sending raw power through her. A snarl came from somewhere deep in her chest.

Protect...must...protect.

She whipped her head around. Who said that?

"Keep your hands to yourself, warlock," Meredith warned.

"The Doctor asked me to read some interesting texts she brought," he stated, drawing his hands back.

"You don't need to read with your hands, yeah?" Meredith shot back. She then looked at Jade. "What's going on? You said you just needed to look at the bracelet."

"Meredith, please," Jade said.

Daric's blue-green eyes zeroed in on Jade. "Seems like you didn't heed my advice, Doctor."

"Advice?" Jade asked. "Will you tell me what this means? What's the source?"

"It doesn't matter now," the warlock said. "When Stefan finds out, he will take you and use you to control the monster."

"The what?"

"Dr. Cross!" Nick's sharp tone cut through the air. "What are you doing?"

Jade shot to her feet, scrambling away from Daric. "Mr. Vrost...I was just...checking on the bracelet."

"You need to consult me before you come in here," Nick reprimanded. "What if you had gotten hurt? Meredith, I told you no one was to come in here without my express permission."

"Sorry, Mr. Vrost," Meredith said, then shot Jade a glare.

Nick rubbed his forehead with his palm. "All right, well, Miller is outside, ready to relieve you," he said to Meredith. "Go and take your break."

"Yes, Mr. Vrost," Meredith nodded. She grabbed Jade by

the arm and tugged her out of the room. "You owe me, girly," she hissed. "Whatever you have to tell me better be juicy."

Jade sighed. "Let's go get some lemon curd muffins." She hoped she wouldn't regret telling Meredith about her and Sebastian.

CHAPTER TWENTY-ONE

The rays of early morning sun streaming through the windows hit Jade's face, waking her up from her dreamless sleep. She blinked, let out a groan and rolled over, carefully peeling Sebastian's heavy arm off her waist. Looking over at Sebastian, she saw he was fast asleep. He looked calm and peaceful, and she was glad. In the past week, he'd had two nightmares. Both times, Sebastian got out of bed, took a hot shower, and then paced around the loft until morning. She didn't say anything but left him in peace instead. During those times, there was an unease from deep within her, an uncomfortable feeling that wouldn't leave her alone and wouldn't let her sleep. She waited in the dark until he came back, and she welcomed him eagerly.

Reaching for her phone, she checked her email and her messages. She went through them in order, reading the oldest first and marking which ones she planned to reply to later and trashing those that didn't need her attention. The last message in her inbox was from Nick Vrost.

Meeting at 9 am at Fenrir with myself, Grant Anderson and

Sebastian Creed. Your attendance is required. We will be discussing important matters.

Jade's heart pounded in her chest. Did the Alpha suspect something was going on between her and Sebastian? *Fudge.* She thought they were being discreet. Since they got back from Tennessee, Sebastian assigned his other employees as her security detail because he didn't need an excuse to see her anymore. She'd been staying at his place since then, going back to her apartment only to get fresh clothes. Did someone see them and report them to Grant?

As her Alpha, Jade had no choice but to follow his orders, if they were for the good of the clan. Human and Lycan relationships were tricky. Finding a Lycan mate was much easier, of course, but, realistically, it wasn't possible for everyone. There were protocols in place, and it was often up to the Lycan to decide when they would tell their human partner the truth. It wasn't a requirement to tell someone, as long as you could keep it a secret. Her stepfather, for example, had no idea that Fiona was a Lycan and they'd been married for a decade.

If a Lycan did want to tell his or her human partner, they would have to petition their Alpha and the Lycan High Council. They conducted extensive background checks and investigations, and then the Council and Alpha would make the final decision. It was a complicated matter, but for the most part, it was a mere formality. In the entire history of Lycan and human relations, there were only a handful of times when a human partner posed a risk of exposing their secret. Usually, they were met with a dose of confusion potion, which made memories unreliable. But, most were happy to sign an NDA and kept quiet. After all, no human wanted to feel the wrath of shifters who could snap them in two, so they kept their mouths shut.

Would she have to reveal her secret to Sebastian? No, it was too early. Besides, she wasn't even sure what she and Sebastian were doing. Well, she knew what they were doing, (namely, each other) but other than that...She shook her head. Going down that path made something in her chest ache, and an unfamiliar sensation was stirring in her middle.

Ignoring the feeling, she walked over to the closet, grabbing her clothes for the day. After a long, hot shower, she made a decision. Denial would be the game. Or at least, ignorance. She was sure Sebastian would agree with her. If anyone from Fenrir was following them, he would have known, too. But, all this time, they'd been careful. They never saw each other at the office nor spent any time in public together. She usually went straight from the office to his loft and back again to the office the next day. They didn't even eat out, preferring to have takeout or delivery at his place. No, she was paranoid. But just in case, she was going to have to be smart.

Sebastian was still fast asleep, and she didn't have the heart to wake him. She scribbled a note, explaining she was going to head home first and that they should arrive at Fenrir separately, so as not to arouse suspicion. Discretion was the key. She placed it over his phone, kissed his cheek, and headed out the door.

———

The private elevator stopped at the executive floor, and Jade stepped out, feeling one hundred percent confident.

"Jade!" exclaimed a familiar voice.

"Lara?" Jade ran into her best friend's arms, pulling the witch in for a hug. "I've missed you so much!"

"Me too! Sorry, we just couldn't get away," Lara explained.

"Hey, Jade." Liam embraced her in greeting.

"Hmph." She pouted as she pulled away from Liam. "I'm

not sure you should stay married to him, Lara. Not if you're going to be moving to San Francisco and leaving me behind."

"Aww, Jade," Lara laughed. "We'll be coming here as often as possible, at least until the baby comes. And you know we can always video conference."

"Fine," Jade relented. "You better be taking good care of her," she said, giving the San Francisco Alpha a warning glare.

"You haven't given me the shovel talk yet, so I suppose I was due," Liam joked.

"How is everything, by the way?" Lara asked as they walked towards the main waiting room of the executive floors. "And what are you doing up here?"

"Everything's...great," she said with a slight smile. "I have a meeting with the Alpha and Beta this morning."

Lara's eyes narrowed at her. "Hmm...there's something different about you today. New lipstick?"

Jade groaned inwardly. "I'll tell you when we're alone, all right?" She glanced around her and saw Nick, Cady, Alynna, and Alex leaving Grant's office. Behind them, a bell dinged, signaling the arrival of the elevator.

The witch's eyebrows shot up. "Did you—"

"What the hell is this, woman?" Sebastian's voice boomed across the room. He strode angrily towards her, waving a piece of paper in the air.

Jade blinked. "It's a note," she said. "A private note," she whispered and shot him a glare.

"I know what it is," he growled. "But what the hell is it about?"

Jade gave an exasperated sigh. "Don't you know what discreet means? I wrote that in the note. I even underlined it."

"Like I said. What the fuck is this shit?"

Jade felt a headache coming on, and she massaged her temple with her palm. Did he hit his head this morning?

Looking around her, she saw everyone was staring at them. "Can we please talk about this later?"

"No, we're gonna talk about this now." He balled up the paper and threw it over his shoulder. "You creep out of my bed without telling me and all you leave is this goddamn note?"

"Sebastian!" Jade warned. She prayed that the earth would swallow her up right then and there. "Please, stop talking."

"You think I'm keeping you a secret? That I'm hiding the fact you've spent every single night in my bed for the past few days? And we're going to slink in here separately like we're ashamed of each other?" He grabbed her by the waist, pulling her to him.

She gasped, her eyes blinking at him in confusion.

"Sweet Jade, you're no secret. And I'm plenty proud."

Jade let out a yelp of surprise as Sebastian kissed her hard, right in front of everyone. She sighed and then leaned into him, opening her mouth so he could dip his tongue into her

Someone in the room cleared his throat to catch their attention. Jade tried to pull back, but Sebastian held on to her for about five more seconds, then turned his glare to everyone in the room.

"Anyone have a fucking problem with this?" Silence. "Good." He let Jade go, and then patted her ass. "Grant," he nodded to the other man, who was standing by the door of his office, his face in complete shock, "ready for that meeting?"

Grant composed himself. "Sure, let's get started."

"Did you know about this?" Alex said to Alynna in a stage whisper.

"No," the brunette shook her head.

"Damn." Lara sighed in disappointment. "I'd have made a killing in the betting pools."

CHAPTER TWENTY-TWO

"**D**aric is definitely being held at the Fenrir Corporation building," Victoria reported. "That means your link to him is still active, correct? Since you were able to pinpoint his location."

"Yes," Stefan confirmed.

"Good. It was too bad those filthy dogs got to our men before they could rescue Daric," Victoria spat. "But at least that fool Marcus is gone. He won't be able to reveal more of our secrets."

"Yes, well, that only means—ARGH!" Stefan suddenly dropped to his knees, his thin, bony hands clawing at his head.

"Master!" Victoria screamed, rushing to Stefan's side. "What's wrong, Master? Talk to me!"

Stefan cried out, his body slamming onto the ground, and curling in on itself as he writhed in pain. He let out a blood curling scream, his hands reaching out to scratch at Victoria.

"Stop, stop!" The witch withdrew from him, pressing her palm against the gash on her forearm. "Master, tell me what I need to do to help you!"

A pasty, claw-like hand reached to her, and his body seized, shaking for a few more seconds before he went eerily still.

"Master," Victoria whispered as she knelt next to him. She cradled his head in her lap. "Master, please, wake up."

Blood red eyes shot open. "The...the..." he rasped.

"What is it, Master? What happened?"

"Daric," he sputtered.

"Did he talk to you? Did he discover some information to help us get to him?"

Stefan nodded weakly. "A vision. He has shared a vision with me."

Victoria gasped. "What did you see?"

"A great...monster," Stefan said. "Fire. Destruction. A monster that would destroy us all."

"Are you sure?" Victoria asked.

"A seer's vision is never wrong!" Stefan spat, pushing away from Victoria. "Daric is telling me something. I saw him. The monster."

"Who is it?"

Stefan closed his eyes. Then, he let out a laugh. "Fools!" he exclaimed. "Those dirty Lycans don't even know!"

"Master?" Victoria was confused.

The master mage got to his feet. "Victoria," he barked. "Gather what men you have. We are hunting down a beast. And, if Daric's vision is correct, we might be able to kill three birds with one stone."

CHAPTER TWENTY-THREE

What Jade thought was going to be a reprimand was actually a discussion about her ongoing security protocols, and how Grant wanted to expand Creed Security's role at Fenrir Corporation.

The Alpha didn't mention anything about her relationship with Sebastian, but at the end of the meeting, he pulled her aside and told her he trusted she knew what she was doing. Nick Vrost, however, warned her to tread carefully.

Lara and Meredith were both waiting for her outside Grant's office, waiting to give Sebastian the shovel talk. And they proceeded to give him said talk, taking turns detailing what they would do to him if he ever made Jade cry. Meredith ended the conversation with a pat on his shoulder, saying, "Good talk." Sebastian didn't get a word in, but despite the serious look on his face, Jade saw just the slightest smile tugging at the corner of his lips. When she was alone with the girls, however, they were both equally excited about her relationship, and they spent most of the afternoon in the lab doing some much-needed girl talk. That night, she and Sebastian had dinner out with Lara and Liam, and Jade couldn't believe how...normal everything was.

The next day, Sebastian had another emergency with one of his contracts, and this time he had to go on-site. He didn't want to leave Jade, but he had no choice. She thought about going back to her place while he was gone, but it seemed so lonely there. Her comfy apartment almost didn't seem like home. So, she decided to go back to his place. Staying there eased some of the loneliness, and she started sleeping in his shirts just to feel close to him and breath in his scent. He came back a few days later, much to her delight, and she welcomed him properly. They didn't leave the house for two days.

Two weeks passed since their meeting at Fenrir and things were normal for the most part. Sebastian was working in his home office, and Jade was in the bedroom, trying to figure out what to wear the next day. As she looked at the clothes hanging in the closet, something struck her. She frowned and walked to the living room, trying to figure out what was bothering her.

"Sebastian?" Jade called. "Have you seen my tablet?"

"It's on the dining room table!" he shouted from his small home office, which was in the far corner of the loft, divided from the rest of the space by partitions.

"How about my hairbrush? I thought I left it in the bathroom."

"Dresser, second drawer on the right."

"And my dry cleaning?"

"My assistant picked it up. It's in the closet."

"Sebastian!" she shouted. "Come out here! Now!"

"What?" he bellowed.

"Now, Sebastian!"

She heard a heavy sigh, chair legs scraping across the hardwood floor, and then lumbering footsteps that became louder the closer they came.

"What is it, darlin'?" he asked.

"My things. They're all over the place."

"Yeah, you're kind of a slob," he teased.

"No!" She stalked up to him, crossed her arms over her chest and craned her neck up so she could glare at him. "I mean...my stuff is *here*."

"So?"

"So?" she asked in an exasperated voice. "Half my clothes must be here. My books are taking up most of your shelves. My hairbrush, my shoes, my makeup. They're all here! I can't remember the last time I was home. Did you trick me into moving in here?"

Sebastian chuckled, and then picked her up, throwing her over his shoulder.

"You oaf!" she cried as the world suddenly turned upside-down. She beat her fists on his muscled back, not that it did anything. He laughed as he walked up the steps to the bedroom, and then plopped her down on the bed.

"Oomph!" The force knocked the wind out of her, and Sebastian dove right on top of her, trapping her lower body with his hips. "Sebastian," she sent him a warning look.

"I like it when you're mad," he teased. "Or pretend to be, anyway. Like that time I picked you up when you fell in front of me in the elevator, wiggling your sexy little ass. You accused me of manhandling you. I guess you don't mind when I manhandle you now, do you?"

She gasped when his hand slipped between them and under her trousers, teasing the edges of her panties. "Don't change the subject," she warned in a breathy voice.

"I also like seeing your things all over my place. And next to my stuff," Sebastian whispered. "They belong here." His fingers eased under her silky underwear, tracing her pussy lips. "Are you mad I tricked you into moving your things in here? Or mad I didn't ask?"

"What?" Her eyes were glazed over.

"I want you to move in here with me, Jade. I don't like being without you."

"Oh, Sebastian," she sighed, wiggling her hips up at him.

"Is that a yes?"

"Yes," she said. He rewarded her by slipping a finger inside her slick cunt.

Sebastian removed the rest of her clothes, then made love to her slowly until she was begging him for release. When he was done, he rolled her over, planting her on his chest.

"Are you sleepy, darlin'? Tired?"

She shook her head. "No, I just need a moment."

"Good," he said, kissing the top of her head. "I'll give you a few minutes, and then we can get dressed."

"Huh?" Her head popped up suddenly. "Where are we going?"

"We're gonna get the rest of your stuff and bring it back here," he said matter-of-factly.

"What?"

"You have suitcases, right? We'll take as much as we can carry. I'll hire a couple guys to bring the rest tomorrow."

"Wait, you want me to move in now?"

He looked at her like she was the one who was crazy. "What are we waiting for? You said you'd move in, why not now?"

"It's eight o'clock in the evening!" she declared. "Surely we can wait for the end of the month. I'm all paid up until then."

"Jade, I'm not waiting, and I'm not giving you a chance to change your mind," he said in a serious tone. "I'll take care of the moving and your landlord. He can have whatever he wants. I'll pay until the end of the year if I have to." He sat up, hauling her with him. "Now, go get that pretty ass in the bathroom and put some clothes on."

Jade got up, grumbled something under her breath about obstinate men, and marched towards the bathroom.

———

"I can't believe you're making me move out of my apartment in the middle of the night," Jade exclaimed as they were in the elevator.

"This is happening, Jade," Sebastian said, smirking at her. "It was only a matter of time."

As soon as the elevator doors opened, Jade knew something was wrong. The garage, which was normally lit by harsh fluorescent lights, was completely plunged in darkness. The hairs on her arms and the back of her neck stood on end. Quietly, she reached for the phone in her purse, her fingers pressing the tiny button on the back that would send a silent alarm back to Nick Vrost and Alynna Westbrooke. The phone vibrated three times, indicating the alarm worked.

"Jade," Sebastian growled. "Stay behind me."

"Well, well, looks like you're trapped." It was a female voice, one that sounded familiar to Jade, but at the same time, different. One of the lights flickered and the woman came into focus. Vivianne...no, it was Victoria Chatraine, Vivianne's twin sister and Lara's aunt. Stefan's right-hand woman.

"Good to finally meet you, Dr. Cross."

"Who the fuck are you?" Sebastian asked in a menacing voice. He reached for her, but stopped when he heard the cocking of several guns.

Victoria tsked. "Uh uh, Mr. Creed. Don't move any of those big muscles of yours," she said, tracing a long red fingernail down his bicep. "Now, if you'll come with me..."

"Leave him out of this, Victoria," Jade said, mustering all the courage she could. She had to stall them, at least until help arrived.

"You know who this is?" Sebastian asked. When she didn't

answer, he flashed Victoria a hate-filled look. "You're the one trying to kill her."

"Oh, smart and handsome!" Victoria laughed. "Almost correct."

"Let him go," she said. "I'm the one you want! Stefan wants me dead, right? Or as an exchange for Daric?"

"Close, but no cigar, my dear." The witch motioned to the men behind her, and nodded to Sebastian. "Get him."

"He doesn't know about us!" Jade shouted in a panicked voice. "He knows nothing!"

"What are you talking about, Jade?"

"Sebastian..." She looked at him sadly. His face turned from shock to anger. "I'm sorry. I'm so sorry." Pain ripped right through her chest. Victoria was going to kill Sebastian if help didn't come soon. "Please," she begged. "Don't kill him."

Victoria let out another laugh. "Oh no, my dear, not at all. He's much more valuable to us alive. Both you and Mr. Creed."

"What is going on? Jade!" Sebastian struggled against the three men who grappled him to the ground. They pushed him onto his knees, and then pulled his arms behind him, strapping his wrists together with plastic cuffs.

"No!"

"Now, Dr. Cross," Victoria continued. "Are you going to come willingly or will we have to restrain you too?"

Sebastian let out a snarl, knocking his head back so it hit the man directly behind him. The goon staggered back, hitting the ground with a loud thud. Sebastian wrenched away from the remaining men who were holding him down, head butting one of them and crouching low to sweep the other guy off his feet. Guns cocked and a shot rang out. Sebastian dropped to his knees, letting out a sharp cry as red bloomed on his shoulder. Two men came forward, holding him down by slamming their boots on his body.

Sebastian lifted his head to to look at her. "Run, Jade!" he screamed.

"No!" Jade screamed. Something inside her was clawing at her, tearing apart her insides and she fell on the ground in pain.

Must...protect...mine...

The she-wolf ripped out of her so fast, she barely had time to breathe before she stood on all fours. She let out a howl, stretching her large head out and then bared her sharp canines. Leaping towards Sebastian, she used her giant paws to swipe at one of the men, clawing him away, while her gaping maw latched onto the other goon's arm. Sebastian rolled to his side to get out of her way, grunting in pain as his injured shoulder hit the cold cement floor.

"You idiots! Why did you shoot him?" Victoria screamed at the remaining men behind her. "Get the tranquilizer dart! The Master wants them both alive!"

The men behind her scrambled, while Jade's she-wolf continued to rip through the other man's arm. She suddenly let him go and howled in pain as a dart hit her back. The she-wolf snarled and then whipped around, stalking towards Victoria, her gray fur dripping with blood.

"Get away from me, you filthy dog!" Victoria screamed. "Put another one in her!"

A second dart hit the she-wolf in the shoulder, but she continued to lumber towards the witch. She could feel the tranquilizer slowing her down, but she fought it. They would die, all of them would die for hurting her mate.

"Jade!" A voice rang out through the garage. She turned her head towards the entrance, where the doors had flown open. Meredith stood in the doorway, dressed in her catsuit, ready to battle. Three wolves, two large ones with brown fur and a smaller black one, stood behind her.

"Lycan scum!" Victoria screamed. "Get them! And get Creed!"

The wolves and Meredith leapt into action, charging the remaining men. There were about a dozen in total, all obviously under the puppet master's spell as they fought the massive Lycan wolves with no fear.

Using the last of her strength, Jade's she-wolf leapt on one of the men who had managed to drag Sebastian towards the door. She swiped a massive paw across his face, shredding the skin with her claws. When the man fell down to the ground, she let out a satisfied snort and turned to Sebastian, wanting to see if he was all right.

My mate. Mine.

But, as she looked at Sebastian, she saw something that made her heart sink and gutted her insides. Getting up from his knees, he stumbled back, as if trying to get away from her. He was staring at her, his eyes wide. It was a look she recognized, the very same ones her classmates had on their faces, that fateful day when she shifted in the bus. Terror. Horror. Revulsion. Hate.

She let out of a howl of pain before the darkness took over.

CHAPTER TWENTY-FOUR

"Jade, honey? Are you okay?"

Jade sat up quickly, her body jolting into consciousness. "What's going on?" she gasped. Looking around her, she saw she was in the back of one of Fenrir medical vans, lying on a stretcher

"Oh, Jade," Lara wrapped her friend in a hug. "Don't you remember?"

The memories were fractured, but they came back. The she-wolf! She shifted for the first time since the bus accident. Seeing Sebastian shot tore her apart, and the she-wolf hacked its way out of her body. She remembered the satisfaction of taking those men down, getting her revenge for...

Sebastian.

The pain came back to her middle, and she doubled over, wrapping her arms around her stomach.

"Jade, what's wrong?" Lara asked.

"I...I..." Sebastian's face came back to haunt her. The look of disgust on his face sent the she-wolf inside her howling in agony. Yes, she was there. The animal in her that she thought was gone, that she had pushed down so deep inside, had come back. And it was in pain. No, both of them were. Sebastian had seen what they truly were and he hated them.

"Is it Sebastian?" Lara asked.

"How...where is he? Is he all right?" She had to know. He may hate her, but she still needed to know he was alive.

Lara's face fell. "Grant and Nick...they took him away. Jade, he's human. You know they can't let him go. He saw you shift, and when you shifted back, he was raving and screaming. We had to hit him with a knock-out potion."

"Victoria!" she suddenly remembered.

"Got away, unfortunately," Lara answered.

"And what about—"

"You should lie back down," the witch said. "Dr. Faulkner and the rest of the medical team are caring for the ones who were seriously injured, so no one's here to look after you."

"Seriously...injured? Oh Lara, did I—" She sat up, trying to get off the stretcher.

"Shhh..." Lara pushed her back down. "Don't worry about it."

"But I hurt them and possibly—"

"You were protecting yourself! Protecting Sebastian!" Lara interrupted. "Just remember that."

Jade sank back down, covering her face with her hands. She almost had it all. A normal life with Sebastian. She had it in her hands and then it crumbled into nothing before her eyes. Sebastian was repulsed by her, and she hurt more innocent people. A sob escaped her chest, and tears flowed freely down her cheeks.

"What can I do to help you, Jade?" Lara pleaded, her arms embracing the Lycan. "Tell me. Whatever you want, I'll do it."

"Take me away from here, Lara," she begged. "Please."

"But, Jade, Sebastian will need you when he wakes up. To explain everything to him."

"No, he doesn't," Jade said, fresh tears flowing down her cheeks.

"What do you mean?"

"Lara...you didn't see him...see his face when he saw my she-wolf!" Jade insisted. "He...he thinks I'm a monster!"

"No, Jade!"

"Yes, he does. It was the same look my classmates had on their faces when they saw me shift! When I started attacking them and hurting them! And now I've ruined more lives!" Including Sebastian's. His world had changed forever. The knowledge of the Lycans would change him. Another life destroyed by her she-wolf.

No. Mine. Ours.

With a snarl, she forced the animal down deep in her. She would lock it away again, force it down so deep so it was like she'd never existed.

"Please, Jade, think about it."

"No," she said, "I've made up my mind. Please, Lara, as my friend, do this one thing for me."

Lara's eyes filled with tears. "F—fine. I'll talk to Liam."

CHAPTER TWENTY-FIVE

It was another nightmare. Yes, that's what it was. Another nightmare. But it was different. Jade, sweet Jade, had turned into a giant wolf.

"Mr. Creed, wake up."

Sebastian's eyes flew open, but he quickly shut them when the lights overhead blinded him. Something was wrong with him; he didn't feel right. It was like he was swimming through thick molasses. His shoulder hurt, too, and he knew that feeling. He'd been shot.

"How are you feeling, Mr. Creed?"

"Like I've been hit by a fucking truck." Sebastian opened his eyes again, but his vision was still blurry. Taking a couple of deep breaths, he cleared his mind. *Jade.* He shook his head to try to clear his vision. "Where is she? I want to see her! Goddammit, she better be safe!" He tried to move, but he realized he was strapped down and restrained. "What the fuck? Get me out of here!"

"Mr. Creed, calm down, please," the voice soothed. "Dr. Cross is fine. She's safe."

He relaxed, the words soothing him. "Who are you? Why am I tied down to this bed?"

"I'm Dr. Faulkner. We've met before."

Sebastian's eyes finally focused, and his vision became clearer. An older man stood over him. It was the same doctor from the night of Jade's rescue. "I don't understand...I..."

"Just get some rest, Mr. Creed. Grant will explain everything once he gets here."

A sharp needle poked into his neck and he struggled against the bonds. But it was too late and the sedative was too strong. Soon, his vision turned to black.

———

When Sebastian woke up again, he was in a different place. He was in a small room with no windows and one door. No escape. Everything was white, from the walls to the sheets on the twin bed where he was lying down. Someone had dressed him in some type of loose gray pajamas and his hands were bound with cuffs. Thank fuck his shoulder wasn't hurting anymore. In fact, it was more like an itch at this point.

Fuck. Did that woman capture him? No. Dr. Faulkner was Fenrir's doctor. His mind was muddled, but he was pretty sure he remembered one detail correctly: Jade had transformed into a giant wolf. And there other wolves too. Fuck. Werewolves were real? The world had gone crazy. But then, considering what happened to him, was he really surprised? He was shocked, and yes, terrified. But, as soon The Beast realized what Jade was, he roared.

Mine. Ours. Mate.

The fucking thing was happy that Jade was an animal, just like him. Fucking ecstatic. All this time...and she never told him. Did she even know? She must have. Because he was sure as shit that he didn't imagine those other wolves that burst through his garage door.

God, what a fucking mess.

The door slid open with a soft swish and Sebastian got to his feet, getting into a defensive position. Grant walked in. Behind him, Nick followed and a brunette who looked familiar.

"Sebastian," Grant greeted.

"What the fuck is going on? Who are you? What are you?" he asked.

"Sit down, Creed," Nick ordered. The blast of power that came from the other man was unmistakable. Vrost didn't even bother to hide it, nor the fact that his icy blue eyes were glowing.

Sebastian staggered back, the back of his knees hitting the bed. He sat on the bed, but remained upright, his bound hands held up to his chest.

Grant let out a long sigh, grabbed one of the chairs in the corner, and placed it in front of Sebastian. "Where do I begin?" he said, sitting down. "What I'm about to tell you is a secret that's hundreds of years old. Normally, I can't reveal this secret to humans without consent from a higher authority, but since you've already seen us, I have no choice.

Sebastian sat there, listening intently to Grant as spoke. His eyes grew wide and a million different questions ran through him. Lycans? Werewolves? They were real? Shit, he should have known. Wait...

"Hold on," Sebastian said, putting his hands up. "You said... there's an animal inside you?"

Grant nodded. "Yes. Our wolves are a part of us, and we learn to control it. Call it when we need it. In most cases, it talks to us, too."

Fuck. Was he a wolf? Is that what that man in the brown robes did to him? "Were you...made into wolves?"

The other man shook his head. "No. You can't make more

Lycans. You have to be born one."

Shit. No, then. "And you know when another person is a Lycan?"

"Yes. We know through scent and we can sense the wolf inside another Lycan."

"Jade—"

Grant nodded. "Yes, she's one too. As you've seen."

"Where is she? Is she safe?"

The man's face faltered, and Sebastian felt the panic rising in him. "Is she safe?" he repeated, the warning in his voice evident.

"She's fine, Mr. Creed," the brunette spoke.

"I've seen you before" Sebastian narrowed his eyes at her.

"My sister, Alynna," Grant explained. "And yes, Jade is fine."

"When can I see her?" he asked.

"Sebastian," Grant began, his face turning serious. "I can't just let you go. You must understand. I have my clan to protect."

"We should have hit him with the confusion potion as soon as we got there," Nick said. "Grant, why did you stop us from administering it?" .

"Because I have this gut feeling," Grant replied. He turned back to Sebastian. "I know you can keep our secret. And you care for Jade, right? If the rest of the world were to find out about us, they will hunt us down. You wouldn't want her to get hurt or get locked up? Turned into a circus show or science experiment?"

"Fuck, no!" He didn't even think of that. Jade was his number one priority now. "I would rather die than see her get hurt. I'll keep your secret."

Grant's face broke into a smile. "I know you would."

"Now, let me out of here," Sebastian said. "I need to see Jade."

"We can't trust him," Nick argued. "He's human."

"Nick," Alynna put a hand on the other man's arm. "We need to give him a chance. Maybe he can earn our trust."

"You can trust me," Sebastian assured them.

"Prove it," Nick challenged.

Sebastian got to his feet, which made Nick stand protectively in front of Grant. The two men stood face to face. "You want fucking proof? Something that will show you can trust me? I'll give you some goddamn proof!" With a roar, he pulled his hands apart, ripping the restraints from his wrists like they were paper. He shocked himself, not realizing the unusual strength he could tap.

Slowly, he faced them, his eyes a burning gold. The power emanating from him sent a shockwave through the small room, sending the three Lycans staggering back.

"Jesus Christ!" Alynna cussed. "What the hell are you?"

Sebastian sank back down on the bed. "I...I don't know..." he said. "I'm not a Lycan, am I?"

Grant sniffed the air around him. "No, you don't smell like a Lycan, but...fucking hell. What is that?" The other man looked visibly shocked. "Can you feel it?" he asked his companions.

Nick nodded. "It's..."

"A Beast," Sebastian finished. "At least that's what I call it. The Beast."

Grant rubbed his face with his hands. "You better start from the beginning."

Sebastian took a deep breath. It was his turn to tell his secret. He told them everything, from the time he was captured up to his rescue and how he struggled to control The Beast afterwards.

Grant's face was inscrutable when he finished his story. "You really don't know what that man put inside you? You haven't transformed into any type of animal?"

Sebastian shook his head.

"He doesn't smell like any animal I know," Nick said. "Maybe you are some type of beast."

"Maybe he didn't complete the spell," Alynna offered. "You said he was in the middle of the ritual and your buddies came in an offed him? That's probably what happened. He didn't finish, and that's why you can't shift. We need to find out what happened to you."

Sebastian shrugged. "I don't really care about that. I've been making peace with The Beast. Being around Jade has helped. It seems to like her...it settles when she's around."

"We should ask the witches," Nick said. "They might have some answers."

"Hold on, witches?" Sebastian asked.

"What, some magical shaman placed a creature inside you and you think witches don't exist?" Alynna asked in an exasperated voice. "You've met the most badass witch I know, by the way. Lara Chatraine."

"Jesus, this day is getting better and better," Sebastian grumbled.

"We're just getting started, I'm afraid," Grant said wryly. "Sebastian, look, I want to trust you. Revealing your secret, that's a step in the right direction. But there are protocols in place. Now, you have to put some trust in me, too. I'm going to do everything I can to get you out of here and keep you safe. But you have to stay put."

"When will I see her?" God, he sounded like a broken record, but he didn't care. He needed Jade. The Beast needed her.

Grant hesitated. "Soon. I promise. And, if all goes well, you'll never have to worry about her."

"Fine," Sebastian relented. "Do what you need to do. But do it quick."

CHAPTER TWENTY-SIX

"C'mon Jade, you can't just mope around here doing nothing!" Lara exclaimed.

"Why not?" Jade asked. "If you don't want me here, just say so."

Lara sighed. "Look, it's not that I don't want you here, but you have a life too. You have you work, your research."

"Do you think Grant will let me set up a lab here in San Francisco?" Jade asked.

"I don't know."

"Maybe I can work for Liam."

True to her word, Lara whisked Jade away from New York and brought her to San Francisco the night of the attack. For the past two days, she'd been staying in one of the guest bedrooms at Gracie Manor, Liam's home in the Pacific Heights District and the headquarters of the San Francisco Lycans.

Jade had holed herself up in her room, refusing to go out or see anyone except Lara. It seemed rude, considering Liam's mother still lived there, but she didn't care. The pain inside her wouldn't go away. Every time she had a free moment or closed her eyes all she could see was Sebastian's face.

"We should order more takeout!" Jade said, trying to change the subject. "I'm starving!"

"Jade, we have a full kitchen staff here, you don't need any greasy Chinese takeout," Lara said in an exasperated tone. "And we just had lunch two hours ago."

Jade frowned. "Really? I thought it was longer than that." She picked up her phone and dialed the Chinese place on Pacific Street. "Hello? Yes, I'd like an order of Beef in Oyster Sauce, Lemon Chicken, Sweet and Sour Shrimp, and—hey!" Jade exclaimed as Lara ripped the phone from her hands.

"Jade!" the witch gasped, her eyes going wide. "Jade, when was the last time you had your period?"

"What? Why are you asking me that?"

"You haven't stopped eating since you got here."

"I stress eat!" she said defensively, trying to retrieve her phone. Lara yanked her hand away, holding the phone high in the air.

"You know, Jade, for a genius, you're kind of dumb," the witch said wryly.

"What are you talking about?"

"You're pregnant."

"I'm not!" she denied.

"And Sebastian is your True Mate."

"Shut up!" Jade put her hands over her ears.

"Did you use protection while you were with him?" Jade's face going white as a sheet answered her question.

"You don't know that he's my True Mate!"

"Well, there's one way to find out." Lara took one of the drinking glasses, bashed it against the table and cut Jade's arm with the jagged end. The sharp glass pierced her skin, and blood flowed down her arm

"Are you insane?" Jade shouted at Lara, reaching for a napkin to cover the wound.

"Look at it," the witch ordered.

She sighed and removed the napkin. The gash quickly sealed and within seconds, the skin healed and looked like it had never been touched at all. Just like all the pregnant True Mates, she was indestructible now.

"Still don't think you guys are True Mates?"

Jade groaned. "Oh, mother fudger truck a duck."

CHAPTER TWENTY-SEVEN

For two days, Sebastian stayed in the cell. Sure, it was a nice cell, but it was boring. Alynna Westbrooke was kind enough to bring him books and a set of playing cards. Dr. Faulkner also came by to examine him. The old doctor was quite shocked when, after peeling of the bandage from his gunshot wound, saw that it was almost completely healed. He'd never healed so fast before he met Jade. Whatever The Beast was, it had also given him the healing and metabolism of a shifter. He asked Dr. Faulkner how he could heal so fast when he didn't before, and the older man was as surprised as he was. Perhaps, the doctor explained, being around other shifters had brought some latent capabilities. Dr. Faulkner asked him for a sample of his blood, which he was happy to give if it would help them find out more about what The Beast was.

Grant insisted that he stay in the cell until he could get clearance from this High Council. Grant (who, as he learned, was head honcho of the New York Lycans) also got him up to speed with their enemies, including the mages and their leader, Stefan. The woman who tried to kidnap Jade was Stefan's most trusted confidant, Victoria, who was, again, another redheaded woman who reminded him of Lara, like Cady. Alynna had explained they were all related, and it made his head hurt trying to remember who was who. Also, there was something Victoria said that he was trying to remember, but couldn't. It was something important and it kept niggling at the back of his mind.

"You're free to go," Grant announced as he strode into the cell, Alynna right behind him.

"Thank fuck!" Sebastian got to his feet. "I need to get some of my own clothes. These are just not me."

"Wait, we have to go over a couple of things." Grant motioned for him to sit.

"Fine, but make it quick." He'd been waiting for this day, aching to get out and see Jade. Touch her, smell her, make love to her.

"First, you keep our secret and we keep yours. The Lycan High Council has been informed of your existence, though this knowledge will not be released to anyone else. And they agreed not to give you the confusion potion or send you to Siberia to our detention center."

"Lucky me," he said sarcastically.

"Next, they want to keep you closely monitored. You'll be registered with High Council, just like us, and we have to keep them informed of anything that happens to you. Now, if Alynna's theory is correct, you might never shift into whatever animal is inside you. But we're not taking any chances. If they determine that you pose a risk to us or the humans, then you'll have to face the consequences."

"Fuck, no!" Sebastian protested. "I'm not gonna be under the thumb of people I haven't even met!" He wasn't in the Marines anymore, and he didn't take orders from anyone.

"Sebastian," Alynna said. "This must be confusing for you.

Believe me, I know. But this is for the best. The Lycan High Council won't meddle in your personal affairs, but they need to know what's going on with you to keep us all safe."

"Besides," Grant interjected. "As a Lycan, Jade has to follow all the rules the High Council has set. We all do. If you were human and you wanted to be with Jade, you would have had to pledge to follow all the same laws we do."

"Fine," Sebastian grumbled. "Now can I go?"

"Yes," Grant said. "Go home and get some rest."

Sebastian followed them out of the cell. Physically leaving the room made him feel much lighter. Frankly, he wasn't sure how long he could have held it together. The Beast was growing restless, roaring to get out. First thing he was going to do once he got his hands on his phone was call Jade. Or, knowing her, she was probably already waiting for him as soon as he got out. He couldn't wait to touch her again.

"You dickhole!"

Sebastian turned his head. A blinding fast blur came at him, hands going to his neck and pinning him on the wall. He was so surprised at the speed of his attacker; he didn't have time to defend himself.

"Meredith! Stand down!" Grant ordered. When the young woman didn't budge, the Alpha pulled her off Sebastian himself.

"What's the matter with you?" Alynna admonished.

"That bastard!" Meredith hissed.

"What the fuck did I do?" Sebastian asked, rubbing his neck. The wildcat was quick and strong. Or should he say she-wolf?

"You drove her away!" the blonde cried, her face twisted in hate. "My only friend! She cared for you, and you only saw her as a monster! Well, let me tell you this—Jade is the most incredible and sweet woman you'll ever meet and she's too good for you! You're the monster, you asshole!"

"Hold on!" Sebastian growled. "What the fuck are you talking about?"

"Jade told me everything! She finally found her she-wolf and saved your sorry ass, and then you rejected her!"

"Rejected her?"

"Stop acting like you don't know!" Meredith huffed. "You were fucking there that night!"

"I don't know what the fuck you're talking about! And where is Jade? I want to see her now!" His eyes shifted into their gold color, the anger rising in him. The power burst from him again, this time, much stronger than before.

"Jesus fucking Christ!" Meredith reeled back. She grabbed at her chest, as if she were having a hard time breathing. "What the flying fuck are you?"

"Shit!" Grant cursed. "No one else is supposed to know! Creed, simmer down!"

Sebastian felt the anger subside, and his eyes returned to normal. "Someone tell me where she is. Now."

Grant and Alynna looked at each other. "She left," Alynna said.

Meredith's brows knitted in confusion. "She told me you hated her, what she was!"

"What the fuck gave her that idea?"

The blonde Lycan shrugged. "Jade said when she came to check on you, you tried to get away from her! She said you looked at her like she was some disgusting animal!"

"Oh, for fuck's sake, I was shot in the shoulder! I was falling on my ass from the blood loss, not to get away from her. And I had just seen her transform into a giant gray wolf!" He rubbed his hands down his face. "Shit. Where is she? I need to explain everything to her."

"She went to San Francisco with Lara and Liam," Meredith said.

"Fuck!" Sebastian had to get to her. Now. He couldn't stand it, having her think that he was disgusted by her, when it was the opposite. Jade's she-wolf was fucking impressive and he could never think she was a monster. If anything, it was him who was the monster. He marched out, heading towards the elevators.

"Where are you going?" Grant called out as Sebastian stalked away from them.

"Where do you think?"

CHAPTER TWENTY-EIGHT

The morning after their discovery, Lara kicked Jade out of bed. She shoved the Lycan into the bathroom and stood guard outside until Jade finished showering and got dressed in clean clothes.

"Seriously? You're kicking a pregnant lady out of the house?" Jade pouted.

"Oh, so you're ready to admit you're pregnant?" Lara countered. "And I'm not kicking you out of my home. I'm encouraging you to go out and get some fresh air."

"I don't want fresh air!" She threw her hands up.

"Your baby needs it!" Lara countered. She let out a resigned sigh. "Look, I'm tired of you locking yourself up and feeling sorry for yourself." Taking Jade's hands in hers, she led her outside of the room. "We're going for a picnic brunch." The witch picked up a heavy wicker basket that was on the floor. "I have chocolate muffins in here. I'll give them to you if you're a good little Lycan, okay?"

"Fine," Jade grumbled. "Let's go."

With the basket between them, Lara and Jade walked down to the Marina Green Triangle, a park in the north end of San

Francisco. There was a wide expanse of soft green grass at the park that was perfect for picnics and sunbathing, not to mention viewing the gorgeous Golden Gate Bridge. Lara spread out the red and white checkered blanket and unpacked the massive lunch that could feed ten men or two pregnant Lycans. They ate and watched the people around them playing frisbee, walking their dogs, playing soccer, and flying kites.

"What are you going to do?" Lara asked finally. They put the dirty dishes back in the basket and then lay back on the blanket.

"I don't know," she confessed. She'd been up all night, trying to come to terms with it all. Pregnant. With Sebastian's child. Her hand immediately went to her stomach. Looking over at Lara, she saw the witch smile as her hand did the same thing to her own belly.

"You have to tell him," Lara said. "He has a right to know."

"You weren't there, Lara," Jade reasoned. "I just can't...I can't..." She swallowed the lump forming in her throat.

"But you can't raise the baby alone."

"Lara, this isn't the Dark Ages. A woman can raise a child by herself."

"But you don't have to. You have a mate."

"I think I've proven that just because you have a True Mate, doesn't mean you'll end up together," she replied bitterly. Sebastian's rejection was still gnawing at her, and she used all her might to push away those feelings.

"You don't know that," Lara pointed out.

"Do you know where he is?" Jade couldn't help it. She needed to know he was safe.

Lara shook her head. "All Liam told me is that Grant is keeping him at Fenrir until the Lycan High Council decides what to do."

Jade shuddered. They wouldn't kill Sebastian for knowing

their secret. But they could make his life difficult. Her stomach dropped, thinking of all the trouble she caused him. How she destroyed his life.

"I'm tired," Jade said, turning away from Lara, not wanting to talk anymore.

"Go on and take a nap," Lara urged. She took a book from her purse. "I'll be here."

Jade closed her eyes, feeling the sun on her skin and the cool wind whipping around her. By the time she woke up, the sun was already high in the sky.

"Lara," she called, her eyes fluttering open. She put her hands in front of her face, shielding herself from the harsh sun "What time is it?"

A large shadow blocked the sun, and she put her hand down slowly. "Lara?"

"Jade."

Her heart slammed into her chest with such force she thought she would faint. She scrambled off the blanket, grabbing it as she stood, clutching it to her chest. "S—s—sebastian? How did you find me?"

"You can run, but I'll always find you." He stood there, looking handsome as ever, his face drawn into a frown. "Why did you leave?"

"I..." She stood rooted to the spot. "Where's Lara?"

"Liam brought me here, she's over there," he jerked his thumb to a black town car sitting at the edge of the park. "Now, answer my question."

She took a deep breath. "You...you saw me. What I am."

"Yes, I did."

"I'm a monster!" she cried, her hands holding onto the blanket so tight her knuckles went white.

"You're not!" he scolded. "And I won't have you calling

yourself that!" He stalked over to her, placing his hands gently on her shoulders. "Look at me. You're not a monster."

"I don't understand." She shook her head. "When you saw me, you were—"

"Meredith told me what you thought you saw. That you thought I was repulsed by seeing your she-wolf."

"Weren't you?" she asked.

He shook his head. "No way. I was losing a lot of blood and going delirious. I couldn't stay on my feet. I'm sorry you thought I was trying to get away from you, but I wasn't. I don't think you're a monster. Your she-wolf is fucking gorgeous, and she saved me."

Jade let out a soft cry, and Sebastian crushed her against his chest. He let out a big sigh of relief as he wound his arms around her. "Don't cry, darlin'. You don't know what it does to me."

"But I ruined your life now," she said sadly. "Just like I destroyed my classmates' lives." She told him the full story of what happened during the bus accident and what happened to the children's lives afterwards.

"You didn't ruin my life, Jade," he said as he held her while she sobbed. "You saved it."

"I don't understand."

Sebastian let go of her, and then tipped her chin up. She gasped as she saw his eyes turn from stormy gray to bright gold.

Mine. Ours. Mate.

Her she-wolf knew. She acknowledged his animal, whatever it was. It was like she reached out to Sebastian, to the creature trapped inside him. The power that burned through him made her knees weak. "Sebastian."

"I'm the monster, Jade," he confessed. "Not you."

She shook her head. "No. You're not. She...my wolf...she's calling to you. Your animal. Can you feel it?"

His eyes burned brighter, as if acknowledging her she-wolf's presence. "Yes," he nodded, closing his eyes. When he opened them again, they were back to their usual color. "I can feel her."

"What is it, Sebastian?" Jade asked. "What's your animal?"

"I don't know," he shook his head. "But let's take a walk. I'll tell you everything." He took her hand and they walked down to the pathway right next to the bay. Jade listened as he recounted the story, the horrors of his capture and the man in robes who put The Beast in him.

"So, you can't shift?"

"I don't even know if I'm supposed to," Sebastian shrugged. "Maybe I'm just meant to live my life, sharing my body with The Beast."

She looked up at him sadly. Truth be told, ever since the she-wolf came back, Jade never felt more whole. Her animal wasn't even angry at her, as she thought it might be. Despite vowing she would push the animal away, she was ready to embrace it.

"Like I said, it doesn't matter." He stopped, as they had reached the end of the pathway. "Come back home with me, Jade. And don't run from me again."

Jade swung her gaze over to him. "Yes, I'll come back home with you."

————

After their talk, Jade and Sebastian walked back to the car where Liam and Lara were waiting for them. The witch had a big, smug smile on her face, while the Alpha welcomed them warmly. He invited Sebastian to stay the night at Gracie Manor before they left in the morning. He accepted and that night they all had dinner, along with Liam's mother, Akiko. Afterwards, Sebastian declined the nightcap Liam offered and hauled Jade back to bed, but not before asking Liam if Gracie

Manor had modern soundproofing, much to Jade's embarrassment.

They made love the whole night, as if they'd been apart for years instead of just three days. Still, they couldn't get enough of each other. Jade was exhausted, but happily so.

They spent the next morning languidly lying in bed, wrapped up in each other's arms, talking.

"Um ... porcupine?" Jade offered when Sebastian asked her what she thought The Beast was.

Sebastian guffawed. "What? Why would you think that?"

"Because you're so prickly and cute!"

"I'm not cute! Try again, darlin'. You know it's probably something badass."

Jade thought for a moment. "How about a lion?"

"I bet you'd like that, Future Cat Lady." He grabbed her hips and hauled her on top of his chest.

She let out a laugh as he tickled her sides and she wiggled around to get away from him. He rolled them over and pinned her to the mattress.

"Sebastian..." she warned. "We need to get ready. I want to have breakfast with Lara and Liam before we go."

"Fine." He gave her a quick kiss on the mouth. "But once we get back to New York, I won't be letting you out of bed for at least a week."

Jade showered and got dressed, putting on her last borrowed outfit from Lara. She came to San Francisco without any luggage at all and had survived by borrowing clothes from her friend. Sebastian finished getting ready, and then they headed downstairs for breakfast.

After their meal, Lara and Liam walked them to the curb, where the town car was waiting to bring them to the private airstrip holding Sebastian's jet.

"Are you headed back to New York right away?" Liam asked.

Sebastian shook his head. "No, we're making one more stop in Tennessee to see my momma."

Lara hugged Jade, and then let out a laugh. She bumped their bellies together. "Pretty soon, we're not going to be able to hug each other."

Jade froze. She brought her lips close to her friend's ear. "Lara, please. Don't say anything."

"Jade!" the redhead admonished in a whisper. "You didn't tell him?"

How could she? When was she going to tell him? Yesterday was a blur, with so many things happening between them. She wanted to tell him, but couldn't find the right time.

"Everything OK?" Liam asked.

Lara grabbed Jade's hand. "I think I saw your tablet in the living room, Jade. We'll be right back," she said to the two men before dragging the Lycan back into the house. "Explain," she demanded when they were alone.

"There wasn't any time!" she reasoned.

"So, tell him now!"

"I..."

"What's the real reason you're not telling him you're pregnant, or that you're True Mates?" Lara asked, her green eyes narrowing at her.

"I'm just...I'm not sure!" Jade shook her head. "He's...he says he wants to be with me, but..."

"Has he told you he loves you?"

"No," Jade admitted. And that was what was bothering her. Despite her protestations about love, her own views on marriage and relationships, it still stung that Sebastian hadn't told her he loved her, especially since she was 100 percent sure she was in love with him.

"Jade," Lara began. "Maybe he's just not the type to say it. Why don't you tell him you love him?"

"I can't," she cried.

"At least tell him he's going to be a father! You're making a mistake not telling him right away. Believe me, I know!"

"Jade! Lara!" Liam called out to them.

"Coming!" Jade said. "Look, I'll tell him when the timing's right."

"You tell him right now!"

"I'm not ready." Jade gave her friend a quick hug. "I'll call you when I get to New York, okay" She walked out before Lara could say anything else.

"Everything all right?" Sebastian was frowning at her.

"Yes," she lied. "Let's go home."

CHAPTER TWENTY-NINE

"Have you received any more visions from Daric, Master?" Victoria asked.

"No," Stefan shook his head. "And every day, I feel my influence over him weakening."

"Are the Lycans turning him against us?" Victoria suggested. "Could he be making a deal with them?"

The master mage grew quiet, his bony fingers stroking his chin. "I can't ignore that possibility, but he will never dare try to harm me." Thin, gray lips curled into a smile. "Not while I have her."

"Master? Who are you talking about?"

Stefan stood up, his black robes swishing around him like a dark cloud. He extended his hand. "Come with me."

The redheaded witch placed her hand in his. She held her breath, knowing what was coming next. The coldness blanketed her, then her body shimmered and vanished, only to reappear again in another location. The master's powers were great, allowing him to travel great distances and take whomever he wanted with him. Victoria had never seen such a gift. Stefan and Daric were the only two magical beings she knew who had such power.

They were standing in a cold, dark cave. Electric lamps were strung along the stone walls, and Victoria followed Stefan as he led her down the long path. They stopped at the end, right in front of a metal door. With a wave of his hand, the locks clicked open and Victoria stepped inside.

"What is this place, Master?" Victoria asked.

"In here, I keep my greatest asset."

"A weapon?" Victoria echoed.

"Not quite, but close." Stefan reached for a switch on the left side and flipped it on. A light overhead flickered, then bathed the room in an eerie light.

Victoria's eyes were drawn to the middle of the room. Sitting on a single chair was a figure, hunched over. Long dirty blonde hair covered the figure's face. It was a woman, as far as she could tell. She was wearing ragged brown robes that hung over her frail body and her feet were bare.

"Signe."

The woman's head slowly looked up. She had a pale face and her turquoise eyes were filled with hate as she looked at Stefan. "Magus," she rasped.

"It's time to go, Signe."

CHAPTER THIRTY

The jet took off from San Francisco and landed in Knoxville a few hours later. Connie was surprised and, of course, delighted that Sebastian and Jade decided to visit. Jade was happy to see the other woman, too, and it gave her an excuse not to tell Sebastian about the pregnancy. After all, how could she reveal the news when they didn't have a lot of privacy? Plus, Connie lived all by herself in the big house and hadn't seen anyone since the funeral. Jade couldn't take Sebastian's attention away from her, not when she was enjoying her son's company. This trip was about Connie, not her.

They only stayed one night, but they made plans for Connie to come visit them in New York the next month. Jade was happy to stay in the big log house again, this time under much happier circumstances. She and Sebastian also made good use of the jacuzzi tub in the bathroom. She enjoyed it so much he declared that he was going to install one in the loft in New York.

So, here she was, nearly a week after they arrived back home and she still hadn't told him. He still hadn't said anything about their relationship either. Sure, he did move her into his loft as he had planned right before Victoria's attack, but, they didn't talk of marriage or (though she hated to be a cliche) defined their relationship. What was she to him? Girlfriend seemed too trite. Whatever they were, she needed to know.

"Everything okay?"

"Oh, Sebastian, you frightened me," Jade said, placing her hand over her chest. Grant had given Sebastian access to her lab, and he came and went as he pleased (which wrecked her productivity, since he always found ways to distract her). He'd been spending more and more time at Fenrir, helping them with their security strategies and preparing them in case of another attack. The Alpha was happy they now had a new ally in the fight against the mages and took full advantage of Sebastian's expertise and resources. According to Sebastian, he and Nick were trying to find ways Creed's security team could help them in the future without exposing their secret.

"Sorry, darlin'," he said, moving closer to her. "It's lunchtime, did you forget?"

Her stomach gurgled loudly, despite the two burritos she had scarfed down an hour ago. This baby was going to eat her out of house and home.

"Well, someone's hungry," he chuckled, placing a kiss on her forehead. "Let's go then."

"Jade! Sebastian!" Meredith burst into the inner lab. "You have to come to the basement, now!"

Sebastian's body went rigid. "What's wrong?"

"It's Daric!"

"Who?" Sebastian asked.

"Fuck, they haven't told you about the warlock!" Meredith slapped her palm on her forehead.

"We'll explain later," Jade said. "Mer, what's going on? Is it the bracelet?"

"We don't know, but he's going crazy! At first I thought he was just trying to get some attention, but he wouldn't stop screaming and then he started trashing his cell! He won't calm down and he keeps shouting he wants to see you and Sebastian!"

"Us? Why? He doesn't even know Sebastian."

"I know! But he called him by name! Everyone's on their way. Let's go now!"

Sebastian and Jade followed Meredith all the way to the basement levels. As they approached Daric's cell, they could hear the shouting. The pained screams made Jade's skin crawl and, as they drew closer, her she-wolf began to stir, digging her claws into her middle as if to warn her.

Grant, Nick, Alynna, and Alex were standing outside the door, their heads together in hushed conversation. When they got closer, all four of them stopped talking and swung their heads toward Jade and Sebastian.

"Do you know what he wants with you?" Grant asked.

Jade shook her head. "No, Primul, I don't."

"And you don't know anyone named Daric?" he asked Sebastian.

"No, never heard of him. But, then again, I should probably check him out," Sebastian said. "I've dealt with a lot of people in my job. He might be using an alias."

"All right, but we should be careful."

"Is the bracelet holding?" Jade asked.

"He hasn't tried to escape or hurt anyone yet," Alynna reported.

"Let's go see what he wants," Grant said, nodding to Alex.

Alex punched in the code to the room and the moment it opened, Daric's shouts stopped. They filed in slowly, one by one.

Daric was in the middle of the room, the chain that

connected him to the wall stretched to its limit. The sheets were ripped up into shreds, the strips of fabric scattered all over the floor. Two chairs were turned on their sides, and one of them had its legs smashed completely. The single table in the corner had been turned over. The warlock was on his knees, his head hung low.

"We're all here, Daric," Grant said. "You have our attention. Now, what do you want?"

Slowly, his head lifted. "Alpha. I wish to make a bargain."

"A bargain?" Grant asked, crossing his arms over his chest. "All right. I'm listening. What do you want?"

"If you let me go, I will ensure no harm comes to Dr. Cross." His piercing gaze bore into Jade. Then he turned his gaze to Sebastian. "Or your monster."

Jade felt Sebastian stiffen beside her and she grabbed his hand, giving it a reassuring squeeze.

"And what makes you think we can't protect them?"

The warlock let out a sardonic laugh. "Stefan will use all his power and might to go after them. He will burn the world to get his hands on your monster and use him to enslave both Lycan and human kind."

"How do you know about me?" Sebastian asked. "Do you know the man who did this to me?"

Daric shook his head. "No, Creed, I do not know him. I only see what the visions tell me. I have seen the destruction you will bring should Stefan get you under his control."

"Fuck Stefan and all the mages," Sebastian spat. "I'll kill myself before I let him control me!"

"But that is why he wants your mate." His eyes looked back at Jade, specifically, her stomach. "And the child she is carrying."

The room went silent. Sebastian slowly pivoted towards Jade, his eyes burning gold. "Jade?"

Jade let out a sharp cry and she grabbed onto Sebastian's forearms. "Sebastian, I meant to tell you! I just...I couldn't! Can we please talk about this later? When we're alone."

Sebastian opened his mouth to protest, but when he everyone was staring at them, he clamped it shut. He turned back to the warlock. "What the fuck do you want?"

"I want my freedom. Let me go and I will finish Stefan himself."

"You've got to be kidding," Alynna said. "Let you go back to your master? Why would we do that?"

"Because..." Daric hesitated. "I will tell you everything. How Stefan acquired his powers, how he's been controlling the humans. I will give you all the information I have. But I need to go now."

"And what exactly will you do once you leave here?" Nick asked.

"I will kill Stefan."

His words hung in the air, heavy like a thick curtain. Finally, Grant spoke. "We should keep you locked up in here. You're switching sides now? You're either crazy or you think we're stupid. Why should we believe you?"

"Because he has my mother!" Daric screamed. "He's had her from the beginning, and is using her to control me! I never wanted any part of this, but he forced me to do his bidding!"

The Lycans all looked at each other, trying to absorb the information. Alynna, Alex, and Nick seemed at a loss. Meredith stood there, her body tight as a bowstring. Jade stood next to Sebastian, but it was like she wasn't even there at all. He didn't acknowledge her, keeping his eyes on Daric. It was like he put up a giant wall between them, keeping her out.

Grant sighed. "I think you're going to have to start from the beginning."

Daric's shoulders sagged. "I grew up in a small village built on the shores of a fjord in Norway," he began. "Our coven was isolated and we survived by fishing, hunting, and trading, but mostly we kept to ourselves. We didn't mingle with other covens and few knew of our existence. It was better this way because our clan had several blessed witches and warlocks." He paused, as if the memories were too much for him. "One day, a man came to our village. I was twelve. He was tall and pale, and brought his followers with him. They were all armed with weapons, both human and magical. He said his name was Stefan and he demanded we bring out our blessed witches and warlocks. Our coven could not fight him, so we had no choice. There were five of us and he made us line up and kneel in front of him."

"What happened?" Grant asked.

"First, he killed Ulric. Ulric could heal himself and others. Next, he killed Mona, a woman who knew the secrets of fire. Then, there were three left. My father, my mother and myself." Daric's breath hitched, but he continued. "He killed my father, Jonas. He had the power of transmogrification."

"The power of what?" Alynna asked.

"The power to transform matter," Jade answered for Daric. "Why was he killing the blessed witches?"

"So he could absorb their power." Daric stated. "Stefan was a warlock with no special gift himself. He barely registered any magic of his own. He hated that he was so mediocre and wanted more power. Somehow he discovered the secret of how to absorb other witch's and warlock's powers by becoming a mage. And once he did that, he scoured the world, looking for blessed witches and warlocks so he could take their magic."

"Why did he let you and your mother live?" Nick asked.

"Well, for one thing, I had the same power as my father, he didn't need mine. And my mother...well she was a seer. She had visions of the future, and Stefan was smart enough to know that was one power he didn't want. Seeing the future is a curse, to watch helplessly, knowing you cannot change it. Many seers go mad and kill themselves. That was one reason we remained isolated in the village. I should know, for I share her talent too. So, Stefan took us, instead. He locked up my mother and he trained me to be his right hand man, dangling her life in front of me, threatening her if I did not obey."

Alynna let out a gasp. "So, what changed?"

"My mother and I share a link. Stefan has been using this to communicate with me. That's how he found me the first time he attacked Fenrir and killed Marcus."

"But the bracelet should stop your powers!" Jade exclaimed.

"My active powers, yes," Daric replied. "But the link to my mother, something we have as seers, is an innate power. So, I'm afraid, dear doctor, your bracelet isn't as powerful as you think."

"Why the change of heart?" Grant asked.

"Stefan has grown desperate. I...I inadvertently sent him visions of Creed the other night. He wants the monster. With him on the mage's side, he won't need puppet masters or human slaves. So, he gave me an ultimatum. Deliver Creed and Dr. Cross or he will kill my mother."

"Then why didn't you just do that?" Grant countered.

Daric grew quiet, then drew up to his full height. His turquoise eyes blazed in fury. "Because I am done with Stefan. This is the last straw. He has threatened me and my mother for the last time. Let me go and I will kill him. This, I vow to you, Grant Anderson, Alpha of New York. On my father's grave and my mother's life, I pledge myself to your clan to keep yours safe from now until my last breath."

"Daric," Grant warned. "Do you know what you're saying? What you're invoking?"

"The pledge to a Lycan clan. Yes, I know," Daric answered.

"You must see how desperate I am. I want to save my mother and time is running out."

"If you do this, if I accept you as part of the New York clan, you know what that means, right?"

He nodded. "I will be forever in your service, Alpha."

"Grant," Nick warned. "Don't trust him."

"This vow is sacred," Grant said. "You cannot break it."

"Accept my pledge or kill me now," Daric said. "Because I will die if I have to, in order to save my mother's life."

Grant let out a sigh. "I can't believe I'm doing this," he ran his fingers through his hair. "I accept your pledge and your vow."

"Then it is done. Release me."

"Oh no," Grant shook his head. "It's not done." Daric's eyes flashed in anger. "As part of my clan, you also have my protection. Stefan will be defeated once and for all, but we will defeat him together." He turned to Nick, Alynna, and Alex. "Gather up our forces and call Vivianne. I have a plan to end this tonight."

"You tricked me!" Daric raged. "You fool! You don't know what you're doing!"

Grant tsked. "Daric, you should show more respect for your Alpha."

"Why do this, Grant?" Daric asked. "Just let me kill him! I will destroy him!"

"And die along with him?"

"If that's what it takes!"

"Sorry, Daric," Grant said. "Pledge or not, I cannot let you go, knowing you would die."

"But why?"

"Because you do not deserve it. You don't deserve any of this," Grant reasoned. "You were a mere boy when you taken, forced to do unspeakable things by an evil man. Stefan may have started this, but we will end it."

———

Sebastian's mind was reeling. His brain was trying to process too much information at the same time. His head buzzed, trying to make sense of it all, but he kept circling back over and over again to the same thing. Jade was pregnant with his child. And apparently, she'd known, but never told him.

The Lycans and their warlock continued to talk. Or fight. Or negotiate. He wasn't sure what the fuck was going on. What he did know was he needed to get out of here. His chest was constricting, and he couldn't breathe. The Beast suddenly became restless, scratching at him for attention. He had to get out of there or he didn't know what would happen.

Sebastian stormed out, not caring if the others saw him. The hallway outside Daric's cell was familiar, and he realized that this was where he had been detained. His old cell was three doors down from Daric's, and he strode into the room, breathing in relief as he was finally alone.

"Sebastian."

He didn't move, and kept his gaze on the white walls, the same one he had gazed at for hours, worrying about Jade.

"Please, Sebastian." He felt Jade move closer to him. "Talk to me."

Time stretched on and on as she waited for him to talk, and even then, Sebastian could only muster two words. "You knew?"

"Yes."

"Since when?"

"Since San Francisco," she admitted. "Please, don't be mad! I was waiting for the right time!"

"When?" Sebastian's voice rose and the tension in the air

grew thick. He whipped around, gray eyes shifting into blazing gold. "Why would you hide this from me?"

"I was afraid!"

"Afraid of what? That I wouldn't be a good dad? That I would turn out like my father—"

"No, Sebastian, please," she sobbed. She tugged at his shirt. "I can't...I can't."

"Can't what?"

She stood there, her mouth pressed together. "Sebastian, believe me, I wanted to tell you. There was so much going on and then you came to San Francisco and we were so happy."

"And you didn't think this news would make me happy? Why?"

"Because you don't love me!" she cried. "I didn't want you to stay with me just because we were having a baby. I couldn't do that to you."

"Dr. Cross, Creed," Nick Vrost came into room. "We need you now. Both of you. There's no time to waste. Are you all right, Dr. Cross?"

Jade wiped the tears from her eyes and nodded at Nick. "I'm fine." She left the room, her head hung low.

"Creed," Nick pinned him with his gaze. "We have a plan in place, but we need you and Dr. Cross to go along with it. I told Grant you probably wouldn't agree, especially if it put your True Mate in harm's way, but don't worry, she's practically indestructible now. I should know, Cady survived getting stabbed."

"My...what? What the fuck are you talking about? And who stabbed your wife?"

"Her mother," Nick said matter-of-factly. "Christ, you really didn't know, did you?"

"Someone's gonna have to bring me up to speed, because I

can't fucking stand feeling my way through this whole shit show like some goddamned teenage boy fumbling with his first bra."

"You have a charming way with words, Creed."

"Yeah? Fuck you too, Vrost." Sebastian strode past him, walking back towards Daric's cell.

CHAPTER THIRTY-ONE

J ade was as still as a rock as she sat in the back seat of the town car. Her hands were tied up, as were her feet, though loosely enough so she could still walk. Daric was in the front, his eyes steady on the road as he drove them down the New Jersey turnpike.

The Lycans had come up with a plan to kill Stefan once and for all. Grant didn't mince his words—he wanted Stefan stopped, dead or alive. They took the entire Lycan security force, plus Alynna, Alex, Meredith, Sebastian, and Nick. Vivianne came as well, and brought along various defensive and offensive potions they could use against the mages. Liam and Lara were on their way, but they would not make it on time. They would follow as soon as they landed in New York.

Daric told them the reason he decided to strike the bargain was that Stefan gave him an ultimatum. The master mage was able to tap into the link between Daric and his mother to send him a message—use any means necessary to escape the Lycans and bring him Sebastian and Jade. The master mage had grown impatient and was tired of waiting for his protégé to escape.

So, the Lycans crafted a plan to trick Stefan. They made it

look like Daric had kidnapped Jade while she was examining the bracelet and used her as a hostage to escape Fenrir. He "stole" one of the company cars and was now driving to southern New Jersey. Daric had sent a message through the link, telling Stefan to meet him at a specific location. The Lycans had picked a spot that was isolated, to reduce the risk of being seen by humans.

"Has Stefan answered back?" Jade asked from the back seat.

"No," Daric answered. "Will you not remove the bracelet?"

Jade shook her head. "Alpha's orders. Even if I wanted to, I can't. I don't have the right equipment with me."

"That is unfortunate," Daric said.

"What if he doesn't show?" Jade asked.

"He will," Daric assured her. "If he wants your mate bad enough, he will."

"What is he?" Jade finally asked the burning question in her mind. "Can he even shift?"

The warlock shook his head. "You don't want to know."

Cold fear gripped her. No, Sebastian couldn't be a monster, could he? Anyway, it didn't matter. Stefan would never succeed. Changing subjects, she decided to make the most of her time. "So, how does it work? How are the mages controlling the humans?"

"Curious little scientist," Daric commented. "Since I may not live past tonight, I supposed I can reveal this secret, in case I do not kill Stefan. You were very close, you know, when you asked me about the source. I'm quite impressed you got that far. Stefan himself took years to gather the information, even with my father's powers."

"So, what's the source?"

"The puppet masters act as channels for Stefan's power, like conduits, if you will. Stefan is the source. It takes some talent to become a puppet master and not all mages have the strength or stamina for it. It drains them and they lose their power over their slaves. Stefan found a way to share his power with the conduits, so they can keep their control over the human slaves."

"How can we stop him?"

"There are two ways—one is to kill him, and the other is with the right spell, one that would break his control over them."

"Tell me the spell then?"

Daric shook his head. "I do not know. Stefan—if he even knew what it was—never shared this with me. But perhaps, you could figure it out."

Jade chewed on her lip, filing the information away for later. She would try to get whatever information she could. "And how do you get the humans for your army?"

Daric's lips tightened. "That's where he needs me. I find them and take them."

Jade's brows wrinkled. "Take them? How? Where?"

"With my powers of course. You know what I can do. I can change and move anything made of matter, but I can also transfer it from place to place. I go to Army camps, training facilities and other places where the best soldiers are, and take them."

"How does your power work? Can you change anything and anyone? Does it have any limits?" Jade's scientific curiosity was fired up and eager to get answers.

"We would need hours for me to explain everything to you, dear Doctor," Daric said. "Unfortunately, we're here," he declared as the car skidded to a halt.

The Lycans had chosen an empty field deep in the most rural area of New Jersey. Frankie had assured them this place was miles from civilization and no other clan claimed the territory. It was dark, and the only the glow of the full moon high above them provided any type of illumination. Another tactical advantage for the Lycans, as they could see much better in the dark than the mages.

Daric opened the door and pulled Jade to her feet. He dragged her a few feet from the car until they were standing in the middle of the field.

She wanted to ask Daric more questions about his powers, as well as Sebastian and what he had seen in his visions, but she couldn't. After all, she was a prisoner, and Stefan could arrive at any moment.

Just as she thought those words, the master mage appeared suddenly from out of thin air. She would have found the whole transmogrification thing fascinating, if her heart wasn't threatening to break her ribcage.

Stefan stood in front of them, tall and pale. With a wave of his hand, two men dressed in black, as well as two dozen more wearing black combat gear and sporting weapons appeared behind him. The master mage waved his hand one more time and two figures materialized next to him. Victoria Chatraine was holding on to another woman with long, matted blonde hair dressed in dirty robes. Her hands were tied behind her and she had a gag around her mouth.

"Mother!" Daric cried. "Are you all right?"

"She's fine, Daric," Stefan said. "Don't be so dramatic. I knew you could escape from those abhorrent creatures, given the right incentive. Now," he peered at Jade. "What have your brought me?"

"Creed's True Mate," Daric said, giving Jade a push. "Just as you instructed."

"Excellent! Soon, he will come for her and we will have the monster under our control."

"What's the plan, Master?" Daric asked. "How will we get Creed to join us?"

Stefan laughed. "I thought that would be obvious, especially to you, Daric." His eyes flickered over Jade. "She will join your mother in her prison. And then I shall have you and Creed by my side, and we will destroy the Lycans and enslave the humans!"

"You monster!" Jade cried out.

"Take her away," he said to the mages behind him. One of them waved his hand to the group of men assembled behind them. Two soldiers jogged over to Jade, grabbed her arms and pulled her towards Stefan. "Your pup will make a nice addition to my forces too," the master mage cackled. "With father and daughter by my side, obeying my every command, I will rule the world."

No! Must...protect...

The threat to her pup awakened the she-wolf, and Jade fought for control of her body. It was too early. She wasn't even supposed to shift into her Lycan form, in case she didn't have full control yet. Where was her clan? They were supposed to be here by now!

Kill him. Now.

Jade let out a piercing scream as the she-wolf tore through her body, her limbs elongating and thick, gray fur sprouted all over her. She snapped her giant teeth at the men who held her, her canines ripping through their flesh like tissue paper.

With the two men writhing on the ground, she turned her attention to Stefan. Someone screamed her name, and while she didn't know who it was, she knew what it meant. The New York clan had arrived in full force.

"Get them! Kill all of them!" Stefan ordered.

The two puppet masters sent their troops to battle. A dozen or so Lycans were charging at the men, claws and fangs bared. Gunshots rang through the air, as well as growls and screams.

The puppet masters had to be stopped. But in her she-wolf form, she couldn't convey the message to her clan. Instead, she jumped at the first one she could reach, knocking him down and pinning him to the ground. The mage cowered and cried out, and the she-wolf snapped her teeth to keep him at bay.

"Daric! What are you doing?" Jade heard Stefan shout in horror. She wanted to look, but the she-wolf kept her attention on her prey.

"You've used me for the last time, Stefan!" Daric shouted.

"What are you...fool! You can't kill me with that toy! Traitor!"

"No!" Daric shouted. The sickening sound of a body hitting the ground near her startled Jade. Finally, the she-wolf turned its head.

Stefan was heading straight for her, his arms outstretched. Pain tore through Jade, and the she-wolf rolled over. Her limbs were on fire and whenever she tried to move, the pain increased.

"Filthy dogs!" Stefan screamed at the top of his lungs. "Stop or the she-wolf dies!"

The air suddenly became still and silence hung thick in the air.

The master mage withdrew a sword from his robe and placed the blade over the she-wolf's neck. "Now, I know True Mates' pups protect their mothers, but I don't think Dr. Cross could possibly recover from a severed head? Or shall we put it to the test?"

"Let her go!" It was Sebastian. He was here.

"Ah, here he is," the master mage sneered. "Good of you to come, Creed."

"You motherfucker!" Sebastian trained his weapon on Stefan. "Let her go or I'll blow your brains out."

"Do you think your weapon can kill me faster than I can take off your mate's head?" Stefan challenged, pressing the blade harder against the she-wolf's neck. "Put your weapon down and come here. Now. You will do as I say from now on."

Jade could feel the sharp steel digging into her neck, blood slowly trickling out of the shallow wound. No, she couldn't let Stefan gain control over Sebastian the way he did Daric. That was no way to live. Her decision made, she wrenched control of her body from the she-wolf. The animal fought her, but she was able to gain enough power to move her head sideways, the blade cutting a deep gash into her neck. Blood spurted out, painting her fur with red streaks. She rolled away and landed on her paws, and she could feel the gash on her neck sealing together.

"You disgusting dog!" Stefan screamed. He raised the sword high and brought it down on her back, piercing through the fur and flesh.

"No!" Sebastian screamed, dropping to his knees.

Jade let out a gasp as she watched Sebastian's body become engulfed in flames. She let out a pained growl as Stefan pulled the sword out. The flesh was healing quickly, closing up completely. She would live, but Sebastian...Stefan must have used his powers to burn him alive. Anger, grief, and heartache surged through her, and she forced the she-wolf's massive body to stand.

The flames around Sebastian grew larger, higher. The she-wolf let out a howl of pain, watching her as her mate was consumed by the fire.

No. Our mate. Alive.

A deafening roar rang through the air, and a burst of power sent a shockwave across the field that knocked everyone off their feet. Sebastian didn't burn. Instead, he had turned into a monster. A dragon.

Sebastian's dragon was bigger than a building, probably a hundred feet tall. Its scales were gold, overlapping his body like thick armor, and big spiny horns ran down its back and all the way to the tip of its tail. Its limbs—two short back legs and two longer forearms—were the size of trucks and tipped with large black talons. The dragon's head was covered in thorny spikes, and its golden eyes burned with anger. The long snout opened, as it threw its head back and let out another roar, spewing fire and lava straight up in the air. Terrifying and massive wings stretched out, flapping and creating great gusts of winds that shook the trees. Jade stood there, rooted in her spot. Sebastian was terrifying and magnificent at the same time.

"He really is a monster!" Victoria cried.

"We must get him under our control!" Stefan trained his bloodshot eyes back at Jade. "Come here, little she-wolf!" He raised his hands again, and Jade could feel coldness wrap around as Stefan willed the matter in her body to come to him. She felt her body fly through the air and braced herself for the fall.

But her body never hit the ground. Air rushed around her, and gigantic talons wrapped around her body. She looked up at the dragon's massive body, its wings beating as they flew through the air. The ground got smaller and smaller and the atmosphere was so thin she could hardly breathe. *Don't fly too high, my dragon*, was her last thought before she passed out.

———

Sebastian slowed his wings down, laying Jade down gently on the soft grass before he landed next to her. The Beast's body was humungous, but pure instinct must have kicked in as he didn't have any trouble maneuvering it. It was a strange sensation, being in such a body. As far as he could tell, he had complete control over it, but the being he called The Beast was in there with him.

Seeing Jade hurt had snapped something in him. After years of fighting with The Beast, Sebastian finally relinquished control. His body felt like it was on fire, and it probably was, but it didn't burn him. No, instead, it let The Beast out. A motherfucking dragon.

The Beast let out a snort. *Our mate. Safe.*

Sebastian nodded in agreement. Jade had passed out from the flight, but she was safe. She wasn't bleeding and he could hear her heartbeat with his enhanced senses. Then, he felt something else. A small pulse of life from her belly. Their child.

The Beast roared one last time, then gave up the body he shared with Sebastian. It tucked itself deep inside him, and Sebastian dropped to his knees, letting out a gasp as he breathed the cool air into his lungs. As soon as his head cleared, he leapt over to the she-wolf.

"Jade," he whispered, stroking the soft, thick fur which had begun to recede back into the wolf's body. Her limbs shortened and the massive snout began to turn back into a human head. His Jade was back.

Clear green eyes opened slowly. "Where am I?"

Sebastian gathered her into his arms, the emotions that he had held back were now threatening to break free like an overflowing dam. "I thought I'd lost you."

"Sebastian?" She looked up at him, her face breaking into a shocked expression. "You...you're a..."

"Dragon," he finished. "The Beast is a dragon. Are you scared of it?"

She shook her head. "I know I should be...but..." She took his hand and put it over her chest. "She knows. The she-wolf knows. The Beast is her mate."

"And you're mine, too, right? My True Mate?"

She nodded. "Sebastian, I'm so sorry I didn't tell you right away. I was scared."

"Why? Why would you think I don't love you?"

Jade's back grew stiff as a board. "You never said anything."

"I didn't think I had to," he reasoned. "Good God, woman, I

got rid of all those men, took you on a romantic date, listened to your damn cat videos, introduced you to my mother, moved you into my home, and chased you across the country!"

Jade let out a small laugh. "But you didn't say it."

"I thought...you just knew." Sebastian frowned. "And that you could feel it, the way I feel you love me, too. You love me, right?"

She sobbed, placing her head on his chest. "Yes, I do love you."

"And I love you, Jade," he answered back. He tipped her chin and gave her a soft kiss.

She leaned into him, demanding more, opening her mouth so he could taste her. His little she-wolf. All his.

Sebastian broke away after a few minutes. "As much as I'd like to keep doing this, darlin'," he said, grinning at her. "We're sitting in the middle of nowhere, naked as jaybirds."

Jade chuckled. "I kissed a dragon and I liked it," she sang.

He rolled his eyes at her and got to his feet, pulling her up with him. "C'mon, maybe we can find some leaves or something. I don't want anyone looking at your sexy ass when they find us."

CHAPTER THIRTY-TWO

They weren't sure where they were exactly, so they picked one direction and started walking. After fifteen minutes, they stumbled upon a farmhouse. Sebastian told Jade to hide in the bushes as he knocked on the door, explaining to the very shocked farmer and his wife that they had been robbed and was hoping he could borrow their phone and perhaps some clothes for him and Jade. After getting dressed, Sebastian called Grant's cell phone. The Alpha was able to trace where they were.

"You're a motherfucking dragon?!" Meredith exclaimed as she ran towards them, Lara not far behind.

"That's what I said," Jade told the other Lycan.

"You did not say motherfucker," Meredith joked, then pulled her friend into a tight hug. "Jade, I'm so glad you're okay."

"Of course, she is," Sebastian said proudly. "She's got a motherfuckin' dragon for a True Mate."

Meredith squealed. "Oh. My. God. You've got a bun in the oven? Yay! I'm gonna be an auntie! Hey, have you thought of names? How do you feel about Meredith for a girl?"

"Mer!" Lara admonished. "You said *I* should name *my* baby Meredith if it was a girl!"

"So? Meredith is a wonderful name," the blonde said in an exasperated tone. "We'll call yours Meredith 1 and Jade's Meredith 2!"

Jade rolled her eyes.

"At least she didn't make any Mother of Dragons reference," Lara quipped.

"Jade, Sebastian," Grant greeted as he walked towards them. "Glad to see you're safe."

"Stefan?" Sebastian asked.

The Alpha shook his head. "Got away. As soon as you flew off, he disappeared, along with Victoria, his mages, and the remaining slaves under his command."

"Daric?" Jade asked. "And his mother?"

"Alive. He's one tough warlock," Meredith said, her lips curving into a smile. "Pretty badly injured though. Without his powers, he wasn't any match for Stefan."

"We have Signe, as well," Lara interjected. "My mother is with her now. She's been badly traumatized, but my coven will do everything we can to help her."

"Sebastian," Grant began, his face turning serious. "Did you know what you had inside you?"

He shook his head. "No, I didn't. I've been fighting The Beast for years, and when I thought Jade was going to die...it broke free."

"Well, I'm glad it did. Otherwise, who knows what would have happened?" The Alpha let out a long sigh. "I have to warn you, though. This is only the beginning. There will be consequences and possibly more trouble along the way."

Sebastian placed an arm around Jade and pulled her close to his body. "I'm part of this now, Grant. I'm going to do everything in my power to protect what's mine."

"Me, too," Jade proclaimed. "I'm a motherfucking badass she-wolf, remember?"

Sebastian threw his head back and laughed.

EPILOGUE

A FEW MONTHS LATER ...

"C'mon, darlin' you can do it," Sebastian encouraged. "One more push, okay?"

A string of expletives ripped from Jade's mouth, the likes of which Sebastian had never heard before. Sure, there were a few naughty words in there that he was familiar with (he was rubbing off on her, after all,) but there were also some names and expressions that were truly only Jade Cross-worthy. As he wondered what a kitten-fudge-ripple-donkey-wanker was, his thoughts were interrupted when Jade's hands bore down on his.

"Fucking hell, Jade!" Damn Lycan strength.

"You'll heal!" she snarled, sweat trickling down her face. She let out another pained groan.

"That's it, Jade," Dr. Faulkner soothed, looking up at her from between her knees. "Almost, there."

Jade let out one last scream, holding onto Sebastian's hand like her life depended on it. He bit his lip as her hand crushed his fingers, desperate to keep his mouth shut. Nothing would compare to the pain Jade was feeling right now, bringing their child into the world.

A loud cry rang through the delivery room, and Jade fell back down on the bed.

"It's a girl!" Dr. Faulkner declared, holding the tiny, squirming infant in his hands. A nurse quickly wrapped up the child and began to clean her.

"You did it, Jade," Sebastian kissed her forehead. "She's here."

"How is she?" Jade asked in a weak voice.

"Strong. Healthy," Dr. Faulkner answered.

"Here she is," the nurse said, handing over the small pink bundle to Jade. She took her daughter, nestling her into her arms as Sebastian moved closer.

"Beautiful. Perfect. Like her mother." He bent down and breathed in the baby's scent. Cherries. Vanilla. And...burnt marshmallows? He let out a silent laugh. Mother Nature had a sense of humor.

"We'll give you a few moments," Dr. Faulkner said, leading his team out of the delivery room.

The new parents looked in wonder at their baby. She was so small and fragile. Would she be a wolf like her mother or a dragon like her father? Sebastian didn't know, but it didn't matter. And in this moment, he knew he would do anything to keep her and Jade safe. But first...

"I love you," Sebastian said, leaning over to kiss Jade on the forehead. He told her everyday, sometimes several times a day, so she wouldn't forget. He took her palm, and tickled it with his fingers.

"I love you, too," she said with a laugh. "What are you doing to my hand?"

"You've got something on your cheek," Sebastian said, trying to keep the smile from breaking out on his face.

"I do? What is it?" She placed her left hand on her cheek, then gasped. Her eyes zeroed in on the gold band on her ring finger and the single yellow diamond in the middle. "Sebastian…"

"I'm not good with words," Sebastian began. "But, I'll try. Jade, I want you to be my wife. I want to be by your side, protect you and our baby, and have your she-wolf protect me. I want you to be mine, but I'll belong to you, too. Will you marry me?"

Jade's eyes shone with happy tears. "Yes, Sebastian. I will marry you."

He bent down and kissed her gently, careful not to crush their daughter. Inside him, The Beast rumbled in happiness.

———

Turn the page to get a preview of the last book in the series,
Tempted by the Wolf
featuring…well, you'll have to see for yourself!

Want to read some **bonus** scenes from this book, featuring Jade and Sebastian's **dirty, hot, and explicit** adventures?

Sign up for my Reader's Group now! You'll get access to ALL the bonus materials form all my books AND two free
Contemporary Billionaire Romances.

Head to this website to subscribe: http:// aliciamontgomeryauthor.com/mailing-list/

I love hearing from readers and if you want to tell me what you think do let me know at alicia@aliciamontgomeryauthor.com

Meredith sighed for the 137th time that hour. She shifted her stance, finding a comfortable position to stand. Here she was, wasting her talents by playing babysitter to a warlock. This wasn't what she signed up for. Of course, forced servitude to the New York Lycan clan wasn't part of her life plans either, but she made her bed and now had to lie in it.

She thought she had it all figured out. Fenrir Corporation was a target that was ripe for the taking. The conglomerate was worth billions of dollars, and they wouldn't miss a couple of million here and there, right? Meredith was trained by one of the world's top cat burglars, and this is what she did. Steal things and sell them for money. Lots of it, as her secret bank account in the Cayman Islands could attest. Never mind that its CEO, Grant Anderson, was the Alpha of the East Coast's most powerful Lycan clan. It should have had her own she-wolf running the other direction. Actually, the bitch did warn her, but she couldn't help it.

Fenrir was the ultimate prize, and she spent six months of her life staking out the place, finding weak spots and then springing into action. Months spent planning the perfect heist, only to be ruined by a little witch and a brainy little scientist. She thought the 33rd floor research facility would be empty and she broke in one night after she was sure its two primary occupants were gone. How was she supposed to know that they'd come back—after office hours— to check on something. They caught Meredith in the act of stealing a few pieces of tech and had her detained. The nerve!

Of course, said witch, Lara Chatraine and Lycan scientist, Jade Cross, were now her best friends, but that wasn't the point. Out of options, she struck a deal with the Alpha of New York— ten years of serving the clan. It was that or imprisonment in Siberia. Well, the choice should have been obvious, although, for a Lone Wolf like her who'd never been part of any clan, it was a tough decision. All her life, she'd been independent and never had to be under an Alpha's thumb, and frankly, she preferred it that way. But then she also preferred not freezing her ass off, so she took the bargain.

Ten years of serving the clan. She'd already had a couple of months under her belt, but the rest of her time seemed to loom overhead. Her she-wolf was also dying to break out of her skin. The New York clan had outfitted her with a tracking device that could not only track her across the planet but would explode if she tried to remove it. Shifting into her wolf form would mean breaking the ankle monitor, and she wasn't sure if Lycan healing could regrow a limb.

Patience, she told the wolf.

I didn't get us into this mess. Why should I have to suffer?

Oh, shut up, bitch.

Stop calling me a bitch!

Well, technically, you are a one, so...

The she-wolf whined, then lay down and pouted.

Meredith knew her relationship with her she-wolf was... special. According to the only other Lycans she talked to, none of their wolves spoke in complete sentences, nor conversed with them. Lucky them. Some days, she couldn't get the animal to shut the fuck up.

A low moan caught her attention, and her head snapped towards the figure in the bed. Daric, the prisoner she'd been guarding for the last two days. The warlock had been injured badly in their latest confrontation with the mages, the Lycans' enemies. Daric couldn't use any of his powers, so he had apparently tried to stab the mages' leader, Stefan, with a knife. That didn't go so well, and Daric ended getting hurt.

Meredith sighed again. Witches and warlocks were biologically human, and thus didn't have the same speedy healing and metabolism Lycans did. She didn't know how the hell they ended up being the dominant species on this planet, seeing as they were all practically walking bags of organs wrapped in skin.

Daric let out another moan and twisted his body, the white sheet covering him slipping lower. Meredith felt her mouth go dry at the sight of his chest—broad and muscled, covered in strange tattoos. His shoulders were wide, nearly taking up the entire width of the small, twin bed. His arms were thick and muscled, like tree trunks. His torso was covered in bandages, but she was pretty sure he'd have a rockin' set of six-pack abs. Daric was about half a foot taller than her 5'10 frame, and probably outweighed her by over a hundred pounds. He could probably pick her up and slam her against the wall and—

The she-wolf growled in appreciation.

Oh, stop it.

Meredith quickly looked away, trying to ignore the rush of heat and desire. She would *not* go there. Again. The first time she saw Daric, he had attacked Jade, and she pulled him off her. The shock of electricity that shot up her arms surprised her, she nearly let go of him. Even in his powerless state, he managed to pin her to the ground. The heat of his rock hard body was something she could never forget, and some nights she woke up wanting and horny, wishing that--

Fuck this shit; she needed to get laid. It had been too long. Almost two years. But, she didn't exactly have the opportunity now. She didn't shit where she ate, and she couldn't go anywhere else except the Fenrir Corp building. Now that Jade had a *motherfucking dragon* for a mate, who also owned a security firm, the Lycan scientist didn't need her as a full-time bodyguard, and thus, Meredith was trapped in the basement, guarding their warlock prisoner.

"Stefan. Mother!"

Daric's scratchy groan had Meredith scrambling to the side of the bed. This was the first time in two days the warlock had been conscious enough to say anything. Dr. Faulkner, the Lycans' resident physician, had been by regularly to check on him. Daric had suffered a few bruised ribs, but no internal injuries. Still, he needed time to recover and rest.

"Daric," she called softly. "Do you need Dr. Faulkner?"

Turquoise eyes flew open and a large hand wrapped around her wrist. Meredith struggled to break free, but his grip was like steel, and his touch sent tingles across her arm.

"Let go, warlock!" she hissed.

He loosened his grip, a brief flash of surprise on his face. "Where am I?"

"You're back in your cell in Fenrir," Meredith sneered.

Daric struggled to sit up, his fingers massaging his temple. "Stefan..."

"He got away, unfortunately," she explained.

"My mother?" His eyes zeroed in on her. "Where is she?"

"She's safe, with the New York coven."

He relaxed visibly, the tension leaving his shoulders. "I've been hurt."

"Yes, well that's what happens when you try to kill a master mage with a butter knife," she said sarcastically. "What the hell were you thinking anyway? Going up against Stefan without your powers?"

"I had no choice," Daric replied. "It was our only chance to kill Stefan."

"Well, it was a stupid choice," Meredith muttered. "You could have died."

"It almost sounds like you care, Lycan," Daric countered.

"I don't, warlock," she spat, hoping the nervousness in her voice didn't come out. "I was just afraid I'd have to clean up the smear your pathetic little body would leave. I hate getting blood on me."

Daric swung his long legs over the side of the bed and attempted to get up. He stumbled, and Meredith pushed him back down.

"What are you trying to do? You've been in bed for two days!"

"And thus, I'm in need of the facilities." Daric looked meaningfully at the door leading to the small bathroom.

"Ah, well I guess you gotta drain the snake, right?" As soon as the words left her lips, she slapped her hand over her mouth. God, she even surprised herself sometimes. *Don't think about his snake. Don't think about his snake.* And there it was, a mental image of Daric's penis stuck in her mind. Thick, veiny, erect and—Fuck, this would be a long day.

Daric struggled again but got to his feet. He towered over her, but he was still weak, so she could probably give him a gentle push, and he'd fall over.

"Do you need help?"

"Not to drain my snake," he said with a small grin.

Meredith turned bright red. God, she was turning into Jade, who blushed at the mere hint of sex or penises.

"I could use some help with this," he said, rubbing the thick, scraggly beard on his lower face. "Could I bother you for some razors?"

"I'll see what I can do," Meredith grumbled. As Daric disappeared into the bathroom, Meredith left the cell. She walked out of the main detention area and into the main hallway leading to the elevators.

"Hey Tank," Meredith said to the burly Lycan guard standing outside.

"Hey, Meredith," he greeted back. "How's the prisoner?"

"Up and about. Say," she began. "Any chance you can get me some razors?"

"You ready to slit his throat already?" Tank chuckled.

"Ha! Tempting, but no." She shook her head. "He's tired of rocking the hobo Jesus look, I guess."

Tank shook his head. "I don't think the Beta will allow that, but let me see what I can do." The Lycan guard picked up the telephone next to him. He said a few words and then put the phone back into the receiver. "Sorry," Tank said, shaking his head. "Mr. Vrost said he doesn't want to leave the warlock alone with anything sharp. You can offer to shave him if you want. But the Beta was pretty clear about not leavin' him alone with anything he could use a weapon."

"Fine," Meredith shrugged. "Have someone send the stuff. I'll take care of it." She really shouldn't, but she couldn't help it. She had been held as a prisoner in this same facility, so she felt some sympathy for the Daric. God knows, she had needed some grooming herself by the time she had some contact with the outside world.

Tank nodded and picked up the phone again. A few minutes later, one of the Lycan security guys, Heath Pearson, came down with a small paper bag.

"You need help, Meredith?"

She shook her head. "I think I can handle one injured warlock with no powers. Thanks, Heath."

Meredith strode back into the main detention. By the time she got to Daric's cell, he was already sitting on the bed. He was wearing a fresh pair of loose pants, and from the dampness of his hair and the droplets of water on his skin, he probably took some time to freshen up. A small towel hung over his neck.

"Nick Vrost said not to give you anything sharp," Meredith said, holding up the paper bag. "But I got the short end of the stick, so I'm volunteering myself as your personal barber today."

Daric stood up and sat on one of the chairs in the middle of the room. "Then I leave myself in your capable hands."

Meredith smiled wryly and walked over to him. She opened the bag and took out the razor, a can of shaving cream, and a pair of scissors. "I've never done this before, so you need to tell me what you want."

A pregnant pause hung in the air. "What I want," he began. "Is...Just take it all off, I suppose. Unless you have a preference?"

She shrugged. "I'm not Vidal Sassoon, here, mister."

He looked at her like she was speaking another language.

"Right." She picked up the shaving cream and squirted a dollop onto her palms. Working it onto his jaw, she ignored the warmth of his skin, and way his beard tickled her fingers. Satisfied with the amount of foam on his face, she wiped her hands on her pants and picked up the razor.

Daric leaned back on the chair to give Meredith a better angle. She leaned down close enough, placing the razor on his cheek. As she took a deep breath, his scent filled her nostrils. Chocolate. Rich and creamy chocolate. The smell was driving her she-wolf wild, and the little slut was rolling around, howling with delight.

Shut the fuck up, bitch!

"Are you going to start before my beard grows any longer?" Daric asked, his eyebrow raised.

Swallowing a gulp, she pushed the desire away, hoping he didn't notice anything. "Um, yeah." She thought she had some snappy comeback, but her brain somehow froze. With a deep breath, she began to shave his beard, working methodically and slowly, trying to calm her shaky hands. But she was so close to him she could feel the heat emanating from his body and his wonderful scent wrapping around her, making her panties flood with her wetness. Thank fuck he wasn't a Lycan or he would have smelled how horny she was right now. She steadied herself by reaching for the back of the chair, but instead, grabbed his shoulder by accident. Fuck, it was like pure stone, hard and unyielding. Meredith had the urge to withdraw her hand. She wasn't sure what possessed her, but she dug her fingers into his shoulder instead. She thought she felt his breath hitch. Maybe it was just her imagination.

With a last downward stroke of the razor, she finished with her task. She took the towel draped around his neck and used it to wipe away the remaining foam. Sweet baby Jesus, had he always been this handsome? She had glanced at him once before when they first caught him, but didn't give it a single thought. A few weeks later, when he had the beard, he looked like that homeless guy who pushed his cart down 3rd Avenue. And now, clean-shaven and looking refreshed, Daric was heart-stopping, drop-dead gorgeous.

As her hands rubbed the fabric over his jaw, his fingers traced over her the back of her palms. They wrapped around her wrists gently, holding them still. Blue-green eyes looked up at her, not with hate or passion, but expectantly. Like he was waiting for something to happen.

"I don't understand," he whispered, shaking his head.

"Understand what?" she asked. His gaze was hypnotic, and

she struggled to break free. But all she wanted was to get lost in them.

The sound of someone clearing his throat made Meredith jump away from Daric.

"Am I interrupting anything?" Grant Anderson, Alpha of New York, stood in the doorway, arms crossed over his chest, a bemused look on his face.

Meredith shook her head and then grabbed the paper bag on the table, stuffing all the items back inside. "No, we're done here," she said, straightening her shoulders.

"I've come to discuss terms, Daric," Grant said as he strode toward the warlock.

Meredith walked briskly towards the door. "I'll be outside," she muttered. She didn't even spare a last backward glance before the door slid close behind her.

Now available in select online stores

CPSIA information can be obtained
at www.ICGtesting.com
Printed in the USA
BVHW041105090323
660079BV00005B/117